Also by Fredrik

available from Fingerpress.co.uk

WORLD WAR II SERIES:

The Cyclist

Farewell Bergerac

Francesca Pascal

The Fat Chef

BARBARIAN WARLORD SAGA:

Galdir—A Slave's Tale

Galdir—Rebel of the North

Galdir—Protector of Rome

See Fred's books on a Virtual Reality stage at:

inkflash.com/FredrikNath

About the Author

Fredrik Nath is a full-time neurosurgeon based in the northeast of England. In his time, he has run twenty consecutive Great North Run half-marathons, trekked to 6000m in Nepal, and crossed the highest mountain pass in the world.

He began writing, like John Buchan, "because he ran out of penny-novels to read and felt he should write his own." Fred loves a good story, which is why he writes.

Catch Fred online at:

www.frednath.com

The Evil
That Men Do

Fredrik Nath

FINGERPRESS LTD
LONDON

The Evil That Men Do

ISBN (pbk): 978-1-908824-49-3

Published by Fingerpress Ltd

Production Editor: Matt Stephens
Production Manager: Michelle Stephens
Copy Editor: Madeleine Horobin
Editorial Assistant: Artica Ham

twitter.com/FingerpressUK
inkflash.com/Fingerpress

To Anne Lee
My PA, my organiser, my friend

Foreword

We all have psychological baggage, whether we choose to admit it or not.

For some it is a driving force, in others it is simply destructive. In this book I've strived to paint a picture of someone who is troubled by his past yet still functions well enough during dark and terrible times. The key is 'well enough'. None of us gets it right all the time even in the imaginative world of fiction. These days of course Rolf might be offered CBT or Mindfulness training, but they had none of that in those days and damaged people had to cope on their own.

And cope, he does.

"*The evil that men do lives after them; the good is oft interred with their bones.*"

— **William Shakespeare: Julius Caesar, Act 3 Scene 2**

The Evil That Men Do

Part One

Chapter 1

"Only the nation that upholds its honour is capable of enduring as time passes. Germany will endure — thanks to the Führer."

Rudolf Hess

1

Rolf Schmidt was a big fellow even as a child, but it was not until he was thirteen he considered killing his father, Max. Of all the things he recalled about his father, the strongest memories were of the heavy shoes the man always wore. Often, as an adult, late at night, when Rolf had time to muse, the sight of them came to mind. They were bible-black and shiny in his flashbacks; they oscillated like a pendulum in the barn. Rolf was very familiar with those shoes. They were sturdy and supported Max Schmidt's feet, as he drove his tractor, cycled into town, or kicked his wife and children. Those clean and vicious shoes made Rolf feel nauseated whenever the mental picture of them forced itself into his conscious thoughts.

Rolf sometimes questioned how the sight of such mundane articles of clothing could stir up so much fear and submerged anger without it bursting forth for the entire world to see. It was as if his rage could only appear when he was alone; the rest of the time it remained smouldering beneath the surface.

He often remembered the look on Max's face when, entering the barn, he had looked up at his father whose heavy frame swung back and forth at the end of the rough, brown, hessian rope with which he had hanged himself. It seemed to Rolf that it was the only time Max had not scrubbed off the mud, or blood, from those shoes. At the time he misinterpreted the expression on Max's face as one of surprise. Much later he understood that the wide, staring, bloodshot eyes, the open mouth and the purple tongue protruding from it, were only signs that the drop had not broken his father's neck.

He sometimes wished he had happy memories of his father to cling to, but the man's appetite for beer and schnapps and his violent rages when he was drunk, erased any nostalgic thoughts Rolf might have retained. Despite all of that, Rolf knew he could have forgiven his father the outbursts of violence. A boy only has one father and he understood how powerful the bond between a son and his father could be. It was the fact of his mother's fate he found most painful, so painful that thinking about it took him to the brink of his ability to control himself. The thoughts were intrusive and seemed to appear at their own whim, beyond his control, erasing any positive thoughts about Max.

Minutes before he found his father he had stumbled over her body, mutilated and bloodied as it lay in the kitchen, when he returned earlier than usual from school. Dumbfounded with shock, he dropped his books and stared at the body. The bruised face, the torn lips and the neck twisted at this impossible angle, testified to a brutality only Max could have inflicted. The pool of clotted blood on the tiles showed him the outcome. Hands by his sides, chin down, he knelt beside his dead mother and wept. His was no hysterical sobbing; it was a true wail of utter grief. The sound went on, until exhausted of tears, he lapsed into silent shock.

Time passed.

Then he calmed, as if he had expected her death, for indeed he had, or at least feared it in his adolescent imaginings. He had always guessed somehow it would come to this. Anger replaced grief faster than he could ever have understood. He pulled open a drawer and extracted a cook's knife, long, shiny and he hoped, lethal. His neat fingers grasped the hardwood handle as he called for his father. If the man were there, he would kill him. Before Annika, his sister, came home, he would do it and spare her the shock of what he intended.

Thirteen years old, but with the fury of a grown man, he swore death to the man who had brought him up. He searched the house. A blood-trail took him upstairs where the tangled bedclothes and the pillow on the floor testified to some kind of struggle. A bright-green table-lamp lay vivid and broken on the floor and his mother's two perfume bottles lay smashed in a sweet-scented heap in the corner of the bedroom.

Silence.

The house was quiet now, for once. In his mind, he could hear the sound of his father shouting, screaming, and thumping those great fists on the kitchen table, with the crockery lifting inches into the air. This time however Rolf held no fear of the big man. He had the knife, he also felt such rage it consumed him.

His search took him to the barn where the sight of his father's body brought no feelings at all at first. He stared up at the face, absorbing what he saw, and dropped the knife.

The anger left him as fast as it had arisen and a deep feeling of sorrow came to him. It overwhelmed him and waves of it swept up on the shores of his mind until, forgetting his sister, forgetting everything, he lay down on the clean, straw-strewn concrete floor and wept again.

2

Paris, 1942
Rolf paced up and down the hallway. He was a big man, blond and muscular. His movements were economical and the battle, in which he had fought at the Maginot Line, had hardened him beyond anything he would have admitted. His skills in hand-to-hand fighting when training belied his nature and his instructor always said he had no "killer instinct". Rolf accepted that. He had joined the army because he had to, not because of any enthusiasm for violence.

The building was silent and the echo of his footfall reverberated in his ears, as if he paced in a cathedral, not the ground floor of the apartment house, here in Nazi-occupied Paris. His unteroffizier had left him there to guard and watch over the hallway to ensure the escapee did not return. He glanced at his image in the mirror of a mahogany armoire, which stood in the hallway, forlorn and empty of accoutrements or keepsakes. He peered at the face, which looked back at him with its troubled, slate-grey eyes; the stubbly face portrayed an expression of utter weariness. He frowned. Rolf felt irritated with the sight of his too smart, too clean, green uniform and even with the efficient, oiled Mauser rifle in his hands. It was the reflection of a man he had never wanted to become; a man drawn into war with utter reluctance.

Tired of walking up and down, he seated himself in a carved wooden chair next to the dresser. The silence around him seemed oppressive; even the street noise outside was faint and distant behind the tall, heavy, oak front doors of the house. Presently, he drew a book from his pocket and began to read. He tapped the arm of the chair with his fingernails as he read.

'*The Lord is my shepherd I shall not want...*'

The battered white cover with its worn silver print and dog-eared pages gave him solace. Only this one keepsake connected him with the life he yearned for and missed. The first few words of the psalm were enough. He knew and understood the book. It had been a gift from his mother many years before at his confirmation, and it had never left his side. The psalm-book was as much a part of him as it had been part of her, and it was his one anchor to a reality that seemed to have passed him by, now he was part of the Third Reich—as if he could ever believe in its tight and orderly workings.

The dank smell of the faded ground-floor carpet gripped his nostrils and he looked up at the staircase leading towards the upper floors. More worn carpet adorned the stairs, held in place by its brass stair-rods. He wondered what kind of people lived here, in this tall, dilapidated building. He questioned why his unteroffizier had made him waste his time here. The fellow insisted an escaped partisan might return and Rolf would have to arrest him. And what had the man done? Printed a few anti-Nazi leaflets? It made no sense to Rolf, whose belief in freedom and the right of every man to speak his mind seemed sacrosanct. If he could be honest, he hated the cloying Nazi dogma, but it was a simple issue of pragmatism. If he had not joined the Party he would have lost his new job, and he might have been seen as an antagonist to the Nazi state. It made no sense to risk one's life for a principle. He wanted freedom and, in the end, to go home to Dortmund; if he had to pretend to be a Nazi, he would do that to achieve his aim.

He jumped when a woman appeared in the doorway. He cursed himself for being so deep in thought he had not even heard the door open. Rolf picked up his Mauser and pointed it at the entrant. The tall oak door stood ajar for a moment and he watched as she pushed it shut with tremulous hands, entering the murky hallway.

'Halt,' Rolf said.

The woman jumped when she heard his voice. He realised the shadows where he sat had hidden him. She was perhaps forty, slim with auburn hair, wearing a brown crumpled suit. Her face revealed fear, and he noticed a faint glimmer of sweat on her forehead. The expression did not belong on that face. It was a beautiful face and one he thought should portray a smile of happiness instead. 'Hello?' she said.

'Stop there.'

She put up her hands and advanced one pace.

'I'm sorry. I came for my case.'

'Who are you?'

He was pointing his gun at her, so he realised why she seemed nervous. He lowered the weapon, then shouldered it.

'I am Francesca Pascal. I am a conservator from the Louvre. I came earlier to appraise a painting but my bag was too heavy to take upstairs.'

'Papers?'

'In my bag. Here...'

'Keep your hands up.'

Rolf grabbed the bag she wore slung over her shoulder.

He examined the wallet with her photograph and the stamped identity document.

'In Ordnung. What are you doing here?'

'I told you. My suitcase. I couldn't wander round Paris with it; it's too heavy.'

'In the suitcase is what?'

'My belongings.'

Tears formed in her eyes. 'One of your generals took my apartment and I had to leave. They took everything except what I carried away.'

Rolf understood her. It was a momentary connection such as one might feel for a begging child in the street. He softened and reached forward patting her on the arm. He withdrew his hand, realising how clumsy his gesture must have seemed. He felt awkward but didn't know why.

'It is a bad war. I'm sorry for you. I am just an ordinary soldier, I cannot help you. I will have to check the contents and I apologise for that.'

'There are some family pictures I painted before my daughter died and a few other belongings. Nothing which could obstruct the German war-machine.'

Even the tone of her voice made him want to help her in some way. He wanted to say to her, 'I am a good man. I don't believe in what the Nazi Party have done to our country. I am educated. Please forgive us.'

But it would have been nonsense. It may have been what he felt, but it had no meaning here in this hallway, here in the epicentre of the German occupation where even Rolf knew there was worse to come. Besides, it was sedition, and for all he knew she would report him.

He picked up the case, which he had not noticed before, where it stood hidden from view behind the dresser.

'Heavy,' he said.

He opened it and glanced inside. His fingers probed for a few seconds, then he shrugged. Did he really care what the woman owned? The act of running his fingers over her personal possessions embarrassed him. It was a kind of voyeurism and he hated it. Rifling through her things seemed a violation to him.

'You can go. Where will you stay? You have money?'

'I will be alright. Do you care?'

'Me? Not every one of my countrymen is heartless. You look a little like my sister. I often think how she would be if France had overrun Dortmund, in the Bundesländer, where we lived. There is no end to this. All I want is for it to finish so I can go home. I'm a Catholic, you see.'

'I see,' she said.

Rolf carried the case to the door realising it was too heavy for the woman.

'I'm afraid I cannot carry it for you. I must stay here. I wish you good luck.'

He watched as she struggled with the case down the stone steps. He knew from her papers who she was, but he wondered what would become of her. He had liked the look of her and had she been younger, he would have wanted to spend time with such a woman. But there was no time for such things now, here in Paris, in a country he had helped defeat and which he did not understand. He spoke French, but possessing the language was no key to comprehending the culture and of all people, Rolf understood that. One of his Philosophy Professors had been full of it, until they arrested him, then sent him away.

Chapter 2

"He who has faith in his heart has the greatest strength in the world."

Adolf Hitler

1

To Rolf, the street outside the apartment block seemed untidy in the afternoon sun, with its dustbins on display and the irregular cobbled roadway. Even the café opposite, with the tattered parasols and dilapidated, weatherworn, and faded tables seemed to cry out for order. The boarded up shops and the ramshackle pavement, interrupted in places by entrances to the alleyways and courtyards, did nothing to suggest the sort of orderliness to which Rolf was accustomed at home. Inside, he approved of the lack of tidiness. It held a charm that struck some kind of chord within him and made him feel like a man who, released from an institution, discovers how disorder in the world equated with freedom.

He heard pigeons cooing above him where they sat upon the ledges high above as he shut the tall door. Rolf stood for a few moments leaning his backside against it, looking around the gloomy hallway. The woman had gone. He pictured how she had struggled with her case making her way on the untidy cobbles in her brown suit, until she disappeared around a corner. None of his business. It was not his job to show concern for the French, only to obey orders, however pointless they seemed to be.

He crossed to the chair and leaning his head against the hard high back in the gloomy quiet, felt his eyelids begin to droop. He shook his head. Rolf stared ahead at the stairwell but try as he might, his eyes failed to focus and his lids closed. He thought the nap could only have lasted a few moments when a sound like a car backfiring outside the building pitched him back to reality. He was sure it was a car, or was it? Had he imagined it?

Another discharge. Then two more, then silence. Rolf grabbed his gun and sliding the bolt, slipped a round into the spout. Safety off, he approached the door and opened it a crack. He peered out into the gloom of the now dusk-painted street.

In the advancing street-shadows, he saw two figures. They held pistols in their hands. They wore suits of some dark colour and black hats upon their heads, like some nineteen-thirties gangsters in a Bogart movie he had once seen. Sierra Madre? Key Largo? The names flew away as he concentrated on the two men. They came closer and he swallowed despite the arid state of his mouth.

Easing the barrel of his gun out through the crack of the opened door, he shouted.

'Halt. Don't approach. Who are you?'

The nearer of the two men removed his hat. Even in the gloaming, Rolf could see the black, greasy, slicked-back hair, and the dark eyes. The man continued to approach.

'Halt, I said. I will shoot you.'

The stock against his cheekbone, as his instructor always

insisted, Rolf closed his left eye and drew a bead on the nearer man through the metal sight.

'Wait, we are Special Brigade. Here.'

The man reached into a pocket and withdrew a wallet. Rolf advanced, wondering what "Special Brigade" meant. He examined the proffered identification and realised they were Milice or something similar.

'Sorry,' he said. 'I thought you could be partisans.'

'No, not us,' said the man, 'them.'

Rolf looked where the man pointed. A man's body lay there face down, a small hole in his grey suit-jacket between the shoulder-blades and a pool of blood lengthening under his chest. A woman, dressed in a brown overcoat, lay face down nearby. Her brown hat lay a few feet from her, still rocking with a gentle, diminishing quiver. He approached, though he knew it was none of his business. Why get mixed up in something like this?

He jumped when she lifted her head from the cobbles. Despite the failing light, there was a pleading iridescence reflected from her eyes. Rolf reached out a hand towards her. It was the second time he had made a meaningless gesture that day and he recognised the fact of it. He drew his hand back to his side and looked at the woman.

She began to crawl. The two Special Brigade men watched, but neither reacted. She looked like a huge snail leaving a black trail in the dusk-light behind her, and Rolf backed away. It was involuntary—a reflex. He felt as if the fading of her life could be contagious; as if approaching too close would allow her to contaminate him and bring death to him too. Then shame took him. He knelt by her side, and reaching down, he turned her over. No words came, only a faint groan of pain. Her gaze met his. That glance connected them; it pierced his very soul. The look in her eyes was one of utter hopelessness. It caused him pain, deep inside, but he could not fathom why; she was not his concern. He held her. He watched as her head fell back in a slow and graceful arc. He understood her death as he had understood his mother's and his father's. It was enough. Nausea came. Rolf lowered the woman's limp frame to the ground and stood up.

'I am Guy Boucher,' a deep voice behind him said.

Turning, Rolf said, 'What?'

'Guy Boucher of the Special Brigade. We work with the Milice and the local Police. These two were partisan spies. They fled and we nailed them. You?'

'Me?'

'What are you doing here?'

'I… I'm guarding this building. A printer has escaped…'

'A printer?'

'Yes. My unteroffizier ordered me to stay here in case the rebel came back.'

'I see. Well, you'd better get about your business then. My men will clear up this…' He paused and gestured towards the two dead bodies. 'This mess. We are not usually as clumsy as this.'

'Clumsy?'

'We don't normally shoot spies in the street. We usually take them in for questioning, but the man had a gun, so we… You understand?'

Rolf wanted to say, 'So you shot them both in the back and now you are the brave killer of women.' But those words did not come. His sense of self-preservation took hold instead.

'Yes, I understand,' was all he said.

He turned and began mounting the stairs to the safety

and reassurance of the apartment house. There was no danger of his shooting the perpetrators once he was behind the doors. He still felt a water brash in his mouth. He wanted to vomit. He wanted most of all to demonstrate his revulsion at the woman's death. Entering the building he told himself how he had not joined this army to shoot women. He had joined to serve his Fatherland and further his career, but all he had witnessed since that fateful enlistment had been barbarism and cruelty.

There was no more conversation with the killers. He knew he meant nothing to them. Rolf was aware he was only a tiny loose cog in a machine of destruction and nothing he could do would make him more in these men's eyes.

As the oak door clunked shut behind him he heard a car drive away. He wondered whether the killers would lose even a moment's sleep over the two lives left seeping away on the cobbles of the untidy street. He leaned forward and vomited. The acid in his mouth awakened him and he felt shame over that too. He wanted to clear up the mess, the undigested omelette, the murder his country's allies had perpetrated, the wickedness of which he had become a part.

2

North Rhine-Westphalia, Germany, 1931

The hayloft felt dry and comfortable to Rolf as he and Annika lay on their backs, arms touching, in the gloom of the barn. Outside, the sun departing shed rosy rays across the farmlands and the farm-buildings. Fifty yards from the barn a river flowed, green and blue in the summer, and brown and swollen in the winter. On the opposite bank stood hazel and beech trees, and beyond that a stone wall separating the farmhouse from the wide fields where barley and wheat grew in alternate years. There was a smell of clean hay, and below them a cow lowed to be milked, early as it was.

'I hated him, you know,' Rolf said.

'I don't want to talk about it.'

'We are together now. We are all that survives. We must keep together.'

'And Berlin?'

'They've accepted me. I can't not go.'

'But you'll write?'

'Of course, my little sister. You think I'll reach the big city and forget you?'

'Not that.'

'What then?'

'There are big things happening in our country. I don't want you to leave me to become part of that.'

Rolf raised himself to one elbow. He reached forwards and touched her shoulder. He said, 'We are always together, whatever happens. You will be safe here anyway. I am only going to the University and then I will return and become a teacher. Mutti would have been proud.'

'She would have hated the National Socialists. They have no religion. They don't care about people, only the Party.'

'I will stay out of the politics. It is not my concern. All I want is to study and become a man who shows the way. A teacher can do that.'

'The way?'

'I just think we have a duty to be kind to others. Each little kindness makes the world a little better, doesn't it? I want my pupils to understand that.'

'By teaching them what? All they learn now in school is how to be German, how to be Nationalistic. You will never get anywhere with your views.'

'You know nothing.'

She sat up and looked at him.

'You're an idealist. I'm not going to be like that. I will keep away from all of them. You'll see.'

She stood and then slipped down the ladder leaving him staring out of the hatchway at the purple sky. The lengthening shadows seemed apt, for he felt his mood plummeting now he was alone.

Rolf felt like a man standing on the brink of a cliff spreading his arms, ready to dive into the jagged, gold and green, white- crested waters below, but knowing he might not survive the impact. For the first time since they arrived at Aunt Elsa's farm he felt he was facing the unknown. He was afraid of Berlin. The big city, the place where politics and change flowed like water in a river, where he would have to learn new rules and new codes of behaviour, just to stay afloat. He knew he would get through it, but at what cost? Would he have to sacrifice all his principles to achieve his aims?

No. Like the memories of his father, he would keep his thoughts occult; unrecognisable to any observer like a snake in the grass, always there, but never seen.

Chapter 3

"Loyalty is a matter of the heart, never of the intellect."

Heinrich Himmler

1

The oak doors springing open startled Rolf and he grabbed at his Mauser, jerking it up across his knees to point at the two figures entering the hallway. It took only seconds for him to relax and the relief was welcome; he had been feeling spooked, thinking of his father, or was it a dream? The scene flashed through his mind. He had stood in front of the big man who swayed as he raised his right hand to backhand Rolf. That so familiar movement, the precursor to pain. Then he returned. He realised he must have dozed off again and the two men who entered, shoving and laughing, in the familiar green uniforms of Wehrmacht rankers, had awakened him. He recognised them at once and the caution left him.

Rolf smiled as he spoke. 'Halt. Who goes there?'

A tall thin man, with a small, serious moustache and greasy brown hair replied. 'Suppose you want a password do you, you raving lunatic?'

His companion, a younger man of Rolf's age, with blond

hair and blue eyes, said 'Give him some space, Gerhard. He might shoot you if you don't.'

'You startled me, Johan.'

'Sleeping on duty, eh?' Johan said, smiling still.

'Why are there two of you?'

Gerhard said, 'There aren't. You're just blind drunk and imagining things. Damned intellectuals can't take their drink, that's what it is.'

Johan said, 'I'm off duty. I thought we could go out on the town tonight. Gerhard has promised to return your rifle and we can go straight to Montmartre, where the women are. I fancy a bit of French arse.'

'And if he forgets my weapon? You're crazy. No. We go back to barracks and then go eat,' Rolf said.

Gerhard, said, 'You can trust me. After nearly two years, you can trust me.'

'I can't trust everyone. I trust you though. I don't want to get into trouble, that's all.'

'And what trouble is there?' Johan said. 'We go get dunk and screw some French girls and Gerhard gets his hard on with two rifles. Come on.'

'No. We can go out once I've done my job.'

'Like sleeping on duty?'

'I wasn't asleep, just thinking.'

'About women?'

'No, about what these French secret police are like.'

'Well if it wasn't about women, I don't want to hear it. Come on.'

Johan slapped Rolf on the arm and made to pull him to the door. Rolf resisted; he looked at Johan, his eyes serious now.

'You're all so irrational. We are in a foreign country; anything could happen if we don't stick to the rules and obey orders.'

Gerhard said, 'You're just tired Rolf. Relax, there is no danger in this place. The Frenchies are all petrified of us. We are the conquerors and they are the defeated peasants who do as they're told.'

Rolf stared at Gerhard for a moment. The words stung him, because he would never have said such a thing himself. Without replying, he made for the door, followed by Johan.

Descending the steps, they turned left and Rolf wondered whether they would run into the attractive woman with the suitcase. He thought she was his kind of woman, but he knew deep inside, even if he found her, she would hate him. It was the look in her eyes as he had tried to pat her arm. It had been a look of revulsion, the conquered looking at the conquerors. What was it the Roman poet said? "Let the vanquished weep". He was right, they should weep. Hitler's Germany, of which Rolf had become such a reluctant part, was here to stay and the weeping French people would not drive them away for a hundred years.

'You know that Gerhard is a fanatic, don't you Johan?'

'He's OK in a fight, that's all I know.'

They passed a baker's on their right. It was closed of course. Those places opened for a few hours at a time and were sold out before the queues faded. Next door was a shop, boarded up with a yellow star painted on the rough wood. "Juden" glowed in smudged red below. Neither of them even remarked upon it. The sight was familiar to both of them, familiar enough to make it normal.

'Yes, but he's political. He could be a Gestapo spy for all we know,' Rolf said.

'Well, he's not spying on us is he? Shot three Frenchies one after the other at the Maginot Line didn't he? He's good in a fight and you don't have to fuck him. Forget about him. We're in Paris. Let's have a good time, eh?'

'They hate us you know.'

'Well you wouldn't expect a welcome would you? Besides, quite a few of them are OK. Wolfy's got a regular girlfriend. He said…'

'He'll wake up with his throat cut one night,' Rolf said.

'It's a crazy world my friend, but while we're here, we should try to enjoy it. There's nothing much to go home to except the war effort and the politicos with their rallies, is there? No we're doing well to be in Paris. Officers get sent here for leave and they even fight each other over it.'

'All I wanted was a job and now look at me. I passed the interviews, you know that?'

'Interviews?'

'Yes, I sat there, questioned by six University Governors and they gave me a job lecturing. Then some Nazi just walked in.'

'Just like that?'

Rolf frowned. 'Yes, he said I can't work at the University unless I join the Party, so I did.'

'What's the harm?'

'As soon as I signed up for the party, they said I had to join the army like any loyal German. The job disappeared.'

'Too bad. I joined up because my brother did. He said we'd get food and regular pay, so I signed on the line like everyone else.'

'I didn't know you had a brother.'

'He got shot at Dunkirk. Bullet got him between the eyes. Never knew what hit him.'

'Sorry.'

'I'm not. He was a bastard to me.'

'So why'd you follow him into the army, if you hated him?'

'Couldn't stand the idea of him coming home and being the one everybody admired. He was a bastard, like I said.'

The two soldiers stopped now outside the caserne where their cadre's headquarters stood, in the seventh arondissment. It was a low flat barracks, of red brick with solid, grey, iron gates and forbidding barbed wire along the metal and concrete fencing.

'I'll sign this in and be back in a few minutes. You have the passes?'

'Here,' Johan said, passing a piece of folded card to Rolf, who took it and shoved it into his pocket. 'I'll wait here, and make sure you're quick. I don't want to hang about.'

Rolf left Johan standing on the tramlines outside and saluted a passing officer as he showed his pass to the guard and entered his barracks.

Almost as soon as he relinquished his rifle in the armoury, Rolf's mood lightened. It would be a good night out if only Johan refrained from drinking too much. The lad became crazy when he drank, but not like Rolf's father, not like a bully. He was not expecting intellectual conversation with Johan, but he understood his friend. It was as if Johan anchored Rolf to the real world with his talk of brandy and women, women and brandy. Yes, he thought, Johan keeps Max from my thoughts and so I need him.

2

The meal was a good one. Both of them appreciated the onion soup to start and the duck with redcurrant sauce that followed. Rolf felt content at the end and although the restaurateur seemed elusive when they wanted to order their sweet, they never felt as unwelcome as they knew they were. They were two German soldiers, in uniform, in the quiet Parisian restaurant. Even the surrounding diners staring and often muted at the sight of them, failed to put them off. They dined and they drank. Beaujolais, Armagnac and then sweet German Kummel brought dizziness and languor to Rolf as the evening wore on, and all the time Johan talked. On and on it went, about the war, about Germany and most of all, about the French women he admired and wanted.

By eleven o'clock Rolf wanted to come up for air. He found Johan's conversation too earthy after the drinking; too ground level for him to function.

'Let's go,' he said.

'One more glass of Kummel, our sweet cumin flavoured friend. One more for the long journey home.'

Johan leaned over the table laughing and spluttering. Rolf wondered whether there was something repulsive about his friend, but he dismissed the thought. Was he not as drunk as he was? He looked around the restaurant. At a nearby table two women sat. They were middle-aged and wore dark suits with bright blouses. The one facing him had a lined, worried-looking expression and he could not see the other woman's face. He hiccupped. Behind him, he heard the sound of a man clearing his throat.

Turning, he said, 'What?'

The man behind him wore a beret; his black, dishevelled suit hung limp on his frame mocking his attempt at appearing smart. He had the look of a man who was used to better times but was making the best of the bad times. He wore a rose in the lapel of his suit and an incongruous bright, yellow, patterned cravat around his neck, but Rolf decided the fellow looked untidy all the same. The face was long and creased, showing his age. Rolf thought he must have been about seventy and could imagine a suntan on that face as if the man had come from a warmer world than the one in which he moved now.

'*Bon soir, mes amis,*' Rolf heard.

'You speak German?' Johan said.

The man greeted them again in their own language.

'It is a wonderful night, is it not?' the man said.

'Yes?' Rolf said.

Johan turned to face the stranger.

'Who the fuck are you?' he said.

'Me? I am only a friendly French entrepreneur. You look as if you need help to find the best Paris has to offer.'

Johan said, 'Best? You mean food?'

'Ah, no sir. I know of an establishment nearby where the best of France is available at a price. See her?' He pointed to the waitress, a plump girl with auburn hair and a ready smile.

'Ah,' Johan said, 'women.'

'No thanks,' Rolf said, 'we are quite happy, thank you.'

'But I can show you to a place where there are many beautiful women. They would want to be with you too. I know you German soldiers. You need the "Oou la la".'

'The girls are clean?' Johan asked.

'Of course. This is Paris; all the girls are clean and beautiful. For twenty francs, I can show you the way.'

'No thanks,' Rolf said.

'Rolf, Rolf,' Johan said. 'That's what we came for, isn't it? Lead on, whatever your name is.'

'I am Zedé. You are my guests here in my beloved Paris. I

will take you to a place where the women are so beautiful you will weep at the sight of them.'

'What are we waiting for?'

Johan stood up; unsteady from the drink, he knocked over a glass on the table and began to try to mop it up with his napkin.

'Do not trouble yourself. They will clean it all up. Come with me.'

'Look,' Rolf said. 'I don't think this is a good idea. We know nothing about this man.'

'Ah, you are too suspicious, my friend. Come, let us go.'

'I'll come along and watch your back.'

'You mean my arse? I don't need that, thanks.'

'Johan, we are not at home. Remember that.'

Johan turned to the Frenchman. 'Expensive?'

'No sir. A mere few francs, no more. You can trust me.'

Johan slapped the man on the back. 'Yes, let's go.'

Inside, Rolf knew it was a mistake. He had no desire to sleep with a whore, but he felt he could not abandon his friend. Outside, it was raining and he followed Johan and the man called Zedé, wondering what the night would bring.

Chapter 4

*"As long as an enemy resists on Germany's soil,
hate is my duty and my virtue vengeance!"*

Henrich von Kleist

1

The evening mist made the narrow cobbled alleyway seem
dim and dark to Rolf. He lagged behind, reluctant and
bitten by misgivings. He was not prudish, but his doubts
arose from caution rather than condemnation. As he entered
the back street with its glinting cobbles, he wondered if there
would be consequences or retribution for something tonight.
He thought about what his mother would have said, but it
gave him no solace. He knew she would have condemned
him for any participation, but it was not her likely admoni-
tions that prevented him; it was his own thoughts.

Rolf smelled trouble. He could not shake off a deep inner
feeling that there was something wrong. Perhaps, he
thought, it was a natural caution, but there again and more
likely in his own mind, it was the fact that he was part of an
occupying army and there could surely not be anyone in
Paris who wished them well. He wondered, as his boots
slipped and clacked on the wet cobbles, whether Johan and

he would survive the night. Then came another thought. The vision of his father's shoes, swinging in thin air. He glanced down at his own black boots and wondered whether there could be something symbolic about the click of his heels on the damp, glistening cobbles; a warning perhaps.

The house to which Zedé led them was a terraced building with a gas-lamp outside, as if it were some relic of the last war. The threshold of the house was a single granite block and he halted at the doorstep. He stood for a moment looking in through a window. The hallway across the threshold, bright and lit by a chandelier, thronged with revellers. The customers, some of them German soldiers, jostled shoulder to shoulder, holding wine bottles and glasses. They laughed and gesticulated in merriment. He could hear strands of modern music, "Lily Marlene" and later that sparrow-woman from Paris.

'Come on,' Johan said and slapped him on the shoulder.

Rolf reached into his trouser pocket and extracted a Deutsch-mark. It was worth twenty Francs and he knew his currency was good.

Turning to Zedé, he said, 'Here. Enough?'

'Yes,' the man said. He pocketed the coin and backed away.

Rolf regarded him, askance.

'You go where?'

'Ah, my friend, my job is done. Here is the soul of Paris. Enjoy it. Life is short.'

Zedé grinned showing his yellow teeth, but it brought no humour to Rolf. There was something cloying and sinister in the man and he had half a mind to grab him, to find out what was happening. The music in his inebriate ears confused him and he shrugged off the urge.

Johan grabbed him by the arm. He said, 'See that one?'

They stood on the doorstep peering into the bright hallway. A young woman of perhaps twenty, with brown curly, shoulder length hair gestured to them. Her index crooked and she waved them in with her left hand. Rolf took hold of his companion's arm.

'Look, I'm not interested tonight. We can go? Yes?'

'I want a piece of arse. You can wait outside, but you can't watch.'

'I wouldn't want to,' Rolf said. 'Look I'll wait. You go and don't be too long. I'll see you in a while.'

Rolf stepped back into the alleyway and parked himself beneath the fire escape. The rusty metal staircase loomed above him but he felt protected from both eyes and tongues. He lit a cigarette and pondered on why he had resisted the temptation. He knew it was not some religious or moral objection. Rolf was not a man to shun the realities of life; it was because he had some deep feeling inside that whore-houses in backstreets of occupied Paris might not be all they seemed, and he felt unsafe.

He stamped on the cigarette-butt and looked around. The alleyway in which he stood smelled of refuse and not even a cat stirred. The only hint of activity came from the open doorway and the only audible sounds were music, laughter and an occasional sound of breaking glass. He waited. A faint, dank smell greeted his nostrils from the mossy cobbles and he shifted his weight from one foot to the other with impatience. Surely, it could not take even a drunken Johan this long.

A sound as if the fire escape rattled came to Rolf's ears from above. Under the iron contraption, he could see nothing and he jumped when a sack containing something heavy hit the ground to his left. He stared. Like a trickle that becomes a stream, realisation came to him.

It was no sack. It was a body. Limp, misshapen and still, it lay crumpled in a heap on the cobblestones. A black stain spread around the deformed and crushed head. Rolf approached. Music still emanated from the open doorway. Laughter still came to his ears and he knelt in the wet beside the body. Turning the dead thing over, he recoiled. Rolf rose. He stood looking down. The body wore the same uniform as he did and he recognised the hair and face of his companion. It was Johan. A wide gash across his throat leaked blood.

He looked up. High above him a dark shadow moved. The iron staircase clattered as if someone at the top ran, heedless of the racket, careless of the noise, high above.

Rolf reacted. Reaching above his head, he pulled down the first rungs of the fire escape, with a screech. Mounting the damp, greasy steps, he climbed, up, ever up. Two floors up, he glanced above to see if anyone was there. A scrabbling on the roof alerted him. He ran up the remaining two flights. He climbed, one foot on the railing, clutching at the guttering, pulling himself up onto a pitched and sloping roof. The tiles rattled around him as he stood. A glance downwards revealed the drop. He could see shiny stones, Johan's body, and the edge of the iron staircase below illuminated by the yellow glow of the gas lamp. Casting aside his fear of heights, he looked from side to side, and then he saw it.

The figure of a man outlined against a faint illumination from the street below caught his eye, to his left. He mounted the roof and reached the apex. One foot either side of the ridge tiles, he waddled to catch up. The figure before him seemed to run. He knew he could do this. He knew, with the certainty that anger imbued, he would catch this killer. In the back of his mind, he pictured the look on Zedé's face as the man had backed away and his final words, proclaiming how life was short. For poor Johan it was a self-evident truism.

With boots slipping and sliding on the tiles, Rolf almost fell to one side but he regained his balance and ran on. His trundling gait slowed him but he was still angry and his rage spurred him on. He looked ahead and stopped. The shadowy figure had jumped onto an adjoining roof and stood, staring back, at a distance of twenty yards in front. The roof on which the man stood was lower down than the one on which Rolf trundled along. Rolf paused. It was not out of weariness but caution. He realised, too late, the man held a gun.

The figure ahead, stood with both arms raised and he aimed at Rolf. A shot rang out into the misty, still air. Rolf realised the man had missed and he flung himself downward grasping at the ridge blocks, desperate to hang on.

Another shot. Fingers scrabbling, Rolf began to slide. Grasping in desperation at the moss-bedecked tiles, he scraped away with his nails and fingertips in a vain attempt to save himself. The roof ended. His body flew over the edge and he grasped the guttering. It began to creak and loosen. Hanging there, he heard another pistol-shot and felt a shard of tile scratch his cheek. Still he hung on, and realising his arms and legs were not wounded, he began to feel with his feet. A hard thin metal surface. Another fire escape. Rolf glanced down.

Sure enough, he found he was dangling over another steel staircase. His feet hung only four feet from the platform. It came to him he was hanging in space and the thought, for no reason he could imagine, reminded him of his father.

Max had swung too. There was no rope around Rolf's neck. He let go, dropping to the wrought iron platform below.

Glancing up, there was no one on the roof now and he realised the killer had escaped. He touched his bleeding cheek with the back of his aching right hand and holding the black iron railing, he looked down. Fifty yards away, lay the body of his hapless friend. This was not the first time he wished he could go back in time, change things. Johan and he had been close. There was no one else in the cadre to whom he felt any real closeness, not even Gerhard. Descending the stairs, he had to jump the five or so feet to the cobbled alley. If only he had listened to his inner voice of caution.

From further up the alley, he heard a woman scream and saw a crowd gathering beneath the dull glow of the whore-house gas-lamp.

2

Rolf sat in a linoleum-floored office. It smelled of disinfect-ant and tobacco. The chair was hard and uncomfortable and a bright light shed a withering glare into his face. Outside, through the wood-slatted blinds and the open window, he heard sounds of occasional traffic passing by and he wondered how soon they would release him. Four o'clock in the morning and the questions never varied, on and on.

Rolf looked at the shadowy face behind the light. The interrogator was young, perhaps the same age as he was. He wore a small and grimy moustache, and his receding hair was greasy, slicked back from his forehead, giving his face an appearance of smoothness, as if it was stretched onto the bones of his skull. He could not see the eyes, but the voice, although even and controlled, betrayed faint menace.

'So you left the restaurant together?'

'Yes.'

'But you did not go into the building when your friend did?'

'No.'

'Why? If you were friends, and in Paris together…'

'I've told you. Johan wanted a woman. I did not.'

'You like boys maybe? Why did you not go inside?'

'I was not in the mood, that's all, and I don't like boys. Look, how long will this go on? He was my friend. We fought together and we shared our rations when we ran short at the Maginot line. Can't you leave me alone?'

'Now, now. You know we have to ask you these questions. I have to fill in a form here.' The man gestured to a sheet in front of him, on the table. 'Killing a German soldier is an important crime to us. We are Allies, are we not?'

'Look you've been questioning me for hours. I told you I was under the fire-escape when he fell.'

'Fell? You said someone pushed him.'

'I said it figuratively.'

'Perhaps you were both on the fire-escape. Maybe you argued over a woman, as drunken men do sometimes. Perhaps you slit his throat and pushed him over.'

'No. No, no, no. I keep telling you. We were friends damn it. We would no more argue over a whore than we would have shot our commanding officer.'

'But you understand this man you saw and claim to have followed, to…' he looked down at the sheet of paper in front of him, following the scrawl with his pencil, ' to Rue Pasteur, left no trace. One of our men has been up on the roof. He saw nothing to support your story. Maybe you climbed the steps to watch your friend enjoy himself? Maybe he didn't like that. Maybe you argued and then you killed him?'

'Holy Mother of Christ. You're stupid,' Rolf muttered. Raising his voice, he said, 'You're wasting time questioning me, and all the time the killer is getting away. Don't you care?'

'Of course we care. You are not our only line of enquiry. Rest assured, we will find this killer and he will face justice. You must admit, no one saw you climb the fire escape; no one was with you when this…this Johan died. You understand why you are here?'

'Surely the whore he shagged can vouch for me? What about this Zedé? I've described him to you. Are you looking for him?'

Rolf leaned forward, the strain showing on his face.

'Be calm, my friend. We are pursuing every line of enquiry, but you must admit there is an attraction in the idea that you might have fought on the fire-escape?'

'Are you arresting me?'

'I don't need to arrest you. I can keep you here for as long as I wish. Now tell me about the restaurant.'

'No.'

'If you don't cooperate, you will be detained. Now, tell me about the…'

The door opened behind Rolf. His questioner stood up.

'Sir,' he said.

A deep voice, familiar and dark behind Rolf said, 'What has he got to say?'

Backing away from the table, the first questioner said, 'He claims to have waited under the fire-escape and his friend was killed above him and thrown down. He thinks I will believe he chased an armed man across the roof.'

'Patrice, you must learn to be objective. The chance of the soldiers killing each other seems unlikely considering what we know about this Zedé. You can go, leave me with this man.'

Rolf glanced over his shoulder. The voice had stirred his memory. As soon as he took in the face, he recognised the Special Brigade killer from outside the apartment house. What was his name? Boucher. Yes, that was it.

Boucher was a tall man, thin and angular. He removed his hat and sat down. Looking up at Patrice, he waved him away. The young man left the two of them staring at each other across the table. Rolf blinked in the light. Boucher pushed the light away and leaned back in his chair. He drew a pack of Chesterfields from his pocket and a box of matches from another.

Silence hung like a mist between them, neither man volunteering any conversation. Boucher extracted a cigarette and tapped the end against the matchbox to extract and discard the loose tobacco. Rolf watched. Without any seeming haste, Boucher lit a match and after igniting his smoke, elbows on the table, he held the match up, between the two men. It burned bright until close to the man's fingertips, when he shook it to extinguish it.

'You are the German from the apartment house.'

Rolf was silent.

'Did you catch your printer?'

'Printer?'

'Yes, you were waiting for some partisan printer, weren't you?' Boucher said with a smile. He took a puff of his cigarette and exhaled a plume of grey smoke upwards into the stale air of the office.

'I was relieved before the man came back, if he did.'

'A disappointing afternoon then, all in all.'

'Look, I didn't kill him.'

'I know that. But you did desert him. You were not there when he needed you most. Would a friend behave like this?'

'You're a fool.'

'But if you had been with him at the crucial time you could perhaps have saved him?'

'I didn't desert him and I didn't kill him.'

'If you had wanted to kill him, I suppose you would hardly have picked such a public place I'm sure. The death has the signature of a resistance group working here in our streets. A man comes. He entices you away and death follows. It seems to be a recurring theme. This man who led you to the brothel? He said nothing to give himself away?'

'The last thing he said to me was "life is short".'

'Tell me about him.'

'I...I don't know any more than I've said already. I never saw him before. If I had been sober, we would never have gone with him. He was old. Looked as if he had seen better times. His suit was creased and grubby, though he wore a rose in his lapel. It seemed strange, but we were both drunk and Johan wanted a woman more than he wanted to be cautious. I've told your men this already.'

Boucher leaned back and put his feet on the desk. Rolf noticed how the light glinted on the man's shoes. They were heavy and black, like his father's.

'They are not my men. You think Special Brigade get involved in murder enquiries? No. We are only interested in the resistance. You say he wore a suit. A rose. His face, what do you remember of his face?'

'He was in his late sixties, maybe older. Face wrinkled as if he knew the sun. His lips were thin. I don't know how to

33

describe a face.'

Boucher took his feet from the desk and leaned forwards. He raised his left hand with an open palm.

'But of course. You are not trained in these things. What can one expect? You are just a simple soldier, no?'

'Can I go?'

'Of course you can go. We would never imprison a soldier of the Reich. You can go as soon as you tell me a little about your friend Johan.'

'Johan?'

'Yes, what sort of man was he? Political? A loner perhaps?'

'Johan was the salt of the earth. He thought more about strong drink and beautiful women than most men think about politics. He was a good man.'

'Intellectual?'

'No. Basic.'

'And you...' Boucher looked at a sheet in front of him on the table, 'Rolf Schmidt? You are an intellectual?'

'No. I'm educated.'

'Isn't that the same thing?'

'No. I have no political persona. I studied Philosophy at university, not politics.'

'Philosophy? The Greeks and Zarathustra? And you have no politics? I don't believe you.'

'All I want is peace and to return to Dortmund, where I belong. I hate this war.'

'Yes, just so. We all regret this war, do we not? But it is here and we must make the best of it. Now Johan, he left you behind while he found a whore?'

'Yes.'

'Not very considerate for a friend.'

'I was not interested so I waited. I didn't mind. He was

my friend.'

'You can go.'

'What?'

'You can go. I have no more questions for you.'

Rolf stood up. His knees ached from the prolonged sitting. He reached the door and Boucher said, 'I will be watching you. You understand?'

'No. I don't bloody understand. My friend was murdered tonight and your men seem to do nothing but question me.'

'Not my men.'

'All the same.'

'My men are more efficient. We find things out with greater ease than these little policemen. We have ways...'

Rolf slammed the door behind him. Although Boucher had let him go, he hated the man. There was something about him, with which he could not quite connect. The facade of pleasantness was just that. Rolf had enough understanding of men to know when they were evil. Boucher killed women and in Rolf's book, someone ought to kill him in return.

Chapter 5

"Diligence and hard work alone do not master life if they do not unite themselves with the strength and purpose of a nation."

Adolf Hitler

1

'Take a few days off. That's an order,' the Oberst said.

Rolf looked at his commanding officer, who was a short man, balding with staring brown eyes and a constant smile, which no one could interpret as humorous. Despite the cold grin, he had a reputation for fairness and Rolf always admired him. It was said in the cadre that Benzigger supported his men both in battle and in peace, and Rolf looked up to such men.

The afternoon sun shone through the net curtain behind the Oberst and Rolf squinted to see his face.

'A few days off?'

'Yes. I've read the report from the police and they seem to have given you a hard time. I would no more think one of my men would kill a comrade than I would credit the French police with brains.'

Benzigger smiled.

'I would rather do my duty, sir.'

The Commanding officer frowned. 'Your duty my boy, is to do what I tell you, understand? If I tell you to take four days leave, you will do it. You are not confined to barracks, but at least try to give a bit of breathing space between the local police and us. You know they are pestering to have you in for questioning again?'

'No sir. I did not.'

'Keep your head down and stay out of trouble. If you create any problems, I'll have to have you transferred somewhere for your own good. Clear?'

'Yes sir,' Rolf said clicking his heels and saluting.

'Off you go then, and take this.'

Benzigger handed him a pass with his own signature, a rarity in those days when unteroffiziers did most of the paperwork. Rolf had nothing to do now for four days and as he made his way to the barrack-room where he kept his belongings, he wondered what to do. He supposed that since he was in Paris, he could take in some of the sights and perhaps sample French food, but the absence of his friend Johan put dampers on any such activity. Rolf resolved to make the most of his relative freedom and wander around Paris, seeking museums and art galleries.

He approached the gates of the caserne and a voice came from behind.

'Oi, Rolf.'

Rolf waited and Gerhard caught up with him.

'Bad luck about Johan. He was a good fellow.'

Rolf said, 'Yes. He was my friend.'

'Where you off to?'

'Figured I might go and get drunk somewhere in town.'

'Bit early?'

'I've had a bad time. They questioned me until five this morning. I had trouble sleeping. I can either go sleep or get drunk. What would you do if you were me?'

'Dunno. I can't join you, I don't have a pass.'

Gerhard slapped Rolf on the back, an uncharacteristic gesture; it left Rolf wondering if he had misjudged the man; he had never shown any empathy before.

'Maybe I'll go to the University. They have some Greek texts hardly anyone has seen.'

'Texts?'

'Yes, scrolls from ancient Greece by philosophers like Anaximander and Aristotle.'

'I don't understand. You're speaking a foreign language.'

'Sorry,' Rolf said, and then he smiled. 'Johan was quite the philosopher you know.'

'Oh?'

'Yes. He always questioned why he never questioned anything.'

'Oh.'

'Never mind. Think about it, my friend.'

He left Gerhard frowning in the narrow conduit between the barrack-houses and marched to the gates, where the guards let him through.

One of them said, 'Be careful out there. One of our chaps was murdered by some Froggie bastard partisan the other day.'

'I'll be careful,' Rolf said.

With his hands in his pockets, he crossed a bridge and turned right, following signs to the Eiffel tower. He knew the Louvre was close by and the only thought occupying his mind was to see some of the sculptures by Rodin. Although he had read a great deal about the great sculptor, he had only seen his work in pictures. He could hardly wait to see the real thing. He understood it was not a German thing to do, and some might have seen his desire as un-patriotic, but all the same he thirsted for some kind of cultural relief, for an airing of his soul.

No galleries or museums were open and Rolf found himself wandering the streets, dejected and missing his friend. There seemed no mental escape. As he walked visions of Johan's body falling to the street from above him, came and went. A public library in the eighth arondissment presented itself and he entered like any of the other customers. The domed ceiling reached far above and he looked up at its ornate plastered surface admiring the cherubs and the painted shields.

Behind the desk, a middle-aged woman with permanent-waved hair looked up at him above thick glass spectacles and smiled. It was the first time anyone had smiled at him since he set out into the Paris streets.

'I wonder,' he said, 'if you have books by Ernest Hemingway.'

'Naturally. This is a library.'

'Where…'

'Up the stairs and turn right. There is an area reserved for American authors. Look out for the sign.'

'Thank you,' he said.

As his left foot touched the first stair, he heard her say, 'Excuse me?'

Rolf turned to face her and he said, 'Yes?'

'Are you allowed to read such books?'

'You question my taste?'

'No. I just heard about the book burning. I thought all you German "allies" hated such works.'

'Please, do not condemn us all with the same rules. I have a degree in philosophy. Hemingway is interesting because he uses narrative prose in a concise way no one else does.'

'But not popular at home?'

'No. Illegal at home. I hope you will not identify me.'

'Me? No. I am happy to point you the way.'

Her smile broadened and Rolf made his way up the stairs. He wondered whether he had made a fool of himself. What did he know about modern American writing? But Hemingway interested him. It was the clipped descriptive prose and the use of fast-paced narrative which seemed to make the books come alive. Reaching the aisle he was seeking he took hold of a book entitled "A Farewell to Arms". His professor had recommended it, but they had burned every copy at home and the leather-bound volume greeted his hand with a pleasure he could feel in his soul.

He sat down and read. The story was everything he had hoped for and he wished he could borrow the volume, so he took it downstairs.

'I'm sorry. You have to be a resident in Paris to borrow a book.'

'But I could be here for the rest of the war.'

'I'm sorry,' the librarian said. 'You could come back and read perhaps?'

Putting the book down with his face showing disappointment he bowed and clicked his heels, 'No. I am sorry to disturb you. I wish there was no war and we could all be at peace.'

He felt stupid to say it. He meant it, but he knew if the woman reported him there could be accusations of betrayal and sedition. The librarian stared at him, saying nothing. He turned and walked from the building. He was not behaving as he should. Rolf knew he needed to act with discretion but the loss of his friend seemed to have changed things inside him. He knew his world was crumbling. There was no art, no freedom of expression any more. All he could hope for was a quick end to the struggle, a train home, and a peaceful end to his life in years to come teaching in Dortmund.

Rolf felt his stomach rumbling and he knew he needed to eat and sleep, the latter of which had so been elusive the previous night. He looked forward to sleep even more than assuaging his hunger. Crossing the boulevard with its tram lines and wide pavements, he entered a narrow side street and jostled by a passer-by, he halted at a sign showing a picture of a duck in flight, with a menu displayed beneath.

The restaurant glowed in the basement—a bright light to entice the hungry. Rolf descended the stairs and for once, he held no feelings of danger or the necessity of caution. He was in France, in Paris and he was hungry. The combination of these things conspired to make him want a place where no one would castigate him for his Aryan background. He knew however it was a pipedream. This was occupied Paris. His people were conquerors and oppressors and he knew everyone around acted with either revulsion, or fear. It was fear, making people capitulate. It was hatred making others kill, yet for this one moment, he did not care. He wanted to enjoy far more than he wanted to belong.

Entering the restaurant, he removed his tunic, hoping to appear informal and relaxed. The room he entered had ten tables with red and white chequered tablecloths. Each sported an empty wine bottle, holding a burning candle, illuminating the grey stone floor and the low, undulating, lathe-and-plaster ceiling. On his left as he entered, he noticed a bar behind which a mirror made the room look bigger.

Rolf chose a table in an alcove facing the door where he had a good view of anyone entering. It was perhaps a sign of his inner caution, though nothing rang alarm bells in his brain. He took a seat and glanced at the menu. His first thought was how they could manage, in this war, to provide such splendid fare.

"Canard au Cerise" he read. He could almost taste it.

As he perused the menu, he thought about Johan and his appetite began to wane. His stomach rumbled all the same, so within minutes he gestured to the waitress who stood by the bar. She had wide brown eyes and mousey, long hair. As she crossed to him, he noticed how her petite, curvaceous figure seemed to move with the grace of a dancer. Jean Harlow came to mind. Her face, with its high cheekbones, was attractive, but showed no pleasure when she regarded him. He knew it was because he was an occupying soldier, with whom no one dared express what they felt.

'Yes?' she said.

'Can I have some bread and…'

'We have no butter.'

'Just bread and oil then.'

'Yes?'

'Can I have the duck with cherries, please?'

'No. there is no duck tonight.'

'Oh. What do you have, then?'

'Cassoulet is good tonight. You have to understand supplies are not normal.'

'I understand. Cassoulet will be fine, thank you.'

She turned and he called to her, 'I want some wine please.'

'Yes?' she said, returning to the table. She looked up at the ceiling, her gaze returning to Rolf's face. The stare was adamant, unyielding. Rolf hesitated. He had now seen all of her to three hundred and sixty degrees and the sight of her body aroused him. She was a beautiful girl.

'You recommend?' he said.

'I recommend you and all your compatriots return to Germany where you belong.'

'Please, Rolf said, 'I only want a bottle of wine.'

'The Bergerac is good enough for you,' she said.

'Thank you. That will be fine.'

'Pay in Deutsche Marks?'

'Yes, if you wish.'

She gave him no reply, nor did she spare him a second look.

He thrummed his fingers on the table and looked around. His table had a clean tablecloth otherwise all around him, the place seemed spartan and bare. He took in the grey stone floor, the plain walls without pictures or hangings. Bleakness stared him in the face, but he knew it was the war and nothing could be as it was before. It broke his heart to know he was one of the men responsible for all this drabness and emptiness.

2

The little white beans made sense to Rolf. They were succulent in their own special way and the flavour, masked by some herb he could not identify, although elusive, seemed to soothe him. Little meat found its way into his portion, but all the same when he finished he felt content. He wondered whether it were his thoughts about Johan inspiring his maudlin mood as well as remorse. Johan was not a man to take life seriously and it may have been that fact attracting Rolf to him in the first place. Johan required no effort on Rolf's part. The man never questioned whether what he said aloud might be offensive. It was as if his friend was detached from the real world, existing in his own bubble containing women, beer and brandy; he was like Max but benign.

A phonograph played a waltz in the background as he ate. Rolf did not recognise the music: it was not German. The thought was a relief. He hated Bruckner and detested Wagner even though he knew it made him unpatriotic. He preferred the modern music. He enjoyed "Lilly Marlene" and even those songs by French singers like Piaf. He ate and he thought.

Rolf felt he had learned something: hunger stimulates depressive thoughts. Now, with a full stomach he felt more optimistic, and he ordered another bottle of wine from the reluctant waitress.

Why not have a drink? He had the wonderful sight of the gorgeous waitress to enhance his night although he knew she would never make demands of him, physically or mentally. He knew she hated him; he was getting used to the idea of being a pariah in Paris. The more wine he drank, the less he cared.

The restaurant was becoming crowded, and he looked at his watch. It was a fine watch, he thought. Swiss. They seemed to have the knack of making efficient things. Was not their banking system the best in the world?

To his left, three workmen sat eating the same bean stew he had eaten and he noticed how, after a few mouthfuls and a few glasses of wine, they began to speak louder and smile more often. To his right was an older couple. They spoke seldom, and when they did they did not smile. The woman wore a hat with a lace veil folded up over her head. Rolf examined her face. Beneath the wrinkles and the down-turned mouth he thought he could discern a woman who once had been beautiful. He imagined her as a young woman and then looked at the waitress. She caught his eye but shifted her gaze as soon as she realised he was looking her way. He sipped his wine and did not stir. People-watching. He enjoyed it and it took his mind away from where he was and who he was. Two young men drank brandy from small balloons at the bar, laughing and drinking, drinking and laughing. It felt to Rolf as if he had not heard the sound of pure, unfettered laughter for a long time.

Then the three men entered. They wore the black uni-forms of the SS and Rolf recognised they were not officers as there were only two flashes on their collars. He had nothing against them. He had, after all, once enquired whether he could join the SS, only to be rejected as soon as they found out about his background. A father who killed himself and a Catholic mother who was not from Germany mitigated against his joining the "elite". There were times when he had looked back and felt only anger at the rejection. When he analysed his thoughts he realised it was all a form of jealousy. In his most lucid moments, he knew he was better off out of the SS. They were brutal and indoctrinated to a degree to which he could never have succumbed. Besides, whether it advanced his career or not, he had an intellectual revulsion for these people now, because he knew they were his inferiors even though he was not allowed to join them.

Rolf doubted whether any of the three men was older than twenty-five. It was clear they were drunk when they entered and he began to feel irritation at their arrogance as they sat down and shouted for service.

The waitress came at once. She knew what was good for her.

'Yes?' she said, standing next to the men, pad poised, and pencil in hand.

The music drowned out the following conversation but Rolf watched as she bent forwards to catch what the man said. The German smiled, glancing down the front of her blouse. Then he made a grab for the girl. His arm encircled her neck and the kiss he aimed landed on her chest as she withdrew. The girl had dropped her pad and pencil and fought to free herself from the soldier's embrace. She placed both hands on the man's chest and shoved, extricating herself only with force. She landed on the floor by the table with the three workmen, one of whom leaned forward to help her to her feet.

The girl straightened her clothing, a brown hip-hugging skirt and a white lace-decorated blouse, and stood glaring at the SS soldiers. Rolf watched as the SS man to his right knelt from the table and scooped up the pencil and paper. He looked up. A mischievous smile laced his lips.

He said, 'Here. You dropped something. Come and get it.'

The girl, fury written in capital letters on her face, stood her ground. After a full minute, she turned to the bar and made her way to the barman. Hushed conversation ensued between them and this time the barman emerged to take the order.

The man nearest Rolf stood up. He swayed a little as he spoke. This time Rolf heard what he said.

'Get the woman. Get her back.'

'She does not wish to serve you. Do you wish to eat?'

'Eat? Yes. Get the waitress and go hide behind your Maginot bar.'

The man indicated the bar with an unsteady forefinger. Rolf began to experience an increasing sweat. He drank a mouthful of wine; his mouth was dry. His heart beat fast, but he dared do nothing.

'Let me take your order. Please, there is no need for trouble. We are a quiet, friendly auberge. No need to...'

The nearest SS man stood up and grabbed him by his shirt-front.

'Get the fucking waitress and do as you're told, Froggie.'

He raised his right hand and slapped the man across the face. The other two laughed. When she saw this, the waitress approached and tried to extricate the barman. Both of the seated SS men stood. One grabbed the girl by the shoulders. The other ran his hands over her thigh.

'We'll have you for the main course, I think.'

It was enough. Rolf stood up, the table in front of him cockled over, spilling the wine and the plate and the candle-holder. He looked at the three workmen. They looked down at their plates. He understood their impotence. There was silent surprise from the young men at the bar.

The three soldiers looked at him. This was not Rolf's battle and he knew it. It was just that he could take no more. It was as if the submerged anger always seething beneath the façade of his otherwise placid exterior became unleashed, as if an eruption took place. It was uncontrollable.

With the speed of an express-train he crossed the five or so feet between him and the nearest man. His right fist connected with a crack on the man's jaw. The soldier released the waitress as he fell.

Open mouthed, the other two seemed frozen to the spot. Rolf pushed the girl away and confronted the other two. The man to his left tried to hit him, but in the drunken haze in which Rolf knew the fellow was floundering, he had no chance. Rolf deflected the blow with his left and struck again with a heavy right hook that lifted the man in the air and slewed him across the table. The remaining soldier stood still, staring as if the world around him was changing and he remained isolated within the bubble, speechless and immobile.

'You'd better get your friends out of here,' Rolf said, panting at the sudden exertion. 'You are a disgrace to the German army.'

The unharmed man knelt at the side of the man on the floor. He looked up at Rolf.

'You've broken his jaw, you bastard.'

'You're lucky it wasn't his neck. Now get out before I do lose my temper.'

Staggering, the three men left, the unharmed man supporting his colleagues.

'You'll get a court martial for this,' he heard as the door slammed shut and the next thing Rolf became aware of was a hand, patting his shoulder and one of the workmen proclaiming in his ear that he was a hero.

Calm came to Rolf. He felt as though the release of his violent temper, his tiger in a bottle, had cleansed him. He felt relaxed and his mood lifted. A glass appeared in his hand and the old woman at the adjoining table rose and filled it with wine. He turned to the waitress.

'Are you all right?'

She regarded him with a cold stare and said nothing, then retreated to the bar. The barman shook his hand. 'Thank you. You saved us. I could not react. They would have put me in prison for assaulting one of them. What could I do?'

Rolf looked at the man. 'Nothing. I lost my temper. I am sorry about my countrymen. Please,' he said, raising his voice, 'I am sorry. They are not Germans. They are scum.'

He wanted to ask the girl her name. He wanted her friendship, but she remained behind the bar and he felt an urgency to leave. He knew military police would arrive in moments and there was no time. Rolf grabbed his tunic. He pushed his way to the door and their eyes met. The question was on his lips, but the look on her face was still one of utter disgust, so he had no chance to say what he wanted.

Outside in the dark of the alleyway, Rolf looked down into the basement and watched for one last moment as the girl began to clear up. Her backside wiggled as she bent to pick up the broken glass on the stone floor. He swallowed with regret. If only things were different. If only he was a tourist and there was no war. The inevitability of her rejection measured as nothing against his certain knowledge that he could change nothing. He knew he would never see her again.

3

It was raining hard outside as Rolf stood to attention in the Oberst's office. The spattering raindrops made a noise like machineguns on the windowpane. Two soldiers in green stood behind him. Benzigger looked up; he was frowning.

'You know why you're here?'

'No sir.'

'You would never make it in the SD. You can't lie convincingly. You know why you're here.'

'Potentially.'

'Potentially, sir.'

'Sir.'

'Look, I give you a few days off as a personal favour…' Benzigger looked up at the two soldiers standing to attention behind Rolf. 'Get out,' he said.

'Look Schmidt,' he said, as the two men left, 'I give you some leave personally, and you do what? Assault three SS rankers in a restaurant.'

'I didn't…'

'You're a philosopher yet you tell lies?'

'There are many layers to an onion I suppose, sir.'

Benzigger smiled. 'I've known you since you first got posted to my unit. I've watched as you trained and became one of our best fighters. When you saved my life in that trench, I knew I owed you a favour. You even got drunk with us that night after the fall of the Maginot line. Don't play me for a fool.'

'No sir.'

'Well?'

'There were three of them. They were assaulting a waitress and a barman who could not protect themselves. I lost my temper.'

'One of the men got a broken jaw. This is possibly very serious.'

'Sir.'

'As it happens, you're lucky. They can't identify you specifically and the complaint coming direct to me indicates they aren't certain it was one of my men. If they come sniffing round here though, they might find you. I'll have to have you posted where they won't find you.'

'Sir?'

'No, not Russia. I've had a request for some men for

guard duty at the Police headquarters here in Paris. An easy job and I can't see how you can possibly get into trouble doing that. You'll get instructions in the morning. Meantime you're confined to barracks. Now get out and control your temper, or it's a court martial for you.'

Chapter 6

"In the end, all ups and downs can be endured, all blows of fate overcome, if there exists a healthy peasantry."

Adolf Hitler

1

The Prefecture in the fourth Arondissment was a huge building. It stood upon an island in the Seine and access existed from the Pont Michel to the south and the Pont au Change to the north. Rolf looked up as he entered, his gaze greeted by inset statues in the frontage and the big rectangular windows. He thought there was nothing forbidding about the building itself, ancient and well-kept as it was.

A wide boulevard by the Seine backed by the façade of the grey, stone building with a grand entrance, seemed excessive for a place where Vichy-French policemen and German soldiers kept their vigil over the supposed dangerous, peaceful population of Paris. Despite the feel of the exterior he had no illusions about the place. He understood what they did. They bowed to his army's whims and wishes. On his first day, they ushered him to Room 35, home of the Special Brigade Section 2. The anti-resistance squad. Allied to the police, their jurisdiction and their powers exceeded anything normal policing required. By the third day, he realised they had carte blanche to do anything they wished to captured partisans and accused traitors. Guard duty meant standing, endless standing, but it gave him time to think, and thinking is a philosopher's backbone.

Rolf was pleased that Gerhard accompanied him, that first day. What surprised him was how Gerhard had volunteered for the secondment. They mounted the stairs shoulder to shoulder and Rolf asked him why he had volunteered for this duty.

'It's better than sitting around the barracks all the time. At least we are in civilian territory. The hours seem generous. One night in four. Not bad.'

'What are we to do here?'

'Guard duty, they said.'

'Standing about. No fighting at least.'

'No fighting.'

'That's why you volunteered isn't it?'

Gerhard said nothing. Rolf understood. Gerhard was political, he was not a natural fighting man, and any peaceful duty would suit him. They had that wish to avoid violence in common; at least Rolf had it, when he was sober.

There were no cells in room 35. Two large rooms separated by a heavy wooden door made up the main quarters of the SB2. They were of generous proportions, with concrete floors and wide, high windows. It was not until they entered the Room 35 interview room he realised where he had heard of the Special Brigade. It was a long room with barred windows marching along the right hand side. Lined up opposite the window were benches with an iron rail behind them. Across the grey, hard floor at the far end of the room a man sat, black-suited and with slicked-back hair. Seated behind the rough wooden desk, Boucher looked up at him. The dark eyes showed no humour, but the man smiled a smile, thin as a knife slash.

'You?' he said.

Rolf experienced a jolt of mental discomfort but said nothing. Boucher spoke in German, each syllable enunciated with a precise slowness that made Rolf shudder.

'Rolf Schmidt. I never forget a name. Unfortunate what happened to your colleague was it not?'

'Yes. Unfortunate.' Rolf was uncertain what he should feel, but he knew what to say.

'Maybe we will catch the fellow who did it. You may have the pleasure of helping him to confess, who knows?'

The man smiled but this time humour showed in his eyes. It was his little joke. Rolf remained silent, wishing he could be elsewhere. Of all the places for them to post him to, this was the one he would have fought to turn down, given the opportunity. How could Benzigger have sent him here? Rolf was a soldier, not a torturer. He looked at the floor. Bloodstains marked it and Rolf understood where he was. It was a place where Frenchmen destroyed other Frenchmen. He recalled how Boucher killed women; perhaps he tortured them too.

'Schmidt. Pay attention will you? You are here to guard the prisoners. I expect you two to remain at their sides at all times when they are out of their cells, and to accompany them to their accommodation below. They are often dangerous and desperate men. If one of them escapes, I will hold you personally responsible. *Compris?*'

'Yes.'

'Yes. Sir.'

'Yes sir.'

'You say nothing,' Boucher said, regarding Gerhart.

'I understand my orders, sir. Is there more to say?'

'No. Here.'

Boucher picked up a sheet of paper on his desk and proffered it. Gerhard stepped forward and took it.

There was a name typed across the top and a number of scribbled observations below. "Spartaco Dolenz" it said.

Boucher said, 'Fetch this one from the cells, basement floor. I need to question him.'

They stood to attention, clicked their heels and turned to the bottle-green painted door. It shut behind them; as they descended the stairs Gerhard said, 'He's the one who questioned you?'

'Yes. There is something cold about the man. He shot a woman.'

'You know this? How?'

Rolf explained.

'He was just doing his job. We are here to do a job and ask no questions. Let's not ask questions. Let's do the job and when the war ends we will leave this place and forget all about these evil little policemen. They are worse than the SD. At least the SD aren't pursuing their own men.'

'Yes. You're right. I just don't like this man. He's French, but he acts like he's a Nazi.'

'So he's a French Nazi. We're all Nazis. You said you were in the party like me, yet you don't have any of the hallmarks.'

'No. I joined to advance my career, but I'm not one of you.'

He heard Gerhard laugh.

'What's so funny?'

Gerhard still laughed. It was as if the private joke held

55

such humour Gerhard was unable to voice his reply.

In the end he said, 'I'll tell you because you are not one of them. My father was a communist. I admired my father. I was lured into the Social Democratic Party because they preached freedom for all Germans whether they were workers or aristocracy. It turns out they are not the people I thought they were, but my time will come one day. They have done a lot for Germany, you know. After the First War, our country was crippled. They provided a crutch, which let us stand on our feet and walk. I just, like you, think their methods are of no social value. And you know, I'm a Lutheran like you.'

'I'm Catholic. My mother was Greek.'

'The story of Rolf Schmidt gets worse and worse.'

Gerhard chuckled but they had descended the stairs to the basement. Turning left, they walked down a concrete corridor, to where a German soldier stood to attention in front of a heavy iron door. He was a stranger to Rolf. A small window with iron bars glared at Rolf from the door.

Handing the paper to the guard, Gerhard paused long enough to comment on the weather and the man let them through into another long corridor some with open, barred cells, others with heavy steel-reinforced doors lining either side. There was a smell of disinfectant in the air and Rolf looked at the prisoners as he walked past their cells. Some lay on their wooden bunks, others stood at the bars, watching as they passed by. The striking feature to Rolf was that no one spoke. The corridor, with its tiny cells, was alive with silence. The atmosphere depressed him and reinforced the oppressive silence.

The German guard, whose name was Kurt, smiled as he opened the cell door, and said to the prisoner, 'I'm sorry. It's time.'

Rolf regarded the man. He was short and dark, his curly hair an untidy mop above an aquiline face. His eyes, dark and darting, held a questioning look and Rolf reached forward as he emerged, clutching the prisoner's upper arm. Gerhard took up the opposite side and they walked, three abreast, along the smooth, grey concrete tunnel to the iron door at the end. Rolf could feel how the prisoner's arm trembled as they mounted the stair and he saw sweat on the man's face. He began to wonder what questioning they would subject him to, but knew it was not his responsibility. He was only obeying orders. What else could he do?

2

Berlin, May 1933.

They called them "corrupting foreign influences" and Rolf had smiled when he read the leaflet. The German Student's Association pasted posters, handed out the leaflets, and as far as he could understand, issued threats to enforce their forthcoming event. To be German. That was their driven philosophy. They could never have understood what an intellectual might have made of it. "To bring an end to Jewish pseudo-intellectualism" and establish German values and German morals in the Fatherland seemed to be their cry. But to Rolf, all books were a means of communication, whether stories or deep-thinking academic works and they made the world safe. There was security in their diversity— he knew this. It was a safety protecting the world from extremes, for extremes threatened liberty, his Professor had said. Rolf believed that too, and it had become embedded in his mind. His father was, after all, an extremist in his way—

extreme in his violence and extreme in his drunkenness.

He stood there in the spring night, surrounded by shouting, gesticulating young people in brown shirts, white blouses and brown skirts, the colour of shit, as they listened to and cheered the tall thin man on the podium. Wind took away much of the speech, though that brought relief to Rolf. They all sounded the same, these politicians. They wasted their rhetoric on him. Had he not read his Zola? Had he not enjoyed his Hemingway? Yet despite his own beliefs, he was here anyway in the dark wet, windy night.

Rolf wore his raincoat, a heavy gabardine affair, but it was for a reason. The coat had deep pockets and he needed them for what he intended. He looked to the west at the State Opera House, the ancient facade reflecting the flames before him as he stood in the queue. He hoped it was a sign that some semblance of culture and decency would prevail in the end. At least they had not destroyed that with fire, like the Reichstag. To the north was the Unter den Linden Boulevard down which he had walked to gain access to the square. It was familiar territory because, opposite the Opera House stood his University, the Humboldt University, where he was learning to be discriminative in what he read and to analyse without prejudice, in this strange world where prejudice was the major driving force.

In front of him was a huge blaze. Wooden struts created a glowing frame onto which they were slinging the books. Some of the students had started already, walking past and throwing volumes into the red, satanic flames. To Rolf, the fire reminded him of his own first vision of Hell. Hot, bright crimson and yellow, the heat destroying flesh and blood; tormenting the dead souls of the damned. He thought this was something similar but instead of burning dead people's souls, they were trying to destroy the thoughts and intellects of great scholars and writers. He pulled his hat down so the brim shaded his eyes and wiped away a droplet of moisture from his eye with the back of his hand.

In the distance, the politician was still flinging out his fiery rhetoric. 'No, to decadence and moral corruption,' he heard. The band that played military tunes earlier was now silent, waiting for the man to finish.

'Yes to decency and morality in family and state.'

The queue was shortening. A fellow, looking inappropriate because of his age, dressed in Hitler Jugend uniform, pulled at his coat.

'What book will you burn? Let me see.'

Rolf pulled the book from his right-hand pocket. It was a copy of a play by Heinrich Heine, "Almansor". He smiled at the fool who looked at it. Had he ever read it? Had he enjoyed the lines, which Rolf kept repeating to himself? He doubted it. It seemed obvious when the man looked down a list and smiled.

'Good. Very good. Burn it my friend, burn the filthy Jewish shit.'

Rolf smiled back and nodded. He passed the invigilator and approached the flames. He could feel the heat on his cheeks. Hellfire must be hotter than this, but the damage here was just as great in its wicked destruction, he thought.

Almost at the flames, he heard in the distance, 'I consign to the flames the writings of Heinrich Mann, Ernst Gläser, Erich Kästner.'

He made the switch without difficulty. No one watched him. It amused him now as he withdrew his hand. It was sleight of hand like a magician and it delighted him as much as the jugglers in the circus when he was seven; as much as the old man who lived on the neighboring farm who produced coins from behind the children's ears and pink handkerchiefs out of thin air. The book felt light in his hand. It was going to be easy. These people around him were fools. Blinded by stupid rhetoric, by lies and national fervour. There was hatred in his grip then. He wanted to burn the book burners. He wished he could spray them all with a flame-thrower and leave their smoking bodies lying on a bed of books, unchristian as the thought was.

He looked at the book and he smiled as he threw it, deep, deep into the inferno. It needed to be burned, it was a wicked travesty and a lowbrow meaningless, thoughtless piece of drivel and it was the only book he had been able to get, of which he thought thus. Watching the flames curling the outer cover, the thought struck him that he was perhaps just as bad as all of the fools who surrounded him. At that moment, he knew he was a prejudiced book-burner like the rest. All the same, he enjoyed his last glimpse of this copy of Mein Kampf as the flames took it. His smile remained pasted on his young face as he walked away southeast towards St Hedwig's Cathedral, the church where he had prayed days ago and where he asked for forgiveness for his sins.

As he walked, he repeated in his mind the mantra, which had been with him most of the evening. It was a line from Heine's play. "Where they burn books, they will in the end, also burn people."

It began to rain as he rounded the corner and he pulled up the collar of his coat as he walked towards the tiny apartment where he lived.

Chapter 7

1

Dolenz sat on the bench in the long, bright, sunlit office, the blinds creating stripes across his face and chest. Handcuffs grasped his hands behind his back holding him tight against the long metal rail. Rolf knew this because he had the keys. The man was sweating. His eyes darted in a nervous dance from one face to another. His left leg trembled and his knee moved up and down in a reflex jumping movement.

Boucher got up from behind the desk and indicated Rolf and Gerhard to stand by the door. The gesture was one of command as if he was their commanding officer. It irritated Rolf. Who was this Frog to tell him what to do? He stayed standing by the prisoner. It was a silent gesture of resistance and one, which he began to question, the more he thought about it.

'You don't seem to understand,' Boucher said

'Sorry?'

'Look Schmidt. I am not a soldier, but while you are here

as a guard, you do as I say. In allied cooperation if nothing else. Understand?'

Rolf sidled over to the door, hefting his Mauser. He watched as Boucher stood in front of the prisoner.

'Spartaco Dolenz?'

Silence.

'Spartaco Dolenz. You are part of a resistance group belonging to the FTP?'

Dolenz remained silent, looking up at Boucher.

Boucher raised his right hand and slapped the prisoner backhanded across the face. It was a hard blow and it drew blood from the man's lower lip. Dolenz refused to speak and Boucher turned to Rolf. There was an expression on his face as if he was looking forward to something. There was neither anger nor guile and Rolf saw only a cold anticipation in Boucher's eyes.

'Take him next door.'

Gerhard and Rolf released the prisoner and each taking one arm, guided him to the heavy wooden door. Rolf opened it. He saw another room of similar proportions to the office-room. Three men stood in the room, each of them dark-suited with jackets off, white shirt-sleeves rolled up, each of them the same age as Rolf. They did not acknowledge Rolf and his companion. There was no greeting and they stared at Dolenz, as a cat might observe a bird.

There were two large mahogany tables in the centre of the room and several chairs. Two low tables stood to the right, one with some objects covered by a blanket. The other held a gas torch and a cylinder such as welders used.

He guided Dolenz to the nearest chair and Boucher who followed behind, gestured the door.

'We won't need you for a while. Wait outside.'

Standing outside, the door ajar, Rolf heard Boucher ask questions. He always came down to the same one however, "Where is Manouchian?" it sounded like, though Rolf was uncertain since the door only remained open a crack. He heard the sound of moving furniture and more questions. The silence from the prisoner screamed in Rolf's ears.

Dolenz broke his silence. Rolf heard him scream. The sound was an animal howl and he glanced at Gerhard, the expression on his companion's face telling him everything. Gerhard's face showed what he too was feeling. It was a revulsion so deep, the temptation to leave must have been overwhelming.

Then, scream after scream after scream. Rolf pushed the door to and the cries through it were masked by the thick wood. It was as if the heavy door was now a protection for him, a way of blotting out what he could hear but not see. Despite closing the door to, he could not shut out what his ears evidenced and he became desperate for relief. He sweated and noticed he breathed hard.

He took out a tin of Lande Mokri and offered one to Gerhard. He noticed his companion's hand shook when he took one. Rolf tapped the end of his smoke against the tin and perching it on his lip he offered his friend a light. Inhaling the rough, strong tobacco smoke, he almost retched.

'I wouldn't mind an American,' he said.

'Some of the French ones are good too,' Gerhard said, exhaling a thin blue line of smoke upwards.

'French? What ones?'

A louder scream than before interrupted them and they fell silent, neither of them wishing to voice what they felt. In the end, Rolf shifted from one foot to the other and turning towards Gerhard said. 'It makes me feel sick.'

'The cigarette?'

'No. This whole set-up. It stinks. They are torturers. It isn't what I came here for.'

'But we have to follow orders. You know that. What are we supposed to do? Release the prisoner and say we didn't like the way they interfered with his rights?'

'No. I just don't want to be here.'

'I didn't know guard duty meant this. I'm asking for a transfer to better duties.'

'Benzigger sent me here as a favour to avoid facing a court martial.'

'This is a favour?'

'It's a purgatory. You came here because?'

'I just thought it would be...'

The door flew open. Boucher emerged. He looked excited. He had taken his jacket off, rolled up his sleeves to the elbow and the sweat showed as dark patches in his white shirt.

'You,' he said nodding to Rolf. 'Take him back in the cells. We'll get him back later. When you've done that, you can have a break for half an hour.'

Boucher seemed to Rolf to be breathing hard, from effort or excitement he could not tell. The two of them entered the room. There was a smell of burning. The prisoner lay spread-eagled on one of the tables and Rolf noticed the three men sat at a table at the far end of the room, smoking and drinking beer despite the early hour. One of them stood up. He smiled.

'Get this piece of shit out of here. He knows nothing.'

Rolf pictured in his head how two of them must have held the man down and the third applied the flames. Although Dolenz still wore his clothes, he realised they must have undressed him and put his clothes back on. The smell came from Dolenz's body. As Rolf began to drag the man to the edge of the table, Dolenz screamed again.

'Sorry,' Rolf said.

Wild eyed and with tears running down his cheeks, the man looked Rolf in the eyes. He said nothing, but the look was enough. There was an animal fear there, as if this man knew what was to come would be worse and Rolf shuddered to think what that might be.

Dolenz could not stand when they extricated him from his torture table and the descent into the cells became a frog-march more than an escort. Rolf took one arm and Gerhard the other. They deposited the man on the bunk in his cell and backed away. The iron-barred door swung shut with a clang and Rolf and Gerhard went outside to the courtyard in front of the building.

They stood looking at the greens and the browns of the Seine as if flowed by and a fresh breeze blew through their hair as if cleansing them. Rolf knew, however, there could be no such simple way of washing off the guilt he felt at the evil with which Boucher's mob had made them entangled. He looked at Gerhard.

'You think following orders is enough of an excuse?'

'No,' Gerhard said, lighting a cigarette, 'nor do you. You know it already.'

'I don't know what to do. This isn't my war anymore.'

Gerhard slapped him on the back. 'Off duty in four hours. Cell duty tomorrow. Maybe that won't be so bad.'

'You know what is happening. So do I. There's nothing we can do. I can't go back to the barracks either. You can. I wish you God speed.'

'I won't leave you here on your own. I'll stay. But you'll have to provide the cigarettes. They'd better be more smokeable than the ration smoke you offered me before.'

'All right. I'll get some different ones here in town when we finish.'

Standing at the door to the SB office for the next three hours did nothing for Rolf, apart from making him wish he could at least read to occupy his mind. He felt in his pocket for his mother's book several times but dared not withdraw it in front of Boucher. He felt it would be like standing before Satan himself and offering holy water. By dusk he felt only relief to be out of the place. Gerhard accompanied him and they melted into the streets to find a place to eat, before they returned to barracks. The rustic chicken stew, in the restaurant where he now felt he might be welcome after the fight, attracted Rolf, and it gave him pleasure to show Gerhard that he had found a place in Paris where the food and wine were good. They made their way to the restaurant though neither of them felt at ease.

2

Their standing orders were that none of the soldiers was allowed to wander the streets of Paris alone. It was not a rule they obeyed all the time and for Rolf on the one day when he did not have to attend the Prefecture, it was something of a relief to be out on his own. His evening with Gerhard had been a failure, because Gerhard was not Johan; he was too serious for Rolf. To cap it all, Rolf had failed to find the beautiful waitress, to his utter frustration. When he asked the barman, he discovered she was not on duty. He found it hard not to show his disappointment, but managed to pry her name out of the man though it took two deutsche marks and a few apple-brandies. Her name was Sandrine.

By the end of the conversation, Gerhard became impatient and threatened to leave, so the evening ended. Today however, Rolf was alone. Gerhard declined his offer of a walk and a meal, so Rolf wandered the streets on his own. He was a big man and he had no worries about anyone assaulting him, as had happened to a number of Wehrmacht soldiers in the streets. Besides, Rolf could not find it in himself to blame the Parisians for their bitterness. He knew the occupation was fraying the tenuous collaborative links, even in daylight.

He sauntered into a small cobbled street. The tenements rose to either side and along the roadway various shops and cafés displayed signs and billboards. Overhead, metal fire escapes lurked and the memory of Johan's body flying from one like those above, came into Rolf's mind. He stopped outside a small café, where a poster on a board advertised "Thé Dansant". He squinted at the poster, which sported a large photograph of a hall with tables around the edge and a railed-off area where men and women were dancing. A young couple pushed past him, laughing, and smiling and he watched as they paid at the door. Four francs. Four lousy francs to be happier than Rolf had ever been. It seemed to Rolf, some aspects of life would never change, although these had never been part of his own. Dancing with a sweetheart was far from either his upbringing or his immediate past, so he could not imagine himself in the same role as the boy who entered here.

Hands in his pockets, he sighed and walked on to another run-down café, this time with two metal tables outside a brown hardwood and glass entrance. The nearest parasol stood askew, knocked into its crippled pose by the weather or perhaps a drunken customer. No sign proclaimed any cheery names and no music emerged, so it suited his mood, alone as he was; the place looked dreary. Rolf straightened the grubby cloth of the parasol and brushed the seat of the wooden chair with his hand before he sat down, waiting for service. At first, he stared at the brick wall opposite and wondered what sort of place this could be, and whether they would be friendly or brusque. His uniform gave him away of course, so he held no expectations of passing the time of day with anyone. That is until she walked past.

Sandrine wore a brown beret enclosing her brown hair and her raincoat hung open over a yellow blouse and a tight brown skirt. He heard her high heels click on the stonework and he noted how she held her chin up when she approached. To Rolf there was pride in her gait as well as beauty. How beautiful she was with her neat trim figure and the sway of her hips as she walked. She seemed to Rolf to be a woman to drive men mad.

She ignored him and there was no hint of recognition in her face as she began to draw level with his table. Could he do it? Did he dare? He swallowed hard and stood up.

'Mademoiselle Sandrine?' he said and bowed in that formal German way of his.

Sandrine stopped and half-turning looked at him. There was a flicker of recognition and she said, 'Oh. It's you.'

'My name is Rolf. I am from Dortmund.'

'I see. Good evening to you.'

She turned away and began walking past him.

'Please, won't you join me?' he said.

Sandrine stopped and swivelled around. She looked so pretty, her face powdered and her lips crimson. She said nothing for a few moments as if undecided. Then she said, 'You think I am that kind of a girl? You think I drink with

German soldiers? Sleep with them? I wouldn't sit with you if you were Hitler himself.'

The vehemence of her response took Rolf by surprise. He had expected a refusal, but not with such force. From the expression on her face, he saw the bright, red lipstick not as make-up, but war paint and he realised discretion would be safer than pursuit of this girl. She must hate him. His persistence was borne of desperation. He wanted her. He wanted to be with her and hold her hand in the Paris streets. He needed to hear her laugh, or even just see her smile; it would be enough.

'Please,' he said. 'Only for a moment. I am alone. I won't trouble you again, it's just that...'

'You Germans are all the same. I know what you want.'

'No, please. I only want a moment of your company; to buy you a drink or a coffee, then we can part.' He lapsed into English-American. 'Don't get plugged with me, Honey.'

Rolf smiled. He knew she would not know what he meant but for a moment, he had visions of himself as an American smuggler on a boat in Key West.

'What did you say?'

'Don't get plugged. It's an American expression. You won't know I suppose, but it's from...'

'I know very well where it comes from. It's a Hemingway expression. One of his books. What right have you, a German, to even whisper of the gold flowing from such art? You burn books like that, don't you?'

'It's from a book by Hemingway, "To Have and Have Not". You've read it?'

'What do you want?'

'Only your company, really. I'm as quick at a whip. I'm educated. I won't disappoint you. Won't you give me just a few minutes of your time? I would be so privileged.'

'You'd be so what?'

'Privileged. To be seen in Paris with such a woman, the most beautiful woman in Paris and to enjoy her company.'

'Are you always this inept when talking to women?'

'Yes; but today I'm doing better than usual.'

'Ten minutes. One coffee. I'm going to a... Anyway, it doesn't concern you.'

'Please, none of my business. Come, sit. I will find the proprietor.'

She drank coffee, strong and black and smoked cigarettes from a bright blue pack. He drank Pernod, showing off. He tried to look like an old hand, but failed until she taught him how to add water until the milky yellowness appeared in the glass and the drink became palatable.

'You like these American writers?' she said.

'They know how to write a good story and they have the gift of conciseness. They tell stories about real people and real life yet use few words. I will go to America one day.'

'What, when it's part of the Third Reich?'

'Please. I'm not political. If I told you I'm a Catholic, maybe you would understand.'

'Oh, come on. You're a German soldier, you love Hemingway and you're a Catholic. You think I'm stupid? I'm going.'

She made to stand up and he grabbed her hand. The physical contact felt electric. Contact.

Sandrine tried to pull her hand away. 'You think I'd believe any of this? I know what you're trying to do. Next, you'll say you love me and expect me to fall into your arms like a fool. Well, I'm no fool. I hate Germany. I hate all of you occupying Germans. Let go of me.'

Rolf let go. 'See. Like Harry Morgan,' he shrugged and gestured with his hand. 'Plugged.'

'And how do you know so much about me? You've been asking people, haven't you?'

'No… Yes.'

'You admit it?'

'Please; sit down. I mean no harm. I'm not like that man in the restaurant. I asked the barman your name, that's all. If they showed American films in Paris, I would take you to see one, but I never mistreat women.'

As if swallowing some jagged pill, she sat down again and smoothed her skirt with both hands.

'They really did burn books didn't they?'

Rolf regarded her with sombre eyes. 'Yes. They did. My professor insisted we all take a book to the festivities. He even advised what book to burn.'

'Don't tell me, Baudelaire.'

'No. He told us to burn either Das Kapital or Mein Kampf. He was more in the middle himself and he hated extremists. He accused them of bringing war and destruction, but you know, he often talked like that.'

'A philosopher?'

'Yes. I'm a philosopher too. I have a degree in it.'

'German philosophy, I suppose. Nietzsche and the like.'

'No. My teachers were eclectic. Well, until some brown-shirted bastard informed on the first two and they were carted off to the east.'

'Look I have to go. I'm meeting someone.'

'Your husband?'

'No. My brother, if you must know.'

'Can I see you again?'

'No, not in this life.'

'Please. I know so little of France. The real France. I promise, I only want friendship.'

She looked undecided. 'Well, only if it is somewhere no one will see me. There are informers everywhere and some of them inform on their compatriots.'

'I'll leave a message at the restaurant. I will go anywhere.'

For the first time, she smiled. It was a radiant smile; it lit up her face and Rolf's only thought was that it made her more beautiful.

He watched as she walked down the cobbles. Even through the raincoat, her hips swayed and it was as if he could not draw his gaze from her. He felt like a man who had taken communion; his soul felt cleansed. He paid the waiter and stood to go. Then, as if a black hand had grabbed him by the throat, he reminded himself where he was going in the morning and he shuddered.

Chapter 8

"The reward of the common sacrifice shall be the freedom and greatness of our fatherland."

Dr. Goebbels

1

Alone in the damp cell corridor, Rolf wondered how long he would have to tolerate his present duties. Returning to barracks, he requested an appointment with the Oberst but the secretary offered a time when he would be on duty and could find no other time for weeks when he could access his commanding officer. On cell duty, he sat on a wooden straight-backed chair, feeling restless and irritated.

Occasional groans or cries came through the door dividing him from the cells and when he unlocked it to let other guards in and out or to check the prisoners it was always with a feeling he would see something unpleasant. There was a smell of disinfect and faeces in equal proportions and the cold concrete floor was discoloured in places by fluids whose origins he preferred not to think about. Two of the cells on the left were smaller than the rest and contained no bunks, though Rolf assumed it was because no one was there for long enough to sleep. The other cells held two prisoners each and contained bunks and chamber pots.

Part of his duties consisted of hosing down the empty cells and brushing the water to the drains along the centre of the corridor. The lighting was bright enough though there was a feeling of gloom despite the glare of the bare light bulbs. To Rolf, it was a miserable place and the only relief from his gloom was the thought that he would see Sandrine when he came off duty.

He had seen her twice since the café and they discovered a mutual love of contemporary cinema and a shared grief over the current censorship banning anything that was not German to its core.

After his inspection of the cells, there was nothing to do, so he sat and tried to concentrate on his book of psalms. Spartaco Golenz was not there. He had disappeared the previous week and Gerhard and he knew quite well where he had gone. He wanted to disappear himself. The place was obnoxious. Closing his eyes, he drifted away at times to somewhere better. It was a mental place to which he could always retreat and one which brought solace, reminding him of his mother. He recalled how her suffering seemed only to make her gentler and kinder, to his mind. He sometimes pictured how she would take him in her arms when he had fallen or tucked him in at night as a small child. He pictured her cooking 'hunter's stew'. It was the way she fried the beef and let him taste the meat before she added stock and vegetables prior to placing it in the oven. It always tasted superb to him. He reminisced how he and his sister Annika used to sit at the table after doing their schoolwork and eat the stew with dumplings and dark bread. The taste of the gravy on the bread...

Boucher's voice dragged him back to reality.

'You there. Schmidt.'

Rolf put away his book. He got up and stood to attention. 'Sir?'

'You were reading. What was it? A book?'

'Yes sir.'

'Let me see.'

'Really, sir. It won't be of interest to you.'

'Let me see and I'll know, won't I?'

'It's personal.'

'You want me to report you?'

'No, sir.'

Boucher held out his hand. Rolf remained standing to attention.

'You want me to report you to your commanding officer? Give me the fucking book.'

'With respect sir. I am a soldier. I do not have to take these kinds of orders from a civilian. I do exactly as you say because those are my orders. What I read is not a matter for the French police.'

'If it means you are a Communist spy, I think it does.'

'Communist?'

'Yes. I want to see what you are reading, and you will show it to me, is that clear? You will find I can cause you considerable trouble. I can even arrest you if I wish.'

Boucher stood close, his face inches away. Rolf could smell garlic on the man's breath, mixed with 4711 cologne. He reached into his pocket and held up the book. Boucher took it. A deep feeling of insecurity took him.

Glancing through the pages, Boucher frowned.

He would never allow Boucher to take it away. He would fight for it if it came to it. His lifeline. His comfort.

Boucher said, 'Religious are you?'

On the verge of acting, he relaxed. 'I'm a Catholic.'

'Unusual in your army, is it not?'

'Yes. They are all Lutheran.'

Boucher handed the book back as if a contagion tainted it.

'Why did you resist me? The book is harmless. There are no penalties for reading psalms, even in Germany.'

'It was a gift from my mother. It means a lot to me. I don't want to lose it.'

'You puzzle me, Schmidt. I said I would watch you. That's doubly true now. You don't fit the mould and men who are eccentric often become corrupt. You know this?'

'Not in my case, sir.'

'Next time I tell you what to do, you do it. Is that clear?'

'I always obey orders from my commanding officer. In this case, my duties are to act as a guard and cooperate with the Special Brigade. You will not find I disobey orders.'

'You aren't like the others. You worry me.'

'Sorry, sir.'

Boucher grunted and waited while Rolf opened the door to the cell corridor. Left alone, Rolf wondered if he could take this much longer. He hated Boucher and he hated the screams he heard in room 35. On those days when they interrogated prisoners, Rolf felt as though he was standing not at the door to the interrogation room, but at the very doors of Hell. He felt like a man who after death, thinks he is going to heaven, only to find he stands before Dante's gates.

On one occasion only did Boucher call Gerhard and Rolf through to help. What they saw sickened him. A man lay spread-eagled and naked on one of the tables. Two men struggled to hold him down and Rolf and Gerhard had to hold his legs as Boucher used a blowtorch on the screaming man. He told them nothing.

Afterwards, Boucher instructed them to dress the man and take him away. The prisoner, a boy of perhaps twenty, like Dolenz, could not stand and they almost had to carry the fellow between them.

It became an endless cycle of brutality, screaming and torture. Rolf began to realise his complicity was as bad as if he took part in the evil, perpetrated in front of his eyes. He knew that witnessing evil and doing nothing to prevent it, smears the observer with the same shit as the evildoer. It was implicit in his religious beliefs too. Passivity of sin was a mute complicity in his church's teachings. Obeying orders was no longer an excuse and it preyed on his mind until he felt he would burst. At night, his dreams consisted of violent sexual torments, until he awoke screaming and sweating.

Apart from those short moments with Sandrine, his whole existence here in Paris had become a torment. He wondered whether his Oberst knew it would be like this and was punishing him, though he discarded the thought. His CO was not a man like these French torturers. If he had known, he would not have sent his men here. But to tell him, Rolf had to wait weeks. It was bordering upon unbearable.

2

Gerhard seemed immune. Rolf wondered whether he was a man made of steel, for he never betrayed any emotions over the beatings, the torture with electricity or the acetylene torch. Even when one of the prisoners died in the interrogation room, he said nothing. Whenever Rolf tried to tackle him on the subject, Gerhard rejected him, changing the subject, or walking away. Rolf began to wonder whether he was the one who was wrong. Perhaps he was over-reacting and the French inquisitors were justified in their methods. His conscience, however, always worked against this. There could surely never be anything to justify inflicting pain to the point of death on any other human being, he was sure.

At times he took shelter in his religion. He studied his mother's book, he prayed, though he had never been a fervent Catholic before. In addition, the nightmares continued as the dreadful acts in which he had become embroiled seemed to become worse and more extreme. At times, he felt he was being tortured too, not in a physical sense but a mental one.

It all changed for Rolf in one day. It was a life-altering revelation and one that would shape his life from the moment he heard that first particular scream.

Rolf and Gerhard arrived to relieve two other guards, both of them men from their platoon. Neither of them spoke and the two men they replaced seemed relieved to depart, their faces a pale shade of grey. He and Gerhart took up their positions outside the door to the interrogation room. It was clear the monsters were busy: Rolf could hear muffled yelps and raised voices. He decided his situation was like being ill. He had suffered the fever and now immunity was growing. In the same way, he felt he had seen everything the Special Brigade had to offer and his distress could be no worse than they had made it already. Nevertheless, he was wrong. He was very wrong.

He jumped when the door flew open. Boucher stood there. He sweated as if some great physical exertion was now behind him.

'You there,' he said. 'Get in here.'

The scene greeting Rolf's eyes was one he would never forget. Slumped in a chair, Sandrine leaned forward, vomiting. Electrical wires were attached to her left breast and there was a smell of burning. Rolf stood ossified. Sandrine? What was she doing here?

Anger and frustration took him. He felt impotent in the face of this scene of horror. He felt as if Boucher had robbed him of the only solace he could ever have expected here in this evil place. Sandrine, not the girl he saw when he was in the town, but Sandrine the tortured remnant of the person with whom he had wanted to be. His mind flew in a maelstrom of confusion and he stood stock-still until Gerhard grabbed his elbow. As if from a long way away, he heard Boucher's voice.

'What the Hell are you staring at? Get her out of here.'

Numb and light-headed, Rolf obeyed. He reached forward to take Sandrine's arm and realised she had fainted. Loosening her leather bonds, he took her arm and Gerhard did his half of the resurrection. They walked in step to the door, the poor girl suspended between them. In Rolf, anger grew. This was his beautiful, wonderful friend. Boucher had to answer for this. Yet deep inside there was cowardice emerging too. There was nothing he could do for her, however much he wanted to. They had arrested her and would question her until she talked. But what could she know? She was a waitress, nothing more. He knew that before the war, she was a student at the Université Sud, studying literature, but even the book burning and banning in Germany could not incriminate her here. It was nonsense.

They descended the stairs and she remained unconscious.

Rolf said, 'I know her.'

'Yes,' Gerhard said. 'The waitress.'

'We have to get her out of here.'

Gerhard's face betrayed irritation. 'What are you talking about? Her goose is cooked.'

'No. We must be able to do something. Something, anything.'

'You think I'll risk everything for a woman? You're so naïve. And it's a woman who belongs to someone else. You're mad.'

'Gerhard, surely, you suffer as much as I do?'

'Suffer? No. I just switch off. I have to. I don't care about these Frenchies. Why should I? They never did anything for me, why should I sweat about what they do to each other? I don't care you see, and besides I have to follow orders.'

Sandrine began to murmur. Rolf could not interpret what she said, but the sound of her voice brought nothing but distress to him. They reached the final set of stairs. She mumbled something about the metro.

Rolf said, 'Sandrine? Sandrine?'

They pushed their way past the guard at the first doorway. Still holding her up, they came to an empty cell. Rolf swung the iron-barred door aside.

'No, not there,' he heard the guard behind him say.

He turned his head. 'What?'

'Not there, this one. It's where they took her from.'

He gestured one of the bare empty cells, one with no bunk and only a bare concrete floor, hidden from view by a green metal door with a barred hatch.

'But she needs to lie down.'

'She looks like she'll lie down anywhere considering the state they've put her in. In here.' Gerhard said, 'Why not put her in there?'

He gestured the adjacent cell with its bunk and blankets.

'Sorry. Express orders. Don't fret. I'll give her some water when she wakes. I'm not inhuman.'

The man smiled as if they were carting a sick dog to the veterinarian's. It was as if he was a kind man ready to help. Rolf knew the truth. The guard was as guilty of the cruelty as any of them were.

Sandrine. He had to do something. But what?

He knelt at her side as she collapsed to the concrete floor against the wall. He touched her bruised cheek. Her head hung as if she slept.

'Look will you get out of here?' the soldier said. He grabbed Rolf's shoulder. 'We aren't here to relieve suffering. Get out.'

Rolf looked up at the face above him. He knew it was an illusion, but the face twisted into a gruesome, black face with red eyes—like Satan himself. He shook his head and the world returned. Glancing back over his shoulder then shutting the cell door, he wondered if his world had become some kind of living Hell and the only way out was to accept and acquiesce.

2

The night brought nightmares, the morning brought pain. Rolf awoke with a scream on his lips. Sandrine. She weighed on his mind before he slept and fitful dozing was all he achieved. It was his job, his duty, to guard prisoners and be at the disposal of the Special Brigade, Boucher in particular. His military oath and "Meine ligen pflicht" came to mind but his "holy duty" could not be the torture of young women. Anger, remorse, and guilt combined in his tired brain, until in the end he sat up, abandoning the elusive notion of sleep. The man in the bunk next to his stirred in his sleep and Rolf pulled on his trousers and groped beneath the bed for his shoes. Standing, the tiredness dissipated and he left the barrack-room in silence. Outside, he lit a cigarette and glanced at his wristwatch. Four a.m. Too early to rise and too late to go back to sleep. He stood outside and studied the weekly NSDAP poster pasted over the previous weeks' propaganda. It read, in black and red archaic print:

Each offense against racial purity
Is a sin against God's will
And against the divine
Order of creation.

Hans Schemm

He recalled how Gerhard, Johan and he had laughed at these quotes when they appeared on the wall each week. The poster meant nothing to any of them; the words were not part of their world, a world where comrades died and they killed for their country.

To Rolf the casern's silence was oppressive—it gave him too much space in which to rack his mind. He sat down on the cold, grey concrete step and thought.

It was as if he too was being tortured. He knew every bruise and every welt as if he could feel them on his own skin. He felt as though they had put him in that chair too and burned him with the blow torch. He also knew that if he had to stand and hear her cry and scream it would make him mad. He thought about his mother and her suffering, through which she spent time loving him and Annika, as if the abuse was all a sideshow, a background against which she could still express her love for her children. Yet nothing ever happened. At times, he resented her and even her love. Why had she not left his father? Why had she endured? Even poverty would have been more tolerable than the violence, as far as Rolf could see. Had she loved him? Had she stayed out of sympathy for the tears Max had shed when he was sober? Rolf knew the truth. He acknowledged she had loved the monster. Like a man may love the source of his own destruction—a kind of addiction, like alcohol, like drugs.

What could Sandrine possibly have done? He knew her and there seemed to be nothing she could be involved in that could attract the attention of the authorities, apart from watching an occasional forbidden film. It was absurd. Two hours passed and he was no nearer to settling his mind than when he arose. The camp was stirring; he could smell sausages cooking and heard the sleepy sounds of men awakening all around.

Rolf, showered, shaved and dressed, walked to the prefecture ready for work. Every step closer made feelings of longing bruise his mind. Every few yards, he grew more frightened of what the day might bring. Would he stand it? Could he bear her suffering? If they did it to him, he could endure. If only they somehow could change places he would be satisfied, perhaps happy, but he knew there would be no relief. Boucher and his torturers were at work and there would be no cheap holiday from pain for Sandrine or Rolf either.

This time they rotated him to cell duty, and he determined he would find Sandrine and help her in some way. It was too much to hope for that his help could mean much, because he knew they deported prisoners when they had finished with them, east, to work camps. In the end he determined to speak to Boucher. The man must understand he had arrested the wrong person.

Sandrine was innocent—he knew it. Perhaps there was some chance the man would listen to him.

3

Striding up the stairs of the prefecture, Rolf made up his mind to speak out for once. For Sandrine. How could he stand by as they hurt her? What would he do to prevent it? Would he help her escape? Would he ruin everything he had spent such time to build, for this girl? Sometimes he thought he hardly knew her, and anyway she hated him and his people, but he dwelt on the thought and realised she did not hate him, only the occupation and the war. Had she not been warm and friendly when they last talked? Had she not laughed and chatted on that last night? The problem was that he had come away from their last evening together thinking he could love her. It was the first time he had thought that about a woman, but it remained in his mind. The thought that she was now hurt, injured by Boucher and his evil torture, crushed him. He had to do something.

Boucher sat behind his desk as Rolf burst in. He looked up, a thin smile on his lips, as if there was nothing amiss. Rolf strode to the desk.

'That woman from yesterday. Sandrine Lebeau. She's innocent.'

'Innocent of what?' came the reply. Boucher, unmoved and it seemed not surprised, continued to smile as if they were talking about the weather.

'She has done nothing; I know her.'

'You know her?'

'Yes, we meet sometimes and talk about books. There is nothing in her to arouse your suspicions.'

'You don't know her.'

'I do.'

'No. She is a member of a terrorist group who assassinate German soldiers and cause a great deal of damage to the infrastructure of the state.'

'She told you that?'

'Not yet.'

'She is just a girl; can't you let her go?'

'I will. I will. I just need time to prove she is innocent. We don't just reveal guilt, we prove innocence, and if, as you say, she is not guilty, she will go home soon.'

'You mean that?'

'Of course. I'm not a monster.'

Rolf swallowed, perhaps he had misjudged this man.

'I have a little job for you.'

'Job?'

'Yes, I want you to note down every time and place you have seen this woman. You see, the apparent friendship with you may have been a ruse to get you alone and for her friends to kill you. She's done that many times, believe me.'

'You're lying,' Rolf said.

'We'll soon find out, won't we? What was it Goethe said? God gives us the nuts, but we have to crack them? They all crack in the end.'

Rolf realised how easy it could become to see Boucher as plausible or even reasonable. The man had almost fooled him. He knew he was, in truth, a monster, and he realised, too, that if Boucher could lie about his own view of himself, he would lie about letting Sandrine go free. Aware a confrontation would only cause deeper problems for her he forced himself to relax, unwinding the coiled spring of his emotions.

'She is only a waitress; a student. She has done nothing,' Rolf mumbled, persisting.

'You think you know? Already she has given us the names of some of her people.'

'Under torture anyone would say anything. Let her go.'

'Schmidt, you are so naïve. A pretty girl turns the head and soon someone stabs you in the back. It has always been the same.' He waved a careless hand. 'You should learn from this. Trust no one; anyone out there can betray you. You think this job gives me pleasure? It doesn't. I am a family man and would do anything to preserve my family and protect them, but we are under occupation and all we have left is to work with our German allies. You have heard Petain's speeches? No? Well I'll tell you, all we have now is finding a route to survival. I have children. I value them and would do anything to ensure they survive the war and come out of this conflict with an advantage,'

'Advantage?'

'Yes, when Germany wins this war, I will be elevated and my children will have a good future.'

'I didn't join the army for this... Torturing of women.'

'Well, just grin and bear it, there's a good fellow.'

Rolf said nothing. The ridiculous logic of Boucher's arguments infuriated him but although he was equipped to argue, he was powerless to act. The picture in his mind was of Sandrine and he realised the truth of it all. It reminded him of a saying he had once heard "Responsibility without power is slavery". He knew he bore responsibility for what was happening beneath his very eyes but he held no power to act.

'You're on cell block duty?'

'Sir.'

'Bring me the notes I asked for when you are relieved at midday. You'd better go.'

And go he did.

Rolf descended the stairs deep in bitter thoughts. The situation was unbearable. He had to do something, but racking his brain he could think of no solution. His hopelessness turned to anger and then frustration. As he took up his post outside the cell corridor, he became impatient for the guard he relieved to go. The man seemed to want to talk and it was many minutes before the exchange of meaningless patter ceased.

He shifted from foot to foot, he began to sweat, but the man went in the end, and as he disappeared around the corner up the stairs, Rolf felt only relief. He turned, unbolted the door, then unlocked it. With urgent steps, he approached the cell in which he knew Sandrine languished. He swallowed hard as he came to the door of the cell, then he opened the observation hatch.

Chapter 9

"Every German boy and every German girl: They must be filled with a holy sense of duty to represent our nation."

Adolf Hitler

1

Lighting in the cell seemed dim to Rolf, yet he could make out where she sat, slumped against the far wall. Her head hung down and he saw she only wore a shift; someone had taken away her clothes. At the sound of the hatch opening, she didn't flinch and Rolf wondered whether she was unconscious, but then he saw her move. She shivered violently and he called to her.

'Sandrine,' he whispered.

There was no reaction so he said louder, 'Sandrine.'

She looked up, and then looked back down to the floor.

'Sandrine, it's me,' he whispered as loud as he dared.

This time she looked at the hatch, but made no effort to stand. Rolf unlocked the cell. He knew if they caught him, he would face severe consequences. He didn't care. Crossing to her side, he squatted and reached for her. Her face, battered and bruised remained looking down as if she was unable to look at him. He drew her to him and she tried to push him away, though it was a feeble movement and he overcame her struggles with ease.

'Sandrine, we have to get out of here.'

'What?' she said, her voice a soft murmur in the still air of the concrete cell.

'We need to get you out of here before they send for you again. Here, let me help you stand.'

He pulled her to her feet. She seemed to wobble and almost fell, but his strong arms supported her. They approached the door and Rolf heard footsteps. He drew back and peered around the corner. He saw no one at first, but then identified the tall lanky figure of Gerhard, accompanied by another guard. They had entered the corridor and were walking towards him.

In that moment, Rolf realised he had to trust Gerhard. There was no basis for it and he had received no indication that his friend would help him, but trust him he would.

He stepped out into the light, defiant, still supporting the girl. Gerhard pulled up. No one moved for a moment, then the other guard whose name, Rolf recalled, was Max, like his father, said, 'How did you know we were coming for her?'

A puzzled expression came to his face, before understanding came.

'What are you doing?'

Rolf looked at Gerhard. His eyes showed pleading. Was there no loyalty between comrades? Had they not been willing to die for each other, back there at the Maginot line?

With a speed taking Rolf by complete surprise, Gerhard swung his rifle upwards in an arc from his side. The stock connected with Max's forehead and he fell senseless to the concrete.

'What the fuck are you doing?' Gerhard said. He stepped forward towards them and took Sandrine's other arm. 'We're dead men now.'

'We can make it up to the hall. I need you to create a diversion and I'll slip out with her.'

'You're mad.'

'As mad as you, hitting Max.'

'I counted on him not remembering when he wakes up.'

'You're with us?'

'I always was. We nearly died in battle together; you think I would betray you now? You're a bloody fool though. For a woman too.'

Between them, they supported the girl to the stairs. She groaned but said nothing. Two flights up, the stairway ended beneath the open, wide staircase. Police officers usually wandered the carpeted hallway from time to time, but today, they were lucky; it was quiet. A lone sergeant sat at the desk by the door, scratching away with a pen on a ledger. Beyond his desk stood the massive doors, open and inviting.

'Gerhard, I need you to get him out of there.'

'I know,' Gerhard said, and strode out towards the sergeant.

Rolf watched, heart in mouth, as Gerhard began talking to the man. They were smiling and the sergeant stood up. The pair approached Rolf where he stood hidden around the corner of the stairwell. Gerhard put his arm on the sergeant's shoulder. They rounded the corner and in consternation, the sergeant looked from Rolf to the girl and then back to Gerhard, whose fist ascended to catch the unsuspecting Frenchman on the tip of his jaw. He collapsed like a sack of turnips and Gerhard guided him to the ground. They propped the man up in the corner of the stairwell then moved fast and unobserved out of the doorway and down the stone steps.

Once onto the boulevard, they turned the corner of the building and Gerhard said, 'She hasn't got any fucking clothes, has she? We won't get far like this.'

A woman with a perambulator stopped and stared, puzzlement written in capital letters across her face in the midday sun.

Rolf, still holding onto Sandrine, said, 'We need a car.'

A faint sound reached his ears of shouting and he understood his stupidity. They would catch him and shoot them all. He pictured his rifle standing against the doorway in the cell corridor. He wished he had kept it slung on his shoulder.

A Citroen crossed the Pont Saint-Michel, heading north. Rolf drew himself and the girl back against the side of the prefecture where they stood with low rosehip bushes either side, protected from view by an elm tree. Gerhard, to Rolf's surprise, leapt into the roadway. He levelled his Mauser.

'Stop,' he shouted.

The driver screeched to a halt and sidling around the vehicle, Gerhard indicated with his Mauser for the owner to get out. The driver was a man of medium height and wore a brown suit. He looked like a businessman to Rolf. He looked terrified. Rolf moved as fast as he could towards the car. He had bundled Sandrine onto the back seat, when he heard the first shots fired behind him. A bullet pinged as it ricocheted on the pavement. He leapt into the driver's seat.

Gerhard opened the passenger-side door. As if thrown there, he pitched into the vehicle, shutting the door, and Rolf revved the engine, double de-clutched into first and flew along the road towards the Pont au Change. A black Renault followed. Rolf could see in the rear-view mirror, one of the men in the pursuing vehicle held a gun; he was leaning out of the window. There was no time for more than a glance however, as the Citroen sped away across the bridge. He glanced to his right. With dismay, he saw Gerhard clutching his chest, where blood poured from it. It trickled through his fingers, but Rolf had no time to watch as they came to the end of the bridge. There were a few cars and some military vehicles going the opposite way, but no one in front. Rolf stepped on the accelerator as if he needed to push it through the floor.

Rolf's car shot along the bridge. At the end, where it met the Rive Droite, he turned left. Parallel to the Seine now, he continued to accelerate. He could hear Gerhard's bubbling breath. He knew he could do nothing for his friend. The car flew under the Pont Neuf and Rolf took a right almost immediately. The tyres screeched and he almost lost it as he turned into a wide road, realising he was passing the Louvre to his left. Absurd as it seemed, he was finally sightseeing.

A wagon, loaded with metal pipes, loomed ahead and he swerved around it, narrowly missing an oncoming hand cart. Gerhard slumped forward, his forehead on the dash. He was not breathing. Rolf sped on, checking his mirror to see if he had lost the pursuit. In and out of the traffic, he dodged. They were still behind him. He turned right onto Rue Richer. Then left. He was lost and still pursued. He saw the passenger of the following car lean out again, gun in hand. Rolf pulled on the seat belt with one hand.

He slammed on the brakes. The Citroen slewed to the right and he corrected. The tyres screeched. The vehicle came to a very sudden stop. Rolf braced himself, his foot on the brake, long before the impact, as the Renault slammed into the rear of his car. For an instant, he sat shocked. The mirror showed no movement. Shaken, but unharmed, he released the seatbelt and jumped out of his car. He ran, crouching, towards the rear. The impact had crushed the front of the Renault. He could see steam spiralling up from the bonnet. The gunman hung limp out of the window, his weapon lost somewhere behind. The driver, a man in police uniform, sat leaning forward onto his steering wheel. Bright red blood ran down his face. Rolf's first thought was that seat belts could be useful sometimes. He ran to the Citroen.

Gerhard remained collapsed against the dash. Rolf checked the pulse in his neck. It confirmed what he already guessed. There was none, so he opened the back door and found Sandrine on the floor. She began moving and trying to get up.

2

Rolf's mind had switched off. He gave no thought to his friend, or the two men in the battered Renault.

Focus.

Focus.

All his thoughts were for Sandrine and he knew he had to get her away, get her hidden. But how?

They limped along the city street and passers-by stared and stood rooted as they passed. He took another left and found an empty café. Swerving into the place, he saw a plump, bald man in a grease-stained once-white vest, cleaning a bar. Rolf felt he had no choice.

'Please help us.'

The man frowned. 'I don't help German soldiers. Go away.'

He turned back to his task.

'Please, this girl is one of you. She's French.'

Rolf heard a siren behind him from the street.

'They'll shoot her. Please. Only her then. Take her and hide her and I will face them.'

'French, you say?'

'Yes. Her name is Sandrine. Please.'

The man hesitated, but not for long.

'This way,' he said, indicating a door, up some steps, at the back of the bar.

Rolf half-dragged Sandrine, half-walked her to the doorway. Her head lolled.

'Up the stairs. There is a ladder to the roof at the top. If you can get her out onto the roof, you can rest there. They won't search up there. Pull the ladder up when you get onto the roof. Hurry. I can't delay them long if they come.'

The climb onto the sloping tiles was a nightmare. Sandrine seemed confused and restless and he had to put her over his shoulder, then once through the skylight, drag her roughly onto the mossy tiles. He pulled up the ladder, resting the end of it on the guttering by his feet. They lay there, side by side, on the tiles.

It began to rain, but the freshness of it revived him. He began to think about Gerhard. He had been a friend unlooked for but there for him when needed him and he knew he had underestimated the man's feelings. Of course, having gone through danger and that battle together, Gerhard would not have given him away. He should have known it; he should have trusted him. Yet, who could one trust in this war? Comrades? Civilians? Rolf had no idea who was who anymore. He regretted his friend's death. It fostered deep hatred in him toward the perpetrators and it gave him guilt. Had he not dragged Gerhard into his mad rescue and flight, he would still be alive. But why not die for a purpose? Was not saving this girl some kind of noble cause? Had Gerhard died for nothing? Perhaps it was, after all, only for Rolf's romantic fantasies about a French girl, who in all likelihood, was involved in murdering German soldiers as Boucher said?

Rolf rejected the thought. He knew she was innocent. There could be no circumstance in which this beautiful, gentle soul could kill anyone. He was sure about that. He turned to look at her. Her face, bruised and battered, the lips swollen to a travesty of her normal appearance appalled him. Still she remained silent and he wondered whether she might have struck her head in the crash.

He reached forward and touched her cheek. It was a gentle movement, a soft caress. He pushed her hair to one side and exposed her face. She stirred and her eyes opened.

'They… They…'

'Hush now. We're safe. We are on a roof in the city. They search for us. We have to stay here and wait.'

Her eyes closed again and minutes passed. How long? Rolf envisioned the sunset leaving them here on this Paris rooftop. His body began to relax and he knew he had to be patient. He wished he could close his eyes, but he knew a pitched roof was no place to rest. He reached for the girl and steadied her lest she fall.

Part 2

Chapter 1

"Never ascribe to malice that which can adequately be explained by incompetence."

Napoleon Bonaparte

1

He felt as if he was on the roof of the world. It was not his world, but a world of fantasy and dreams. One in which he had become a hero in his own mind, if not anyone else's. A sinking red sun, peeping out beneath grey banks of cloud above the horizon picked out highlights across the Paris roofs as the daylight faded. Long shadows from the pitched and flat roofs pointed fingers of shadow towards him and he could see the fading light reflected from the tramlines in the wet streets far below. Rolf shivered as the temperature dropped and he moved closer to Sandrine, their mutual warmth comforting him.

'It's gone quiet. Maybe we can go down.'

'Yes,' she said. 'I will try.'

He put down the ladder and climbed down through the skylight's opening, descending to a narrow carpeted corridor below. He supported Sandrine as she too, unsteady and weak, climbed down. For a moment, they stood there, in the dark, he supporting her, she shivering. They made their way down the stairs. Three floors down, the staircase opened out into the tiny restaurant. On the right, a bar stood and six or so tables occupied the room. Diners chatted by candlelight and thick black curtains hung in the windows, either side of the blacked-out, glazed door.

No one looked up as they entered and the proprietor approached as soon as they came into the restaurant. He still wore his black trousers and greasy vest, but now had a clean white apron over the top.

'Here,' he said, pulling a chair out for Sandrine at a small table in the corner. The checked tablecloth and the inadequate smoky candle gave the appearance of quaintness though neither of them noticed. 'I will bring food.'

They sat, Sandrine vague and uncommunicative and Rolf cautious and watching the door. He had no weapons and he knew if the police came he would be powerless. He loosened his collar with tremulous fingers.

An elderly man, dressed in a black jacket and wearing a cravat, turned in his seat and faced them. He swallowed a mouthful and said, 'They won't come back. They've gone. Relax yourselves.'

Rolf stared. Did they all know? Would they inform?

A middle-aged woman was seated at a table by the window, smoking a cigarette. She stood up, extinguished her smoke in the ashtray and picking up a cloth bag from the floor, she approached. She wore a woollen cardigan over a lace-dressed blouse with a cameo brooch at the neck. Her long smooth skirt accentuated her tall figure. She placed a hand on Sandrine's shoulder. As the girl looked up, the woman smiled and said, 'Come, we must clean up your face. You can't go home looking as if your friend beat you up, can we?'

Rolf looked around the tables while Sandrine disappeared with the woman. No one stared at him. An occasional glance came his way, but it was as if none of the diners wished to express any interest in the man and woman, for whom the police searched. He felt as if he was in one of those dreams where he arrived at work and found he had forgotten to dress, standing naked for all to see, yet no one noticed.

Presently, Sandrine returned. She had cleaned off the blood, leaving only the evolving bruises and the lacerated lips to show how the Special Brigade had treated her. From somewhere a dress of yellow, flowery material had appeared and he noticed Sandrine wore shoes. The woman went to the bar and then returned with a bottle of red wine and two round, short-stemmed wine glasses. She opened the bottle at the table as if it was all of no consequence and no effort. Rolf reached forward to help her pull the cork, but she waved his hand away.

'You think there is a Frenchwoman alive who cannot pull a cork?'

A man behind her laughed—a soft, friendly chuckle.

'I'm sorry.' Rolf said.

'You will be if you don't get out of that damned Sauerkraut uniform.' The man in the black jacket said. 'Michel, Michel,' he called towards the hatchway connecting the bar-space to a kitchen at the back of the room.

The rotund restaurateur appeared. 'I'm cooking, Josef. What do you want? You usually help yourself anyway.'

'This young man needs some clothes. All of Paris is looking for him. Everyone knows about the German soldier who rescued a French girl.'

'I'm cooking,' the plump man said, 'You see to it, if you aren't too busy feeding your face. Henri's room.'

He threw a key to the old man who caught it with surprising speed and stood up. He walked to the back stairs with a limp and motioned Rolf to follow. They went up and the old man said, without looking round, 'I'm Josef Jaboulet. I live around the corner, everyone knows me. Michel, the owner, is my brother-in-law. You know if you weren't a Kraut, you would be a national hero. As it is, no one here will give you up.'

Relief swept over Rolf and he realised there was no one here to fear. They entered a bedroom where a neat, unmade bed languished in the corner, and an armoire stood against the wall by the window.

'Michel's son's room. There are clothes. Henri has escaped with others to England. He won't need them. Maybe you will return them after the war is over?'

The old man chuckled as he searched in a drawer, extracting a pair of undershorts and then opened the wardrobe. He selected a plain, grey suit and a checked shirt. 'I'll leave you to change. You know the way down, eh?'

'Will it not be too small?' Rolf said.

'No, Michel is not so big but his son is bigger. Come down when you are ready, there will be cassoulet. It is one of Michel's great strengths.'

It took only moments to discard his uniform and he left it in an untidy green pile in a corner. Descending the stairs again, in the tight suit with short trousers, he entered the restaurant. Everyone there stood and applauded him. Colour rose to his face and he sat down next to Sandrine, too embarrassed to look any of the customers in the eye. Their food sat steaming on the plates before them and although Sandrine ate little, the wine seemed to restore her to some degree.

'You got me out. Thank you.'

'I did it because…'

'Whatever you did it for, I'm grateful. What will you do now?'

'Now I'm a deserter. They will shoot me if they catch me. I have nowhere to go except with you.'

'With me? I will have to hide too. You think every policeman in Paris isn't looking for us both? It won't be safe to be seen together. Separately, we might have a chance, but together they will pick us up in a moment.'

Rolf said nothing, chewing his food and frowning. Josef turned around, moving his chair, so he sat facing them.

'I'm sorry, I heard what you said. You can lie low at my place for a while until the fire dies down. It is too hot in the streets just now for you both. I live fifty yards away. You will be safe there.'

Sandrine said, 'Can you get word to my friends?'

'You want to advertise?'

'I have friends who will come for me as soon as it is safe. I need to warn them.'

'I can still walk, if that is what you mean. So, you accept my offer?'

Rolf said, 'I am most grateful.'

He stood up and clicked his heels. When every face in the place turned towards him, he realised his foolishness and sat down. Sandrine scowled.

'You're a bloody fool. Stop being so… So…German.'

'I'm sorry.'

'And stop apologising.'

The old man watched the exchange with a smile on his lips. 'You must like each other a lot,' he said.

Sandrine glared but Rolf smiled. He knew the truth of it.

It was beginning to dawn on him he would die for this girl; he almost had.

Presently, Sandrine said, 'Were you alone? It is all a fog in my head, but I thought there were two of you.'

'Yes. My friend Gerhard. He died.'

'Died?'

'They shot him and he died in the car. He died for you. He didn't need to help you see, and he made the choice.'

'I see. I'm sorry.'

Again silence. It was as if the day's events had taken away what little they had in common. Neither of them wished to talk and they finished their meal in silence.

Rolf knew he had lost everything. A deserter in an occupied country surrounded by 'enemy' and hunted by his own people too. He discarded the gloomy thoughts. He had saved her and as he looked into those brown eyes, he felt certain it was worth it. He realised now that all he wanted was to be near this young French woman, whatever it cost him.

2

He often thought about Gerhard in the days that came. Johan had thought his friend was political, but that was not who he was. Rolf understood him now; now he was dead and it was too late. Too late to express what he felt. A reluctant hero, yet with a soul of cast iron. Gerhard gave his life for Rolf. True, it was not for some noble cause, nor even to save a young woman from torture and probable death. He died helping a friend in an escapade he thought was crazy, because of loyalty. There could be no other explanation as far as Rolf could see.

There was no chair in the room, so he lay on the double bed in the tiny bedroom, next to Sandrine who was reading a book, and explained.

'Gerhard was a serious fellow, you know. I thought he was an idealist at first and I never understood the strength of his friendship.'

She lowered her book, 'I'm sorry he died to get me out. What was he like?'

'You will think I'm stupid, but I don't really know. He was always serious and I thought he was a staunch Nazi, but he wasn't. It turned out he was a communist at heart, but like me, he pretended to be a Nazi. He didn't talk much, you know.'

'You know my friends will come in two or three days, don't you?'

'Yes.'

'Well, they will get me out, but I don't know what they will make of you.'

'Make of me?'

'You think they will trust you?'

'You trust me.'

'You saved my life, didn't you?' she said, turning and propping herself up on one elbow. The book fell to the floor, with a clunk.

'So you trust me. I thought so. They will trust me, if you do.' He reached out a flat hand and touched her hair.

Sandrine withdrew and stood up. 'What is this? You think we are lovers or something? Never touch me again. You hear me?'

Rolf stared at the grey painted door as she slammed it on her way out. He thought he had over-played his hand and he felt rejected and ashamed. He was no good with women, he never had been. That girl at the fairground. The roller-coaster, the ghost train and then standing outside and his clumsy attempt at putting his arm around her. Her response had been a mirror image of Sandrine's. Why can't women be easier to get on with?

Rolf took in his surroundings. The attic room, in which he and Sandrine stayed, was small but cosy. True, the double bed meant he had to sleep on the floor but all the same, it looked comfortable. The chest of drawers had seen better days but the wardrobe was new and there was a clean rug on the floor. Rolf was familiar with the rug, since he awoke on both the previous mornings with his face embedded in it. A small window under the eaves looked out on another cobbled street, around the corner from the 'Bon Faisan,' where Michel hid them only two days before. He wondered at the contrast between this place and his home, a place of wide farmlands and golden cornfields. He liked France though; he liked Paris and the untidy charm of the streets and the cafés. But most of all, he liked the people. They had a charm of their own and gave him a sense of belonging he had never witnessed before. He wished he was one of them, but knew he was not. This was not his country and whatever happened he knew his link to it was Sandrine; beautiful, angry Sandrine.

He reached down and picked up the book she was reading. It must have come from their host, though he could not recall Josef giving it to her. It was a copy of 'Huckleberry Finn' by Mark Twain. He opened the book at the chapter where the drunk, Boggs, enters the town and he recognised the prose. Reading it gave him a thrill. It smacked of freedom. A freedom to express oneself, a right to be eccentric. Only a man who was free could have written a book like this. Free of Party Dogma; free to choose with whom he mixed.

Sadness came then. What had they done to his homeland? What had they done to his culture?

He put the book down and stared straight ahead. He realised the last few years, toeing the Nazi Party line had wasted time and taken away what sense of self-expression he could ever have had. It made him both sad and determined. Determined to do what he could. His position now was a world away from where he had seen himself that summer in the hayloft. He had burned his bridges too; the future would never be the same.

Chapter 2

"There are only two forces in the world, the sword and the spirit. In the long run the sword will always be conquered by the spirit."

Napoleon Bonaparte.

1

They marked time for four days, communicating well at times; at others, she seemed only to tolerate his presence as a kind of necessary evil. He was not used to women, despite the presence of his sister and his aunt throughout his formative years. Sandrine seemed friendly enough until Rolf spoke to her, when she would clam up as if the very sound of his voice was an irritation. They both spent days reading: it allowed them to be together but meant they did not have to speak. Rolf read his mother's psalm-book at first, but knowing every word already, he also ruminated as he read.

He could picture the look on his mother's face when she handed it to him. At the age of forty few lines creased her plump pink face. She had, despite that, a worn look about her and Rolf often wondered whether the strain of living with an alcoholic was killing his beautiful *mutti*. They stood in the kitchen dressed in their best Sunday clothes. He remembered he wore leather shorts and fiddled with his hat. It held a blue feather in the hatband and he could picture it in his mind still. The snow had come early that year and he recalled how Max had made him clear the path before going to the ceremony. Although he had stumbled over his lines in the little local church, his mother had expressed how proud she was of him. They ate strudel in the kitchen and Max drank schnapps. His memories of the remains of that day were unpleasant and he thrust them from his mind.

Josef had a number of modern books, mostly American, and Rolf discovered that Sandrine was as avid a reader as he was. Rolf wondered whether, like him, she used books as a form of escape from the present. She shared his taste in American writers some of the time, and when alone they spent time discussing modern American films and books.

'Hemingway is my favourite. His narrative prose is—'

'I prefer Steinbeck,' she said, sitting up and becoming animated. She waved her arms as she spoke, her long fingers active, gesticulating. 'For depth and description he is far above the more modern writers.'

'I don't know Steinbeck.'

'You should read "Of Mice and Men". It's a wonderful story about a small clever man and a big stupid one.'

'Like me?'

Sandrine smiled a brief smiled but continued. 'The strength of the story is the pathos of Lenny's character and the sadness with which the book ends. Steinbeck was a master of story and emotion. Heavier going than Hemingway but more powerful.'

'You said you were at university. Was it modern American literature you were studying?'

'Yes.'

'I envy you. It is all closed to me and has been for years now since the Nazis…'

'I know. I thought you were a book burner at first.'

'I am?'

'You are?'

'Yes. When everyone else was burning Heine, I burnt "Mein Kampf" instead. It gave me great satisfaction to throw it onto the flames.'

'No one saw you?'

'Everyone saw me, but they thought it was a different book.'

'If that makes you a book burner, then all the world could admire you. Burning books by book burners is surely the opposite thing?'

'So do you admire me too?

She said nothing and looked away.

They lapsed into silence and regarded each other. Rolf noticed there was a look in her eyes he had not seen before. It was a kind of sparkle. He dared not hope it meant anything and her put the thought that she might at last like him out of mind. He dared not hope.

2

Late on the fourth night, as Rolf wallowed in Huckleberry Finn, he heard a banging on the door downstairs. He peered out of the little window beneath the eaves and saw two men standing on the wet cobbles below. They wore long raincoats and both wore berets. One, taller than the other, stood back and eyed the street, and then the knock came again, harder and more insistent.

Rolf realised from their clothes they could not be police and he relaxed. He heard muffled voices below and headed for the stairs. Sandrine stood next to Josef in the doorway and hearing Rolf's footsteps behind, glanced at him over her shoulder. She was not smiling. She turned back to the shadowy figures at the door.

'He has to. They will find him if he stays.'

A deep voice said, 'He can't go with us. It will endanger us all. How can you be so sure he isn't a spy?'

'He saved my life. His friend died in the rescue. I will vouch for him with André. Anyway, he has now seen your faces and if they catch him, he will talk. It's too dangerous to ignore.'

'André won't approve, you know this. You'd better come now Sandrine, and maybe we'll come back for your... friend. If that is all he is.'

'No. He's coming too, or I stay and take my chances.'

The man turned to his companion and threw up his arms in exasperation.

Sandrine turned to Rolf. 'Come. We're going.'

They said their goodbyes to Joseph and within a minute or two, Rolf found himself in a black Renault, riding bumpy roads across town. The journey took twenty minutes and they drove into a narrow alleyway. It ended in a rough concrete courtyard enclosed by plain red brick buildings, and two large garage doors loomed ahead. Above the doors windows perforated the brickwork, two to a floor, overlooking the courtyard. A truck stood parked in one corner of the yard facing towards them, and in the other corner stood several dustbins, overflowing with rubbish. The taller man got out and hammered on the double doors with his fist. A face appeared at a window above, and after a pause one of the doors opened. They got out and entered the building—a warehouse. It smelled of gasoline and grease. Empty cartons and tea chests spilling wood shavings and old crumpled newspaper littered the floor. To the right stood a glazed and door-less office, and overhead a metal rail ran the length of the ceiling on one side, below, a wooden staircase.

Still in silence, they searched Rolf and then a rough hand shoved him into the centre of the warehouse floor. A light bulb high above his head illuminated him and made it hard for him to identify who stood in the shadows.

'Wait there, Rolf, it'll be alright,' he heard Sandrine say, then the clack of her heels as she her climbed the wooden stairs to his right. It was as if her attitude had changed from one of truculence to the role of protector. He was glad she was here, he would have feared for his life otherwise. Enclosed by silence, he made out only vague figures around him. His one attempt to step out of the light brought the cocking of a weapon and a curt growl from his captors.

'Get back there, where we can see you, Kraut.'

Rolf returned to the spot and waited. A few minutes later, he heard steps coming down and a squat, dark-haired man emerged from the shadows. He wore a grey overall and his curly brown hair sat in an untidy mop above a hard, sallow face, wearing a stern expression. The dark eyes met his and the man said, 'I'm André Gautier. I am the leader here. Sandrine tells me you got her out of the prefecture.'

'Yes.'

'Is that all you have to say? The news is all over Paris. No one has escaped custody from there before.'

'I was working there. I was a guard.'

Gautier stared at Rolf. 'Why did you do it? If they caught you, they would have had you shot, you know that don't you?'

'Court martialled first, more likely,' Rolf said. 'Prison if I'm lucky, but they shot my friend so maybe…'

'If I wanted to plant a spy among us partisans I would have him rescue someone of low importance to ensure he is accepted.'

'They shot at us and killed my friend. Ask Sandrine, the bullets were real enough.'

Rolf noticed he was sweating and his head thumped with a rapid rhythm. He wanted to run, to escape, and get air, but he knew he had to stay there and endure the questions. His own reaction shamed him. Had not Sandrine felt the same when his own people brought her in. She had not cracked or panicked and he determined he would not do so either. He stood his ground.

'I wasn't very aware at the time, but his friend was there and didn't come with us. I believe him,' Sandrine said and she stepped forward to stand next to Rolf. A wave of relief and gratitude spread over him. He wanted to put his arm around her.

A voice, Rolf thought came from the shorter man who picked them up, said, 'He's a Kraut. We can't risk leaving him alive to inform on us, André.'

Gautier turned around and faced the man. 'You give the orders now do you Louis? And if he is innocent? What if all he did was to save Sandrine, eh?'

Louis turned and began walking away. He muttered, 'No bloody use and a huge risk, all the same.'

Rolf, encouraged by Gautier's words, said, 'I know you don't trust me. I don't even blame you for it either. In your shoes I would be suspicious. Let me prove myself to you, I am a soldier and I can fight. I want to fight at your side.

You'll see.'

'Yes,' Gautier said, 'we will find out soon enough. You can't leave this place for a long time anyway and you will be watched twenty-four hours a day until we know the truth.'

'I hope you enjoy watching me eat, sleep and shit,' Rolf said and then smiled. 'You don't need to, but I suppose it is what I would do too. Where do you want me?'

Sandrine took his hand and led him up the stairs. The touch of her hand seemed a sweet balm to his frayed nerves. He knew he would go anywhere she led him. She took him to the third floor where they locked him in a small storeroom with a barred window and a camp bed in one corner where someone had cleared a space among the boxes and debris. The room was warm and dry but too small to even pace up and down. Rolf sat on the cot and considered his options. He could either try to escape or stay and wait for these people to accept him. Neither option was attractive but if he escaped, he had nowhere to go and the chance of capture seemed very high, since he would be alone in the streets of Paris. He lay down, making a pillow of his coat and closing his eyes.

There was no light when he opened his eyes and the luminous dial of his Swiss watch, a gift from his aunt before he left the farm to go to Berlin, said three o'clock. He realised his bladder needed urgent relief, but locked in there seemed to be no way to empty it. He banged on the door.

'Hey, is there anyone there?' he said as loud as he could.

A voice from behind the door said 'Calm down, what's wrong?'

He explained and the door opened. A short man stood in Rolf's way, revolver in hand. Rolf looked down at the weapon, a Walther.

He said, 'There's no need to point that at me. I've got nowhere to run to, have I?'

'So you say. I don't trust you any more than Louis does.'

'I'm Rolf Schmidt,' Rolf said, extending a hand.

The man stepped back, 'I'm no fool, remember that.'

'Your name? I would hate to be killed by a man whose name I don't know.'

'Get ready for disappointment then.'

'Look, I'm not a spy. If I was, don't you think it would be obvious? I'm a deserter from the German army, just a Heer soldier, nothing more. I don't like what the Nazis are doing to our country and I don't like what they have done to yours either. I got the girl out because they were torturing her. Any man would have done the same.'

They walked along a galleried landing, the drop across the railings descending to the concrete below.

'Here. You can piss here.'

Rolf opened the door. When he emerged, the man seemed to have relaxed. The gun bulged his jacket where he had stuffed it in his belt. A cigarette hung from his mouth.

'Can I have one?' Rolf said.

'You won't like it. It's French.'

'I'll risk it.'

The man extracted a battered blue pack from his jacket pocket and removed a plain, unfiltered cigarette. Rolf smelled it. The man offered him a light from the glowing tip of his own smoke, his other hand resting on the butt of his pistol. Rolf exhaled a long column of dense blue smoke.

'You know,' he said, 'these aren't bad. Bit aromatic but quite nice really.'

The man grunted.

Rolf persisted, 'What's your name?'

'Claude. That's all you need to know. Afraid I'll have to lock you up again, we can't have you running back to your army, and telling them where we are, now can we?'

'Food?'

'Not until morning. Giles will go to the baker's.'

'Thank you for the cigarette. What make?'

'Gauloise. French in name and French in nature. They are a symbol of our resistance.'

Rolf heard the door shut behind him and the lock clicked. He was alone again and he wondered where Sandrine could be. Perhaps, now she was with her partisan friends, she had forgotten him. Rolf finished the cigarette and despite rumblings from his stomach, he dozed until dawn.

3

The door to the storeroom opened when he tried it next morning. His wristwatch said nine o'clock. Rolf recalled not sleeping, but as soon as he felt he should arise, he descended the ladder of a deep sleep. He did not feel refreshed. It felt as if he had tossed and turned all night. He staggered to the landing and three floors up, could look down to the concrete floor of the warehouse across the metal railing.

The place was well lit. The light bulb, which had so irritated him the night before, gave a view of what was transpiring blow. He could hear raised voices. Seven or eight men sat and stood around a table. Rolf could smell coffee and noticed they ate bread and cheese. Sandrine was there too.

He recognised Claude. 'I don't think he's the sort to be a spy. If what Sandrine says is true, we could be making a mistake. I know it's the safest thing to do, but he could be useful; he's German. He can go places we can't.'

Louis said, 'No. We do it now. Then there's no risk. Don't you see you are gambling with all our lives? Get rid of him, one way, or another.'

Louis removed a parabellum from his belt and placed it on the table. The gun lay on the table and the assembled partisans seemed to stare at it. It was a statement of intent. No one spoke at first, and then André Gautier stood up.

'You know, Louis, since we recruited you, you've done nothing but kill people or talk about killing. We are here to liberate our country. The deaths we cause are forgivable because we are at war. To take a life only on suspicion is worthy only of the Krauts. It is not our way. Sandrine, you agree?'

Sandrine leaned back in her chair. She was smoking and wore a beige raincoat, no doubt supplied by one of the men around her.

She said, 'I know he's not a spy. I got to know him a little before the escape, don't forget. He's a bookish intellectual, nothing else. You don't need to kill him. Use him. He can fight. I saw him fight three soldiers in the restaurant and he had no difficulties. We need him.'

Claude said, 'Let's vote on it. All those in favour of …'

'Hey. You…' Rolf called from the landing.

All eyes came his way. He began descending the stairs two at a time, and silence reigned until he was down. He approached the table where André sat and he looked around at the faces of the partisans.

'I understand you don't trust me. If I was a spy—a plant, I suppose I would have done all the things I have done so far—like André says. But I'm not. Give me time and you will see. I rescued Sandrine, not for you, but because she is a friend. She matters to me. I had no other reason. And it got my friend, Gerhard, killed. I have to live with that, but all the same, I'm glad I did it. I don't care for the Nazi doctrines. I'm a bloody Catholic. For the sake of Christ, let me be useful to you.'

Silence greeted him. Rolf shifted from one foot to the other and he noticed his heart beating. Out of the silence a voice he had not heard before, said with an accent he could not place, 'He's right. Even if he was a spy, we could use him. In an operation, the slightest problem, and we gun him down. It is only by using him we can be sure.'

The speaker was a short slim man, wearing a brown wide-brimmed hat and a brown overcoat. He stepped forward and lit a cigarette. The cool-looking smoke ascended into the still, stale air of the warehouse.

Sandrine said to the assembled men, 'Lucien is right. Let Rolf prove his loyalties and I swear you'll see I'm right.'

They voted then. Six raised a hand to support Sandrine. Only Louis kept his hand down. Rolf felt as if he witnessed it all from a distance, as if he stood outside himself, looking on, only partially committed. He wondered as he watched the men raise their hands, whether it was a simple denial of reality: he did not want to take in that they had just voted on whether to kill him or not. He realised these men would have done so if they had voted that way. He felt relief at the result, but knew he still needed to be cautious.

Lucien slapped him on the shoulder as he passed, making his way to the doors. 'Don't worry, Kraut. We'll find plenty of things for you to prove yourself with.'

The words were worrying, but the smile on the man's face seemed reassuring.

Sandrine came to him 'You're lucky. André doesn't think you're a spy. He believes me. Be careful of Louis though. He's new and he's vicious. He kills your people in public places and he wants revenge for his wife and daughter.'

'Wife?'

'Yes, they were taken away in the Vel d'hive round up. They say none of them are coming back.'

'I heard. They've been deported to camps in the east. Maybe when the war is over...'

'Don't be naïve. They go to their deaths. You don't seem to understand. Your people are killing all the Jews. You're in their army and you don't know that?'

'I heard rumours about ridding the world of Jews but I've never seen anything to suggest they kill them.'

Sandrine shook her head, 'It's as if you live in a different world from us. Your people are evil.'

'Stop calling them my people. I have chosen my people. My people are your people. I will die to get Germany out of France, if that is what you want of me.'

'I don't understand your reasons.'

'I have always believed in freedom. The Nazis took away all our freedoms at home, now they do the same here. I thought once, I could just shut my eyes to it all, toe the line, you know? When I saw what they have created in the prefecture—French against French, torture and hatred, I came to learn I can stand to witness only so much. Then when they brought you in, I could no longer push it away from me. Nietzsche describes a superman in all of us. My "*Ubermensch*" is here now and ready to grow.'

'We are all fighting for freedom, you know. Freedom to write, to talk, and even to see films which offend the politicians.'

'It isn't even that. It's defence of cultural freedom.'

'Well, if you say so. I guess a world without Bogart and Bacall would be an empty one for us both.'

Her comment brought a smile to both their faces. The smiles subsided quickly as Gautier approached.

'Rolf, isn't it?'

Rolf, out of habit, clicked his heels and bowed a little bow, as was his wont. 'Sir,' he said.

André said, 'You're not in the army now. Call me André, not "sir". I'm not your surrogate officer. Come, we need to talk.'

Gautier led him to the part-glazed office. Sandrine followed. He wondered whether this was bad news or good. What he heard next brought only determination.

Chapter 3

"There are two levers for moving men: interest and fear."

Napoleon Bonaparte

1

'For what it's worth,' Gautier said, 'I wouldn't have let them shoot you, you know.'

'Very comforting,' Rolf said, pulling up a battered wooden chair. Gautier sat behind a worn-looking desk. 'What do you want me to do?'

'Do?'

'Yes. I thought you wanted me to do something. Just ask me.'

'No. We want to observe you first. Your main value to us is as a German, not your fighting skills.'

'You mean I have to stay cooped up here all the time? It will drive me crazy.'

'What's the alternative? You can't go back to the German army. They'd shoot you.'

'I'm not used to being shut up, that's all.' Rolf glanced sideways at Sandrine, her presence reassuring him. He felt as though he had become dependent on her. He rescued her

119

when she needed him; now he needed her. Perhaps it was always like that—one way then the opposite.

'I'll work something out, don't worry. I have a visitor coming in a few minutes. You may not like him, but we have to work with him. He's Armenian.'

'Why wouldn't I like him?'

'Being German and that.'

'We are all on the same side now aren't we?'

'I think that's him,' Sandrine said.

Rolf heard the warehouse doors open, then soon after, a footfall at the doorway. A man appeared followed by another. The fellow was of medium height, but built skinny. He wore a black moustache; his hair was curly and combed back from his high forehead. The brown suit had seen better days and he wore a woollen jumper over his shirt, which he had buttoned to the neck. A small rounded scar on his right cheek and his pitted complexion attested to a hard life and Rolf wondered what sort of man this was. He had heard of the Turkish oppression of the Armenians, read about it in the newspapers, but it had always seemed so far away and irrelevant to his own life. Manouchian's features otherwise looked unremarkable except for his eyes. They were coal-black and burned with a clarity and earnestness Rolf noticed as soon as the man looked at him.

The other man was young, maybe early twenties. He wore a dark jacket and grey trousers, untidy but clean. He wore no hat either, but his hair was neat and brown and combed to the side. The serious face suggested a man who kept his determination deep inside himself, though Rolf wondered whether it was laced with hatred, from the cold glare directed towards him.

'Missak. You came. It is good to see you again. All is

well?'

The man smiled and they shook hands and touched cheeks. 'André. I came as you asked. You've met Marcel?'

'I don't believe so.' Gautier proffered his hand and the younger man took it. 'This is Schmidt, our German soldier. You know about him?'

Rolf stood up. He was about to bow as was his habit, but he thought better of it and proffered his hand instead. The visitor took it and Rolf noticed Manouchian's hand was warm and dry. Their eyes met.

'Missak Manouchian. So. The German. This is Marcel Rayman, one of my men. I'm the leader of a small group of the FTP-MOI.'

Rolf offered his hand to Rayman who did not respond, so Rolf dropped his hand to his side.

Sandrine stood and Manouchian kissed her on both cheeks. Both of them smiled as if they were old friends. There was a smile on Rayman's face as he too greeted Sandrine. Rolf felt he could hardly blame them; he still thought she was the most beautiful woman in Paris.

'Thank you for the poems,' she said.

'I'm honoured you read them. They mean a lot to me.'

Manouchian sat down.

'We have instructions from above,' Gautier said.

'Yes?' Manouchian said.

'Yes. We have to make the newspapers. We need them to sit up and take note.'

'I heard,' Manouchian said. 'I've told them time and again, I don't mind leading but I won't kill anyone. It's against all my principles. I'm better with blowing things up and the like.'

'Petra insists. He's suggested a high ranking German officer.

We will need to cooperate to do this. Can you give me two men?'

'Yes. Two men will be possible. Marcel, one of the others. Preparation is everything you know. You've watched this man?'

'You think I'm stupid?'

They were all sitting now, leaning forward. Rolf saw earnestness in their faces but he felt disappointment too. He wondered whether he had any role in this or whether, as an untrusted observer, they would keep him out. The thought that this was a trap and they could be testing him sat implanted in his mind as the conversation evolved. It could, he realised, all have been an elaborate fiction, to fool him. Perhaps, they wanted to see if he would pass on information to someone.

Rolf stood up. 'Do I have a part to play?'

They were silent and Rayman turned to stare at Rolf. He said, 'He can't be trusted. I won't work with a German.'

Gautier said, unflinching, 'He can be trusted. Sandrine owes him her life.'

Sandrine looked from face to face. 'He got me out of the prefecture. You can trust him.'

No one spoke for a few moments. Gautier broke the silence. 'Colonel Ritter. He reports to Saukel, responsible for the deportations to labour camps.'

Manouchian said, 'Where?'

'Sixteenth arondissment. Rue Pétrarque. He leaves there every morning at eight-thirty in his car.'

'Bullet proof?' Rayman said.

'No, not as far as we can see. I've had him watched for a few weeks.'

Rolf said, 'I could deliver a message, it would delay him

outside the vehicle. You'll need to get me a uniform though.'

'No, we know how to do this,' Gautier said. 'Someone has to walk up to the car and blast the man. There is time. We will plan it in detail. Marcel, how would you like to wipe away a German Colonel?'

Rayman smiled but said nothing.

'I'll do it,' Rolf said.

All eyes turned to him. Silence pervaded the room. Rolf noticed he was sweating. He wished he had remained silent.

Presently, Gautier said, 'You've killed men before? Eh?'

'Yes. On the Maginot line.' It was, he realised too late, the wrong thing to say.

Rayman stood up and faced him. 'So you killed Frenchmen? You think it qualifies you to kill Germans too, do you? Your people are the ones responsible for all this death and deportation. You think we'd let you take part in this? You're crazy. I could kill you where you sit.'

Manouchian got up. He placed a placatory hand on Rayman's shoulder. 'Marcel. This isn't one of the men we are fighting. He's proven himself and is here to help us. *Depéche toi*, my friend.'

Turning to Rolf, he said, 'You must forgive Marcel. His father received a deportation order last week. He went to the prefecture to register and he hasn't come back.'

'I'm sorry,' Rolf said.

'You're sorry?' Rayman said. His eyes narrowed as he regarded Rolf. 'My father is deported and you're fucking sorry? You'll have to kill more than one or two generals before I trust you. I hate all of you. Know that? Look at me again and I'll put you in the ground. I swear it.'

Sandrine stood up. 'I've had enough of this. If any of you had been there at the prefecture to help me, I could understand. Do you know what they did to me? For two days, they beat me. Want to see the blowtorch burns on my thighs? Here.'

She began to lift her skirt. As one man, they looked away. Even Rolf did.

'None of you were there for me. No one came to get me out. You sit here and whine on about your families, your principles and the only person who helped me in that sewer, that hellhole, was Rolf Schmidt, a German soldier. He knocked out a guard; he stole a car and they chased us all over Paris. And they shot his friend. And for what? To be greeted by the resistance with hatred? If you don't accept him as one of us, I'll go with him somewhere else. Hear me?'

Rolf said nothing. He looked at Sandrine with admiration. If he had saved her from the wolves once, she had now returned the favour twice and he knew it.

Gautier stood up. 'We came here to discuss an operation. No one is on trial. Let's stop all this bickering and get on with the matter at hand. I agree with Sandrine. We can trust Rolf, but if it makes you happier Marcel, we'll keep him out of the action on this one. He can drive the car instead. Eh Rolf? You like driving don't you? Especially in Paris.'

There was no further remonstrance or argument. Gautier explained the plan and each of the men in the room accepted the role Gautier gave him. When Manouchian left, he turned to Rolf who was the last to leave the glazed office and said, 'I don't like killing, maybe it's the poet in me, but I think life is precious and to deny that finest of God's gifts to anyone, is a sin. I've told them that although I will fight for freedom, I won't pull the trigger. You understand maybe?'

'I am a Catholic, like these other people around us. I don't want to kill anyone, but this is for human liberty. The freedom to choose one's fate is also one of God's gifts. But I understand. My problem is I have now to prove myself to these people and I want their trust too.'

'Maybe it is also that I risk more than you do. I have a wife. The more I do in the name of freedom, the more I endanger her.'

'Go with God, my friend,' Rolf said and patted him on the shoulder.

Left alone now, Rolf wondered what would happen next.

'They don't trust me. Only Sandrine sticks up for me. It's like that day when I came home late from the woods. He hunted me all around the yard and the barn; belt in hand. I can feel the lick of that leather even now on my back, my buttocks. I remember the tears and the anger. I wanted to be bigger. I wanted to be strong enough to defend myself, but then I was powerless. I was alone with a monster and I am alone now, but I will defend myself this time. If Max taught me anything, it was never to allow anyone to shame me that way again. Who does that Marcel think he is? What does he know about me? Nothing. I need them to accept me; I have no other life now. Germany, the Third Reich, Nazi dogma are all behind me and I will suffer whatever test they throw my way, if only I can be with Sandrine.

Yes, for Sandrine I would walk through Hell'.

2

Rolf sat drumming his fingers on the steering wheel of a dark-green Fiat in a narrow street of the sixteenth arondissment. He noticed he was sweating and out of habit, he ran his fingers round the inside of his shirt collar. It felt too tight. He looked around the street outside. He had parked the car close to the corner where the street ended on its junction with Rue Scheffer. He could see the double iron gates of the Pétrarque Square almost directly ahead. To his right was a café with parasols and tables, basking in the early morning sun that poured down between the tall yellow stone buildings with their balconies and shuttered windows. He stared at the couple sitting at the cafe to his right. The perambulator the woman rocked to and fro was old and rickety, but no sound came from any occupant. He heard a church chime eight thirty and he looked at his watch to confirm the time.

Marcel Rayman and Thomas Selek walked up the pavement behind him and he started the car. The soft drone of the engine soothed him. At least now, he was doing something. Having waited almost half-an-hour already, he felt only relief to be occupied. His anxiety left him, as if, now events were unfolding, there was only the job and no distraction. He knew what to do.

Thomas and Marcel crossed the roadway sauntering towards Sandrine and Louis where they sat at the pavement tables, diagonally opposite the iron gates. The roadway passed the white, well-appointed house on the left corner of the square. A large black car arrived passing the Fiat to Rolf's left. The car turned left and pulled up close to the pavement, outside the iron gates, diagonally opposite the couple with the pram. A German soldier got out. The uniform was green, and Rolf placed the man as a Heer Unteroffizier. The man walked up the drive of the house and the front door opened. Rolf checked his mirror. Nothing.

Thomas and Marcel leaned over the pram. Their backs to the German car, they stood engaging the couple in conversation, though Rolf could not hear what they said.

Sandrine, from the café table, was watching over Marcel's shoulder as a tall, well-built middle-aged Standartenfürer emerged from the house. He put on his cap and smiled to the Unteroffizier. They spoke a few words in German as they descended the front steps walking towards the car. Sandrine, face serious, said something, her lips taught, and her voice inaudible to Rolf, even though his window was open and the group were only yards away. The tall iron gates swung open.

Still nothing. No one moved. The Germans entered the black Mercedes. Ritter sat alone on the back seat. The engine coughed then broke into that soft purr of the powerful, efficient, German diesel engine.

To Rolf, it seemed as if several things happened at once. Sandrine and Louis stood up. They held pistols in their hands: parabellums. Marcel and Thomas turned in unison. Each held a sten. As if rehearsed and now perfect in their movements, they crossed the road in three quick steps. Marcel stood to the left front end of the vehicle. He brought his weapon to bear on the windscreen. Thomas stood further round, at the passenger door.

They both opened up at once. As they did, Sandrine and Louis walked towards Rolf, then took up position either side of the car, ready to get in, pointing their guns up and down the street, in case the partisans needed cover. They waited.

Shot after shot, the rat-tat-tat of the stens rang out. Over and over again they fired, Marcel first at the driver and the Unteroffizier in the front. Then round after round poured into the back seat through the decimated, splintered windscreens. Thomas fired too just as his companion did, first into the front, then the back. Like clockwork. Like automatons. Neither face betrayed emotion, only concentration; if they were scared, it did not show. Rolf understood why Gautier asked for their help. They were unshakeable. Marcel changed magazine first. His hands moved with blurry speed. Then he resumed firing. When both had exhausted two full magazines, they turned and ran to the Fiat.

Rolf revved the engine. They slammed the back doors behind them. The car jerked as it pulled away. To the left, in the corner of his eye, Rolf saw armed soldiers emerging from the building. His foot flat down on the accelerator, he sped the few yards to the end of the road and turned right heading towards the Seine right bank, desperate to distance them from any pursuit.

He heard a shot, then more shots. One hit the rear windscreen. He ducked with a reflex movement and then took a right into Rue de Pasteur, then right again and on, until he was certain there was no pursuit. Ten minutes later, they abandoned the car in a tiny side street and split up. Unlike the others, Sandrine and Rolf stayed together and they made their escape.

As Sandrine took his arm, Rolf reflected it had been a quick, savage operation, the whole thing executed with almost German precision and efficiency. By his side, Sandrine, hugged his arm and smiled.

He looked down at her. 'We are a good team, yes?'

'We are a good team, yes.'

'Back to the warehouse?'

'We can risk a drink maybe on the way. I know a small discrete place…'

'As long as it isn't Absinthe. I prefer schnapps.'

'I thought you liked Absinthe? You drank that every time we saw each other before.'

'I was trying to impress. Now I need a drink more than I need to impress.'

She nodded, still smiling and they walked unnoticed, arm in arm, towards the Pont d'Élena and the Left Bank. Rolf felt his hands were shaking, but whether it was from the danger of the operation or closeness to Sandrine, he could not decide. He knew though he did not care where he was, as long as she took him in tow.

Chapter 4

"The bed has become a place of luxury to me! I would not exchange it for all the thrones in the world."

Napoleon Bonaparte

1

They spent the rest of the day in cafés and wandering the streets, as if she were his guide. She even held his hand at times. To Rolf, he had entered a new world. One in which he was learning all the time as Sandrine told him about Paris, about France and the history of the places they sauntered around. It was as if the morning had never happened, as if they were simply friends wandering the streets, enjoying the smells and sounds of the wonderful city. By dusk, neither of them wanted to go back to the warehouse so they decided to share a bottle of wine in a place Sandrine knew well.

The bar in the Rue Surcouf sported an awning bearing broad white letters, "Au Canon des Invalides," and it seemed crowded when they arrived. Rubbing shoulders with German soldiers who once would have greeted him with open arms made him shudder now. Rolf glanced at faces with trepidation in case someone might recognise him, and kept his head down as much as he could. He experienced fear now, it was true, but there was something else gnawing at him, rubbing him raw. As he reached the bar he began to understand what bothered him and so it ceased to rankle. It felt as if he had alienated himself from his country and his roots, but he also felt as if he had emerged refreshed and clean, rather than filthy and treacherous. He had a good feeling about pursuing a moral path. Sandrine held his hand as they pushed through the revelling crowd, her cool fingers like a gentle balm on sunburnt skin.

Sandrine bought a bottle of cheap red wine with some of her last ration coupons and they found a table after waiting, what seemed to Rolf, to be an age. A smoke haze filled the room and despite the choking atmosphere Sandrine lit a Gauloise. Rolf poured another glass and sat looking at her. She reached across the table and took his hand in hers. For Rolf, it was as if the room was empty and the only person present was this beautiful woman, her smile, her dark eyes and hair. She leaned across the tiny round table, the varnish patchy from long use, and it rocked an unsteady dance, cockling towards her.

'You did well today.'

'I did nothing. All I did was drive a car. Marcel was the one; and his friend—what was his name?'

'No need for names here. Marcel is bitter and angry. He has lost much and seeks revenge. It is the wrong sentiment.'

'Is there a right one?'

'Yes.' She lowered her voice and he had to strain to hear her. 'Resistance is all that matters, but who knows whether it will have been worth it in the end? I think the Germans will win this war and then a German peace will come.'

'German peace is an oxymoron. My countrymen don't want peace. The Nazi dogma is to spread the Aryan cant across the whole world and make us a super-race. Not the supermen Nietzsche had in mind either. All he did was recognise man's greed for power. He was right about the Nazi High Command though. Their appetite for control of others is like a fox in a hen coop—as long as they have power, it doesn't matter to them whether they waste other people's lives.'

She frowned. 'You really want to have this kind of talk at a time like this? Look around. People are laughing, drinking. They want to forget. Can't we distance ourselves from it all for just one, small island of time?'

'I'm sorry. Maybe my nerves are on edge after this morning. Let's go.'

'No. I want another bottle.'

'But why? We have to find our way back.'

'Look at that man's face. Over there, the one with the scar. See how his eyes light up, every time he drinks that Calvados? He's laughing and he's drunk. Tomorrow he will be back in reality. I don't want to join him, but I recognise the voice of inevitability. Let's take this one moment to ourselves Rolf, please. Let's be real people for this one moment. I need some release.'

'As you wish,' he said. He picked up the empty bottle and pushed his way to the bar. He ordered a fresh bottle with Sandrine's last coupons and stood waiting for it, when he noticed a familiar figure in the corner of his eye.

'I know you,' he shouted in the man's ear, above the surrounding hubbub.

'I'm sorry, I don't know you,' Zedé said. He made to draw away.

'Yes you do. You do. And by God, I know you.'

Rolf grabbed his bottle as it appeared in front of him.

Zedé looked unsteady as he backed away and Rolf could see he was drunk, a glass of some clear spirit in hand. The old man wore the same battered suit with the wilting flower in his lapel. The dark eyes still had a piercing quality, despite his inebriate state. Rolf looked past him at Sandrine. He tried to catch her eye but she seemed to be in conversation with a young woman, dressed in a blue overcoat and black beret, on the adjoining table.

Rolf recalled the last time he had seen this man and anger came, unannounced and involuntary. He grabbed Zedé by his lapels. 'You led my friend to his death. You think I'm going to let you lead me to mine?'

'Please, please. You are wrong about me. I didn't know there were partisan killers at that place. Please, believe me.'

The man's face and his whining voice were too much for Rolf to maintain his temper and it struck him that even if Zedé was not who he claimed to be, they might both be on the same side now. He grabbed his bottle with his left hand and with his right, dragged the discomfited Zedé with him. Without letting go of the now very uncomfortable man, Rolf set down the bottle and grabbed a vacant chair from the next table.

'Sit,' he said.

Sandrine stared as Zedé sat down.

'Now tell us,' Rolf said in a barely audible voice, 'who you are and what group you work for?'

'Rolf?' Sandrine said.

Zedé said, 'Please, Mademoiselle, he thinks I led his friend to his death. It is nonsense. His friend was killed by partisans in a whorehouse. I only showed them where such a place might be. I swear I had nothing to do with the death of one of our noble allies.'

'I know you,' Sandrine said.

A glimmer of recognition came to Zedé's face. 'Yes, of course, you are Philippe's daughter. You do know me. You can vouch for me with this nice German soldier. I am blameless. You know me.'

'Keep your voice down, will you,' Rolf said. 'I'm not a German soldier now.'

'You deserted?' Zedé said, shrugging his shoulders. 'But that is fine with me. If you are not one of them, then you are one of us.'

Sandrine looked at Rolf, her eyes questioning.

'I had no choice. He might have recognised me.'

'I remember you from my father's shop,' she said.

'Shop?' Rolf said.

'My father had a hardware shop.'

Rolf turned to Zedé. 'I helped her escape from the prefecture. Room 35. Understand?'

'Room 35?' Zedé said, with a faint slur. 'This situation becomes more interesting by the minute.'

He paused for a moment and took a gulp of his drink. 'Naturally, I won't tell a soul. Where are you staying?'

'It doesn't matter' Sandrine said. 'It is enough to know we are connected with people who can hunt you down if you inform.'

'Inform? I would never do that. At least I would never tell the authorities I have seen either of you. Look, I'll come clean. I am linked to the FTP. One of their men encouraged me to...'

'Encouraged?' Rolf said.

'Well all right, paid me. It was to attract German soldiers

to the L'Oiseaux Bleu. I did my job. Brossolette would vouch for me. You know him if you are connected.'

Sandrine said, 'I've heard of him.'

'Then although your friend, who was German but is not German, soldier then not soldier, seeks to kill me for it, you understand I was doing the same job as you.'

'Where can we find you?' Rolf said.

'Why would you want to do that?'

'If Special Brigade come looking for us by accident, clairvoyance or even by chance, I want to know where you live. You understand?'

'I can lead you there. You would be welcome any time. I am a true Frenchman. You can count on me.'

'We go with him?' Sandrine said.

'Yes.'

They began drinking again. Rolf continued to hold onto the hapless Zedé's lapel. When the contents of the bottle had gone, Rolf stood to leave, dragging Zedé to his feet.

Zedé said, 'I have an apartment twenty minutes' walk from here. You are welcome. If you just let go of me, you can please follow me.'

The weather had changed when they left the bar. A fine drizzle descended and by the time they reached Zedé's home, all three were damp. Darkness had fallen with the rain clouds, and the starless cloud above them seemed plain and dull. The dank alleyway and the refuse they passed added nothing to Rolf but a feeling of gloom. Zedé halted at a narrow doorway and they entered, up some steps to a hallway lit by a single electric bulb suspended high up from the ceiling.

He lived on the third floor and the dark hardwood door creaked as he opened it. Inside, another narrow hallway opened out into a warm, cheerful room, with high windows and a small balcony overlooking a boulevard. There was a faint, musty smell of hay, as if the place needed airing. The furniture seemed to have seen better times but there was a good rug in the centre of the room and a dresser on which numerous photographs stood in wooden and in silver frames. Rolf crossed the creaking floorboards and examined them. There was an old photograph of a young woman; she was dressed in an elaborate costume and a complicated hat. Next to that was a group photograph of actors on stage, taking a bow. More photographs of stages, artists, and theatres adorned the dresser top and Rolf gained some insight into the man Zedé once was.

Zedé picked up the image of the young woman. His small moustache broadened as he smiled.

'My wife,' he said.

'Wife?' Sandrine said.

'Yes. She died. An actress. Her stage name was Ulrika Soltz. You've maybe heard of her? No? Silent movies and stage plays. We had a good life in those days, before this war.'

'I'm sorry.'

'No. Don't be. I am almost glad she didn't live to see what has become of us all. She got pneumonia in the winter of thirty-eight,' he said, looking at the photograph for a few moments more. Then, as if determined not to think of his loss, he became more animated and swept an arm across the room. '*Mi casa, su casa*, as they say in Madrid. I will make coffee. Real coffee, not this chicory rubbish. It is the only perquisite I receive for being known in the world of stage and screen. A gift from a little sparrow only a few months back.'

'Sparrow?' Sandrine said.

'With the voice of an angel.'

'You know Edith Piaf?' Rolf said, his voice higher pitched than normal.

'Before I came on hard times, I owned a theatre. It burned down and now I am as you see. Burned down myself, a smouldering wreck of a man, who gets his money where he can.'

Rolf checked the tiny kitchen before leaving Zedé to make coffee, and sat with Sandrine on the chaise longue. There were more photographs on the walls, some signed by the subject, others not. Neither of them spoke. It was as if they had entered a different world, a place of fantasy and glitter and there seemed somehow to be no other place to go. In some strange way however, Zedé's home gave a feeling of appropriateness as if they were meant to be there.

2

Zedé sat opposite the two of them, sipping from a demitasse.

'I have no wine, only a little Eau de Vie, but I wouldn't offer that rotgut stuff to a guest. You can stay here tonight if you wish. I have some bread and cheese but nothing else, I'm afraid. Not like the old days, when Ulrika and I would drink Champagne and eat the finest foie gras and beluga caviar on those little blinis, you know the ones?.'

'We need to get back,' Rolf said.

'Pity. I have two rooms. You are welcome. To be honest, I would savour the company. I have been alone here a long time.'

'We are perhaps not in such a hurry,' Sandrine said.

Rolf gave her a questioning glance.

'Then I will tell you about my life, and perhaps you will tell me of yours. He was a good man, your father. He often supplied me with props; on loan of course, but all the same...'

He began to talk then. Tales of film stars, theatres and wild parties. He knew gossip and fact but never separated the two and Rolf felt as if he had entered a different place, an oasis of unreality in the middle of a stark and brutal world. They conversed, they ate, and they laughed and Sandrine took Rolf's hand. A tiny squeeze, the feeling of her hand in his, seemed as natural to him as if he had known her for years. He realised this was the escape she had talked about in the bar. Rolf understood now how she needed this time away from war and guns and damp warehouses.

The evening wore on and by the time they had consumed the half-bottle of Eau de Vie and all the bread and cheese, their host began to yawn.

'I'm sorry. You must stay here tonight. It will make an old showman happy to have company.'

'We must go,' Rolf said. 'The others will be worried about us.'

'Others?' Zedé said.

Sandrine interjected, 'We stay with some friends who will be worried if we don't go back.'

'But you are both grown up. Here, you can use the main bedroom. I never use it since Ulrika...'

Rolf squeezed her hand. 'We must get back.'

Sandrine frowned. 'It isn't too important...'

'Ah, I see. You don't trust me. Maybe because I led your friend to his death...'

'Yes,'

'I'm sorry. You have to understand this is a war. All I did was to obey orders. Your people are destroying our country and every man, whether he is an old one or young one must do his bit. I'm sorry he was your friend. Really. But I am loyal only to France.'

'You don't understand. I'm not one of them. Germany as the Third Reich is not my country. I belong to the Länder. Dortmund. I am no longer one of those men in green uniforms, though I cannot forget my friend.'

'I'm sorry for it. I cannot apologise for serving my country any more than you can apologise for serving yours. It was never personal until tonight. If you feel safer, you can lock me in my bedroom with my chamber-pot and let me out in the morning.'

The thought of doing as Zedé suggested made Rolf smile. It seemed a ridiculous idea. He wanted to stay. He wanted to be with Sandrine. Fires were burning in his mind and there was only one way to slake them. If taking a risk was the price, then he had no hesitation in accepting it. He looked at Sandrine.

'We stay?'

She looked up at him. 'I'm tired. We can stay. You sleep on the couch. I'll take the bed.'

Zedé took his leave, with a short, quick goodnight and they stood, still holding hands in the centre of the room. Zedé had locked one of the two doors behind them as he went in and it left one other, which stood ajar.

He pulled her to him and looked at her face. She said nothing, her face betraying neither encouragement nor dissent. As if time meant nothing to him, he leaned forward until he could feel her breath on his lips and still she did not move. Her head tilted a little and her lips parted.

Their lips touched. To Rolf it was electric, a spasm of more intense desire than any he had ever felt. It stayed, it grew, and he revelled in it.

She pushed against his chest.

'Not here, she said.

Rolf noticed how her chest moved, her breathing rapid. She turned and led him by the hand towards the doorway. Her lips were upon him as soon as Rolf pushed the door to. This time their passion grew. The feel of her tongue swirling against his, the touch of her body against his, his thoughts that he lacked experience. It all combined in a heady mix. Overwhelmed by his desire, his fingers trembling and fumbling, he unbuttoned her blouse and she ran her fingers through his hair. They fell on the bed and undressed each other. Rolf winced as his shoes hit the floor, he felt embarrassed that Zedé might hear and understand. She placed an index against his lips and shook her head.

They touched each other, learning the feel, the smell and taste of one another too. They kissed all the while and she guided him as they made love. She pushed him off and guided his head between her legs and she cried out as she reached her peak.

'Oh God,' she called.

'Oh-my-God,' she said, and she shuddered, perspiring and pushing his head away. He entered her then and with each desperate thrust, she moaned and clawed at him, until he could feel such intense pleasure from the weals on his back, it made him finish. Spasm after spasm. Then kiss after kiss. His kisses, desperate now, as if wanting to retrieve some of the pleasure of the moments before—before it faded and was lost in the Paris night. He fell away from her and they lay by side; he was damp with sweat and dizzy with pleasure.

He loved her then. He knew he wanted no one else for the rest of his life and he was not a man to change his mind. Rolf turned towards her and touched her face—a gentle open-handed caress.

'I love you,' he said.

She turned her head away and said, 'Don't'

'What's wrong?'

'Nothing, nothing wrong. It was wonderful, just don't make me love you. Not love.'

He withdrew his hand and she got up, searching for something in the tangled heap of clothes. She extracted a handkerchief, wiped herself, and then strode naked into the living area, returning almost at once with her pack of Gauloise cigarettes.

They lay next to each other, touching and fondling as they smoked. But the closeness had gone and he knew it. Silence remained with them. It hung in the air, like a thin but impenetrable wall between them, and Rolf could not understand, in his inexperience of women, what could bring about such an abrupt change. All he had done was voice his love for her. Was that so bad? Should he have said nothing? Did she not love him? It seemed unbelievable after the moment they had just shared. She called upon God, for heaven's sake. Did that mean nothing?

Chapter 5

"Vengeance has no foresight."

Napoleon Bonaparte

1

Rolf could see the tip of the Tour Eiffel out of the window as he leaned, naked against the windowsill, and he realised they were still in the heart of the city. A tree-lined boulevard, houses and shops and best of all, the river, greeted him as he opened the window. Sandrine moaned a soft murmur as he looked at her. She turned in her half-sleep, and Rolf resumed greeting the blue skies and the new day with a feeling of optimism the likes of which he had not felt for a long, long time.

A song came to mind and he mumbled it at first, then sang in a soft voice, not wishing to awaken her, yet desperate to give voice to his feelings. He knew it must sound odd with his German accent, but today, on this bright and sunny morning, his heart got the better of him.

Bluebirds,
Singing a song,
Nothing but bluebirds,
All day long...

'Irving Berlin,' she said.

Glancing over his shoulder, Rolf realised he had awakened her and he began to feel contrite; he stopped singing and faced her.

'I'm sorry, I didn't mean to wake you.'

'You missed out a bit,' she said.

```
Never saw the sun shining so bright,
Never saw things going so right,
Noticing the days hurrying by,
When you're in love, my how they fly…
```

She wiggled her hips and danced, turning a tiny pirouette, ending in front of him. She was smiling and he wished he could always remember that smile beaming through the crimson lips that so lately were touching his.

Placing his hands on her shoulders, he said, 'You didn't like the word "love" last night when it was on my lips. Has the morning brought a change of heart?'

'I only sang the words of an American song. I doesn't mean I need to live by every word of it.'

Dejected, he looked at the floor. 'No, I suppose not.'

'Rolf,' she said, reaching up with both hands and touching his cheeks, 'either of us could die at any time. Commitment is too much to ask of anyone now. Perhaps when the war ends…'

'I don't understand you. One moment you love me, the next…'

'Why does it matter? We are here together now. Let's enjoy the moment, not think of the future. Just for now. Please.'

He reached for her and held her to him. His hands caressed

her back and his lips sought hers. She pushed him away.

'We have to go,' she said, still smiling. 'It's late. They will be missing us.'

'Zedé…'

'He'll awaken and we'll be gone. You can leave him a note, if you like.'

They dressed in silence. Rolf ached for her. He wished she were less determined. All he wanted was to make love, and to hell with the partisan group. Weighed against his desire for Sandrine, partisans dwindled into obscurity. She seemed to Rolf to be immune to persuasion, however, and he achieved nothing each time he tried. He ceased his attempts at arousing her and complied in the end. He wrote a note to Zedé and they left, through the door and down the stairs, and out into the fresh autumn morning.

They dared not take a cab nor to use the metro. The walk took them an hour before they reached the archway beyond which stood the square with the warehouse. Entering the archway, Sandrine, ahead by a few feet, stopped. She raised her hand. She began to pull back.

'This isn't right,' she said.

'What isn't?'

'The windows. There should be a white rag in the top one. It's gone.'

'What does that mean?'

Sandrine began walking along the street. A dog passed her and cocked his leg on an overflowing dustbin. A fat woman emerged from a doorway and threw the contents of a bowl onto the cobbles. And all the time, Sandrine quickened her step. Rolf walked faster and caught up with her. He put a hand on her shoulder.

'What's wrong? Tell me.'

'It means we're blown. No white rag in the window means the Germans have been here. We must go.'

'But where?'

'I have a number.'

'A telephone, where?'

'The station. If anyone answers the ringing, it isn't safe. If no answer, then I know a safe house where we are supposed to meet.'

'You're sure?'

'No. I'm not sure. What do you suggest? We walk in there and ask if there are any Germans? Trust me on this Rolf. It was planned long ago.'

Silent now, with Rolf half a pace behind, they walked fast towards the railway station, hoping they would be unnoticed, despite the blue skies above.

2

The apartment on the third floor of the building on the corner of Rue Mahias and Rue Tesserant held one main advantage for the partisans. It gave access to the rooftops, high above the Boulogne district and held a prospect of quick escape if the Special Brigade found them again. From the roof, Rolf could see the Ile de Seguin where the biggest factory in France produced Renault cars.

He stood waiting in the drizzle, sitting on a low wall, beyond which was a drop to the street five floors down. They had ushered Sandrine away and sent him up the two floors to the roof, guarded by Louis, who fidgeted with a Luger. He snapped the safety off and on and the sound began to irritate, though Rolf said nothing. Louis did not point the gun at Rolf, but the meaning was clear. Distrust. He understood why they had no faith in him. Would he have reacted otherwise, if the fate had reversed positions? He thought not, and so it caused no offence.

He waited patient and quiet for an hour, until Louis took him down again. The stairwell was wide and well appointed, a green patterned carpet clothing the stairs and pictures lining the walls. They stopped at a dark hardwood door and Louis knocked three times, then twice more.

Claude, Lucien and André stood in the room. Sandrine sat in an easy chair, looking up as Rolf entered with anxiety expressed in her face. Louis gestured a chair next to Sandrine's with the Luger.

'Sit,' he said.

Rolf looked at Louis' face and it was an open book to him.

He wants to be the one to kill me. I know it. It's written in his eyes; even his half-smile, but they won't do it here. They will invite me to go with them. Somewhere quiet, where people will smile as if I can trust them. It began with them not trusting me and ends in the same way. Now I don't trust them either.

André said, 'Rolf. We need to know how the Special Brigade found us. Louis seems to think it was you.'

'Why would I do that?' Rolf said. 'They would shoot me on sight as you all know. We've talked about this before.'

Claude said, 'You see any faces here whom you could accuse of betraying us?'

'No. How can you be so sure it's me? They could have followed any one of you. They might have had another informant outside the group. Besides, I've had no opportunity to send messages to anyone. Have I been alone for a moment? No.'

'Why didn't you return last night as instructed?' Lucien said. 'There must have been a reason why you did not want to be there when the SB came. Maybe you knew they were coming? They brought German soldiers with them, you know. You are a German soldier. Is there a connexion?'

'Sandrine will have told you what happened. I see no need to repeat the truth. We didn't return, because we stayed the night at an FTP operative's place. He offered, we said yes. It is as simple as that.'

'He never left your side, all night?' Lucien said to Sandrine, a smile on his lips.

She flushed then took out a cigarette with trembling fingers and lit one with a match. Rolf wondered what they had said to her before he entered.

Exhaling, she looked at Lucien. 'Look, I've told you what happened. Rolf did nothing to arouse my suspicions. It was my idea to go for a drink. It was my idea to stay at Zedé's apartment. You could check that with Zedé. You said you know him, André. You can ask him.'

'You want to know how you can trust me?' Rolf said.

Louis said, 'We can't trust you.'

'You could, if I did something to show you I am not on the other side. I can do a mission. You don't like the Special Brigade? I'll kill Boucher for you.'

'You?' Claude said, 'How will you do that? No one can get close to him. It's been tried before.'

'I will do it. I will do my homework and once I know all about him, I'll kill him. If I'm a traitor, I won't do it. If they shoot me, you've lost nothing; it will save you the trouble. If I succeed, you will know.'

'Rolf,' Lucien said, 'if I were in your shoes, if I were a traitor; I would say the same, to buy time and look for an opportunity to escape. You have no credentials, no surety. All we know about you is that you helped Sandrine escape from the Prefecture.'

'But I did my job with the operation. I was at risk too.'

Louis, who had said little so far, stepped forward. He took the Luger and waved it under Rolf's nose. 'Know what this is?'

Rolf looked up. Louis slipped the safety. 'Well,' he said.

Rolf said, 'It's a Luger.'

'It's a Luger and it is the last thing you will ever see. You are a spy. This is inevitability, as certain as being born. I'm going to…'

Lucien pulled him away. 'Stupid, Louis. I say we give him his chance. There are many reasons for wanting Boucher out of our hair, not just what they did to Spartaco.'

'Who the hell do you think you are, pushing me around?' Louis pointed the gun at Lucien. It was a mistake. They were standing close. Lucien was smaller than Louis, but he was fast. With a movement so quick, it rivalled the blink of an eye, Lucien raised his arm, arching his back, and sweeping the gun to the side with his left. His elbow contacted the point of Louis' chin and he pitched backwards, the back of his head striking a round, three-legged table behind. He lay still.

André said, 'Oh well done. Now look, we are fighting among ourselves.'

He crossed the room and pushed Lucien aside, kneeling on the brown Turkish rug. He slapped Louis' face until he began to come around. Standing, he faced Rolf, who had not moved. 'Rolf, since you came to us, we've had nothing but trouble. Now we even fight each other. Why shouldn't we just get rid of you?'

'Because you know I'm not a traitor. If something goes wrong next time, maybe you'll know. Let me have Boucher. I've seen what he does to people with his blowtorch. Ask Sandrine.'

Sandrine stood up. 'This is stupid.' She waved her cigarette at him. 'I vouch for Rolf. If he wants to do this service for us, I for one will help him. You know what Boucher did to me?'

Rolf looked at her. He was puzzled. He realised there were no scars on her thighs. The thought dissipated as fast as it came into his mind and André drew his attention.

'Sit down. The only one out of control here is Louis and he won't be a bother for a while.'

He glanced towards his feet where Louis lay groaning and holding his head.

'I will need to follow Boucher and formulate a plan,' Rolf said.

'Someone will be with you every second you are out of this place. You will not be armed and you will stay within sight at all times. If you disobey, whoever is with you will finish you. Understand?'

'I will go with him,' Sandrine said.

'You? No Sandrine, I don't think so. You look at him with affection in your eyes and that is written all over his face. What you do together here is none of my business, but outside, I think watching our German friend here is a job for us.'

'You don't believe me? I've been part of this group as long as you have. If you don't trust me…'

'Yes, we trust you, but where this man is concerned, you could make a mistake. You need to trust us too. I will make sure he doesn't get into any trouble.'

'And what do I do? Sit here on my arse?'

'Yes.'

Fuming, Sandrine sat down and puffed at her cigarette, inhaling a deep lungful of smoke. She said nothing.

'So. It is settled,' André said. 'Tomorrow we talk about where and when and you do some observation. No point waiting outside the prefecture until the evening. You should follow him when he finishes his duties and Lucien will go with you. Remember, if Lucien doesn't return and you do. It will mean your life. Understand.'

'Understood.'

Louis took an hour to come around. He stared at Rolf from time to time and Rolf could almost read the man's mind. He also knew he would need to make sure Louis was never behind him. The Luger could go off by accident and Rolf thought that would be a bad thing.

Chapter 6

"Never interrupt your enemy when he is making a mistake."

Napoleon Bonaparte

1

They didn't know where Boucher lived, so they took a chance. Rolf and Lucien parked their black Citroën on the Rive Gauche facing towards the Pont Neuf on the assumption the Special Brigade commander lived to the west. It would have been foolish to park on the bridge—they would have been too conspicuous—so they settled for parking on the main road where they could see the Prefecture across the bridge.

'You're sure you'll recognise the car?' Rolf said.

'Yes. I've seen it many times. We tried to kill the man six months ago, but he's elusive. Even Manouchian came up with no ideas in the end. Keep watching. I'm going to get some cigarettes, over there at the kiosk.' He pointed across the road.

'I thought you had to watch me all the time?'

'Heh. André is paranoid. I know it wasn't you tipped them off. I can judge a man.'

'What about Louis?

'What about Louis?'

'You trust him? He's a killer.'

'I'll tell you about Louis. He's lost family to the SD and the Special Brigade. He wants vengeance, and who can blame him? If I was in his shoes, I wouldn't trust a Kraut either.'

'Reassuring.'

'No. Not reassuring, common sense.'

Lucien grunted as he elevated himself out of the vehicle. As the door slammed, Rolf concentrated on the prefecture. He had a good view. The Pont au Change with its wide, paved surface stood empty and devoid of traffic and he would be able to see any car emerging onto it. He was looking for a Black Renault limousine. André had described it and it was as different to Rolf's car as a wolf might compare to a mouse.

Lucien opened the door and looked across the bridge before settling himself in the passenger's seat. 'What time?' he said.

'Six-thirty,' Rolf replied, glancing at his watch. He was sweating.

'Should be soon. Maybe he works late.'

'No. When I was there he was usually away by this time.'

'Maybe he's busy organising the search for that Schmidt fellow.'

'Yes. Very funny. Maybe he is looking for you instead?'

'Cigarette?' Lucien said, proffering the blue pack.

Rolf took one and lit it with his own match. He wound down the window and continued his vigil. Moments later the black car emerged from the street in front of the prefecture and turned left, heading along the Pont au Change.

'We're on,' Lucien said.

Rolf started the engine and shifted into first, his foot on the clutch, waiting. The black car turned left heading west and Rolf followed. As instructed by Lucien, he followed one or sometimes two cars behind when there was traffic, and when there was not he held back.

After ten minutes the limousine stopped at a roadside flower stall and Boucher got out. He wore his usual black suit and a charcoal coat, but no hat, his hair shiny and sleek in the dusk light. Crossing the road to the barrow and he bought a large bunch of red and white roses and then returned to the vehicle, before the limousine sped away.

They drove until they reached the Bois de Boulogne where the black limousine turned right. Still following, Rolf turned left onto Rue de Villiers, now heading west. Half-way up on the right where there was a side street, the limousine stopped at a shoe shop with an apartment over. They drove past and pulled off the road into a cobbled alleyway. Hurrying now, they both approached the corner and watched as Boucher emerged from the vehicle. Leaning into the car, he took up the bouquet and spoke to the driver before walking towards the building on the corner. He smiled at an armed police officer standing on the entrance steps and rummaged in his pocket. Rolf and Lucien approached.

Looking up, Rolf noticed the building rose five floors from the street. The windows had shutters and low wrought iron railings at each one. The grey stone façade of the building was designed with ridges in the stonework. Passing the side-street entrance they noticed Boucher standing on the steps at the side of the building. Flowers in one hand and a key in the other, he was opening the door. The policeman, with a

German rifle slung upon his shoulder, looked around as Boucher put the key in the lock. The two partisans walked past, noting the surroundings all the time.

Rolf kept an eye on the entrance as Boucher went in and they stood watching him disappear through the door. Waiting, they saw lamps lit on the third floor, though the other floors remained dark. Luck was with them then, because Boucher came to one of the lit windows, holding a vase, intent on placing it on the sill. Although Rolf could not hear, he saw Boucher turn around smiling as a woman came into view, backlit by the lights. She put her arms around his neck as he put down the flowers; he turned to her, and they embraced.

'That's his wife,' Lucien said.

'He's got children too, he told me.'

'Told you that?'

'Yes. He wants to advance them in life by torturing partisans. Bastard.'

'Eh?'

'He expects advancement when the war is over. He told me. You know, one time I almost thought he was human.'

'Then what?'

'They brought in Sandrine and I realised. He deserves to die.'

'No one deserves to die. No one is completely evil either. We want him dead to warn his successor not to tangle with us. It's business. If you make it so deeply personal, you'll make mistakes. Remember, it's business and nothing else.'

'I don't believe you.'

'Look the light's come on in the other room.'

They continued to watch. They could see Boucher holding a small child in his arms and walking back and forth in front of the window, settling the infant. Once again, he seemed almost human to Rolf, but then pictures came into his mind, visions of what he had experienced as a guard in the prefecture. The vision cleared his mind of sympathy. He focused on how he could get to Boucher. What he hated most was the way the man seemed to feel justified in killing and torturing women. It was the story of an abuser, and it filled Rolf's mind as he watched.

Rolf stepped back from the corner on which they stood. He gestured to Lucien to follow and they made their way back to the car. Seated together in the small Citroën they smoked and remained there, parked in the side-street.

'Well it wasn't a waste of time,' Rolf said.

'No. We know where he lives and we know when he is there. No closer to getting in though.'

'Difficult. There's a guard on the door. However we do it, we have to get past him.'

'Report back eh?'

'Yes, let's go. If we're late, André will probably shoot me.'

Lucien laughed aloud at that. The unlit shops of the Paris suburbs flew by as they drove back to Rue de Tesserant. The streets showed Paris as a sad place. Shops boarded up, graffiti with anti-Semitic slogans, and soldiers coming out of bars and restaurants. He stopped outside one of the shops, its windows boarded up. A slogan written on one of the boards caught Rolf's eye. It said "Travail Famille, Patrie". Beneath it, another sign in red said, "Tracas, famine,Patroille".

'Tracas?'

Lucien sighed. 'It means trouble. Trouble, Starvation and Patrols. It's what your people have brought to us since they invaded. Every man and woman has to resist somehow, don't they?'

Rolf laughed.

'You think it's funny?' Lucien said, scowling.

'No. Not that. It's just that you have your propaganda and we have ours. Every week there was a poster pasted outside our barrack-room. It contained what the High Command think are pearls of wisdom. Indoctrination and propaganda. If I were to translate some of them to you, you would laugh as well. In one, Hitler says you need a healthy peasant population and all will be well.'

'Either way. We need to get back. They will be worried.'

'Worried I have betrayed you to the SB?'

'No. Worried in case we have been arrested. Now drive, will you? I don't want to be stopped by a patrol.'

2

'Oh God,' Sandrine whispered.

Her rhythm slowed and she looked down at Rolf, a slow smile spreading across her crimson lips.

He shuddered beneath her as he came to his last thrust. She collapsed across him, her hands either side of his face. To Rolf the wetness of their perspiration was to be treasured. Leaning forwards, she placed her lips on his and Rolf felt something he had never experienced before. It was a deep feeling of peace. It was as if she had laid all his ghosts to rest: as if Sandrine had confined those swinging black shoes at last to some deep furrow in his mind, where he would never need to go again.

He reached up and caressed her back with both hands, soft gentle fingertips, touching, feeling. 'I don't care whether you think it is dangerous to voice it. I love you. I love you more than life, more than anything in my world.'

She whispered. 'You are unwise, Rolf. It isn't just the fact of it. It is the responsibility that goes with it. Any of us could die or be captured any time.'

'All right then, if you won't say it, you love me.'

'Shut up.'

'I know you do.'

'Please.'

'Don't you believe in fate? God, or fate, or destiny? They have thrust us together and we are powerless to change what we feel. Why do you fight it so?'

'Our love is dangerous. To love and then betray is unforgiveable.'

'You would never betray me, any more than I would betray you.'

Sandrine sat up and swung her legs over the edge of the narrow cot. She sat there and reached to the floor for her cigarettes. Lighting one, she blew a smoke-ring.

Rolf, leaning on one elbow, watched as it drifted away.

It floats in the still air; a slow ghostly circle, hanging for a few moments, then gone forever in a shapeless mass. Like my life. A perfect shape for a time, and then dissipated forever. No trace. If I don't make the most of it, it's wasted. God, how I love this woman.

Rolf touched her back in silence then reached for the blue Gauloise pack and extracted a cigarette.

'You know,' she said, 'being together makes us more vulnerable to people like Boucher than ever. If either of us is caught again, they will use it.'

'How so?'

'To make us talk, they would do anything to either of us. They could use my love for you to threaten you and make me talk.'

'See. You said it.'

'What?' she said.

Rolf, the unlit cigarette, wagging from the corner of his mouth, said, 'You do love me.'

She sighed. It was an exhalation shaped by resignation, as if all she had tried to hide had now become plain. She stubbed out the cigarette in the green ashtray at her feet. He felt as though he had finally triumphed over some impregnable barrier, emerging at last the victor.

'Sandrine, when this war is over, I will marry you. Before then, I need to kill Boucher. After what he did to you, he deserves killing.'

'Perhaps.'

'He burned you.'

'No. He threatened to. Thanks to you, he didn't succeed.'

'You were going to show Manouchian and the others the burns, but I knew there weren't any. I puzzled over it.'

'I was only pretending. It was just that I wanted them to leave you alone.'

'You did that for me?'

'Of course.'

'How could you ever doubt that you loved me?'

'I didn't. I just didn't want to admit it, that's all.'

Her words irritated him. Rolf turned over and faced the wall. 'Women. I don't understand you.'

Sandrine lay down beside him, cuddling into his back, her hands caressing his chest.

'You'll learn,' she whispered.

He didn't see the tear meandering down her cheek and dripping to spread its tiny stain on the white pillowcase.

Chapter 7

"The only conquests which are permanent and leave no regrets are our conquests over ourselves."

Napoleon Bonaparte

1

6 a.m. Rue de Villiers

Claude stood shifting from one foot to another. He stood leaning against a doorway diagonally across from Boucher's building, with his hands in his pockets, wearing a wide-brimmed hat. A cigarette dangled from the corner of his mouth and he coughed as the smoke hit the back of his throat. Looking up, his eyes narrowed. Two men in black uniforms approached, as dawn's early light flooded the wet flagstones, casting long shadows before them.

Rolf, tall and broad, his uniform tight and uncomfortable-looking, nodded towards the building across the street.

'He hasn't come out?'

'No. I've been here since he came back last night. I went for a piss once, but I never lost sight of the front door.'

Lucien, next to Rolf, checked his watch.

'Five past six. Sandrine should be here any minute.' He

looked up at Rolf. 'Sure about this?'

'Of course. We've planned and rehearsed. We will do it.'

They heard the growl of the black Renault's engine as it turned the corner. Sandrine was driving and André sat beside her. They stopped ten yards down the road and Rolf and Lucien approached. André got out and opened the boot.

'We'll need the spare clips as well,' Rolf said, reaching into the car and extracting a Walther PP handgun.

'You're not fighting a war, you know,' André said.

'No, but it is best to be prepared. He might have a gun there.'

'Of course he'll have a gun. We're just banking on him not using it to open the door to the Milice, aren't we?'

'You'll wait down the road?'

'Rolf, will you relax? We've been over it a hundred times. Ready?'

Rolf and Lucien, holding their guns by their sides, looked up and down the deserted street. Not even a cat stirred and as the Black Renault drove up the road, they crossed and approached the steps to the apartment house. There was no guard visible. Rolf assumed it was because it was early, since the guards were off-duty at night. Mounting the steps, he pulled a crowbar from its hiding place behind his back. It was not a quiet process but he did the best he could to muffle the crack of the lock giving way. Followed by Lucien, he advanced, gun first.

Silence. The hallway was empty. A set of stairs to his right descended and another to his left went up. Rays of morning light from a small window above them gave a dim illumination. They stood listening as Lucien pushed the now unlockable door to, behind them.

'Third floor,' Rolf muttered.

They crept up the stairs. On the third floor landing two varnished hardwood doors greeted them. Rolf estimated which door belonged to the outward facing apartment. Lucien flattened himself against the wall by the door and Rolf knocked twice with the crowbar on the dark wood. They waited.

Silence.

Rolf banged on the door again. A dog barked in the street, loud and clear to both their ears.

Lucien whispered, 'He is there, Claude said so.'

'Maybe he's dressing.'

Rolf knocked again. A faint sound drew his attention. It came from below. It was as if someone padded with great care up the carpeted stairs.

'Check the stairs,' Rolf whispered.

Lucien crossed to the stairwell and looked down through the black, wrought iron railings. Rolf had decided to try knocking again when Lucien fired. He jumped, his heart beating a rapid tattoo inside his chest and his ears ringing, the sound seemed so loud and so sudden.

Rolf joined Lucien. Bullets ricocheted around them. Lucien kept firing. No one came up but Rolf could see rifle barrels pointing up towards him. He grabbed the arm of Lucien's coat.

'Up,' He said. 'Up the stairs.'

There were two floors above them and then the roof, or so Rolf hoped. He had no idea whether there might be a skylight or a door, but he knew they would not be going down.

One floor up and he heard a gunshot from above him. The bullet took Lucien in the thigh. He collapsed. Blood flowed through his fingers and Rolf heard someone descending.

Bullets pinged on the stone staircase around him. He leapt up the stairs, keeping the sparse cover of the railings between him and his assailant. Another shot, then another. He took his time. A soldier's head appeared and he fired, two handed.

The body rolled down the stairs and Rolf rushed on. A Heer private knelt on the next landing, inserting a magazine into his Mauser. Rolf took a head shot. The man's helmet rolled away. His brains splattered on the wall behind. No others.

Rolf ran down the stairs to where Lucien was tying a belt around his thigh. Rolf leaned over the bannister and fired twice: blind, random shots. A deterrent, nothing more. He had seen no targets.

He leaned down and grasped Lucien around the waist and they struggled up the stairs.

'You go,' Lucien said. 'You can't get out trailing me along.'

'No. We're in this together.'

'It'll get you killed. Leave me and I'll slow them down long enough for you to get up to the roof.'

'Together. I know what they do to their prisoners. Understand? Now get a move on or I'll shoot you myself.'

Lucien tried to stand, but his leg gave way. Blood still poured out, a pool of it accumulating at his feet. More shots from below. Rolf bent down and pulled Lucien over his shoulder. Carrying him, he climbed up the stairs as fast as he could.

There was an iron door at the top, a padlock holding it firm. Rolf stepped back and fired twice. He snapped off the broken lock and kicked open the door. He emerged into the morning light. Putting down the now semi-conscious Lucien he turned his attention to the door. There was an external bolt, but rust rendered it immobile when he tried it. He leaned into the stairwell and fired three times down the stairs. Anything to delay. He needed time to think, but there was none.

2

Rolf examined his options. Carrying Lucien meant he could not jump far anywhere. He crossed the flat roof and peered over the edge. Another roof six or so feet below ran the length of the adjacent building, but it was not flat, it was a tiled, pitched affair, green moss covering the tiles in places. He returned to the stairwell and fired a couple more shots, then inserted another clip.

Bending forward, gun in hand, he grasped his friend and slung him over his shoulder. There was no time for hesitation. No time to weigh the risks, only action, step by step, to the edge. He dropped astride the ridge tiles and fell to one knee almost toppling, but he was a strong man and managed to remain upright. He looked down and saw a military truck, tiny from this height, though he could identify men with rifles stepping down out of the back. An odd, straggling run came then. One foot either side of the ridge tiles. To the end of the roof, where another began. Then another two feet up. He was heading east. His only hope was to find a way down and hope André and Sandrine realised what was happening. Then the tiles came alive. All around him, bullets pinged into the red clay surface. No time to shoot back. No time.

Exposed and an easy target, Rolf took the step up. He ran again and found a flat roof further on this time. He glanced over his shoulder. Three men in black with rifles were negotiating the drop to the first roof. Holding onto Lucien with his left hand, he raised his gun. Kneeling, aiming with care, he levelled it and fired. The first man down cried out and fell, arms outstretched above him as he dropped, slipping limp and lifeless down the ridge to the street below. His companions lay flat and began firing again.

Breathing hard, Rolf found the weight of his friend almost unbearable. He knew there was no choice and there could be little chance of escape, but deep inside him there was a burning anger. It was like when he found his mother. It was as if that rage he once felt all those years before revisited him. Like some giant hand, it propelled him forwards. He began to feel that exhilaration men feel in battle. Perhaps, he thought, it was his Germanic nature coming out, some kind of crude battle fury. He even smiled as he found a closed door. It would not be closed much longer, though whether or not the soldiers would be on those stairs too, he could not know, nor did he care.

Firing to where he thought the lock would be, Rolf managed to open the door. He wrenched it one-handed until he could get in. He flew down the stairs, still clutching his burden. No soldiers, not yet anyway. Ten flights down, still carrying Lucien. A woman emerged from a doorway wearing curlers in her hair and a blue dressing gown. A look of horror filled her middle-aged face and she retreated indoors at once, slamming the door. Rolf had no time to watch. He gained the ground floor and opened the door. He could see soldiers running in his direction and he saw two peel off, and enter one of the intervening buildings. The other two came straight at him. Whether they did not see him at first, or whether some miracle intervened, neither of them lowered their guns. They were perhaps a hundred yards from the main group. Rolf counted on confusion. How could they know he was now at ground level?

He descended the stairs and went down on one knee leaning around the wrought-iron railings. Again, he aimed. He knew that if he became careless it would cost him his life. He dropped one of the soldiers with a chest shot and aimed at the other as the man knelt, levelling his Mauser.

Rolf fired. A loud click. Then... Nothing.

A misfire. He knew all was lost. He tried to duck back into the hallway as fast as he could but he knew the German was flexing his index finger. He knew he was dead.

Chapter 8

"In today's complex and fast-moving world, what we need even more than foresight or hindsight is insight."

Napoleon Bonaparte

1

The tyres screeched as the Renault rocketed forward. The soldier, his finger on the trigger of his Mauser, looked up. He could not help but see the inevitability of his death as the Renault hit him. The gun flew away and Rolf, hearing the car, understood what had happened. He struggled with the prostrate Lucien on his shoulder. Like a fire fighter carrying some hapless victim, he ran from the steps and opened the car door. Shouts in German came from the area of the truck. He almost threw Lucien's prostrate form into the car and André, who was driving, reversed fast enough to throw Rolf and Lucien to the foot well behind the seats. He swivelled the car round a corner, the gears screeched as he found first, and they were away.

Shots rang out, the rear windscreen shattered and the car slewed to one side.

'They've shot out a tyre,' André said.

Rolf, on the back seat now, breathing hard, said, 'So fucking what? It's not your father's car.'

Sandrine smiled, despite the tension and said, 'No. We just need to get away as fast as we can.'

'What the fuck happened? Did you get him?' André said.

Rolf fell silent for a moment. He looked down at Lucien, a man he now admired. He had followed Rolf, accepted his plan, and now lay dying on the back seat of the car because of him.

'They were waiting for us. Soldiers above and below. They must have known.'

Sandrine said, 'How could they? Only we knew the plan. Maybe they just suspected and covered all options. The truck with the soldiers didn't arrive until long after the shooting started.'

'It was only minutes before the truck came. They knew, I tell you. They knew.'

André said, 'They couldn't have known unless one of us is an informer.'

'What about Lucien?'

'You think he's a traitor? Well, fuck you. He's one of my closest friends. We grew up together. I can vouch for him,' André said.

'No, not that. He's shot. He needs a doctor, maybe hospital.'

'No hospital,' Sandrine said. 'They would find him easily and he would be in room thirty-five before you could blink. We get him back to the apartment and a doctor will come. We have connections.'

'He's shot pretty badly. His leg.'

'Press on it,' André said.

'What? Are you a fucking doctor now?'

'All bleeding stops if you press on it. It's basic first aid.

Do it.'

Rolf cut a piece of his shirt using the knife he wore at his waist. It was the one retained piece of equipment from his Third Reich days. He pressed on the wound though the bleeding was slowing. Rolf looked at the knife. The enamel swastika embedded in the pommel evoked anger and frustration. His people. His countrymen. And now? He was killing them as if they were nothing to him. Yet in a strange way, they were nothing. They were blind followers of a rigid stupid dogma. Indiscriminate and stupid. He took the blade, threw it out of the shattered rear windscreen, and sighed. The world was shit. Or maybe, he reflected, it would be shit without Sandrine.

The car bumped and swerved and he looked at the back of her head. If this was love, following this woman, then love would be his life. It absorbed him, ate away at him and it gave pleasure. The passivity he felt in that moment seemed delicious. He wanted it to sweep him away forever. He knew, as he began to relax into the bumpy ride, he would do anything for this woman.

2

'It's the fucking Kraut,' Louis said, staring straight at Rolf. 'It was all safe before he came and now? There are SB and Kraut soldiers everywhere we look. We can't afford to lose more people. André, you know it.'

They were sitting at the table in the kitchen, Sandrine, André, Claude and Rolf. With the curtains drawn, only a single electric bulb above them illuminated their faces and the wine bottle in front of them stood almost full. No one was drinking; no one dared to relax.

'You're an idiot,' Sandrine said. 'He carried Lucien out of there. He didn't leave him. You're crazy.'

Claude, said, 'I agree. I've never thought Rolf was one of them. Anyway, who ever heard of a Nazi smoking Gauloise?'

He laughed but no one followed his lead.

Andre said, 'This isn't funny. We almost lost two men today. Either way, Louis, where were you?'

'You know I was sick. My stomach…'

'So one could easily say it was because you knew it would all go wrong and you kept out of trouble.'

'Me? You can't…'

'No. Of course not. André's just saying it could be any of us if we look too closely,' Sandrine said. 'I don't think we have a traitor, just a very clever policeman who knows what we are likely to do. Boucher is outguessing us.'

Rolf said, 'I understand how you feel. Until only a month ago, I was one of them. I might have been ordered to shoot any one of you in the street like a dog. I am an educated man. I know right from wrong. There is no one in the room who can teach me morals. I've read it all: I know my countrymen have been led astray by wicked politicians who only seek to enrich themselves. Have you not wondered why the Louvre is closed? It's because if they show any pictures, my countrymen steal them and send them home. I will fight and die with you. I give you my word. Don't misunderstand. It isn't because of some higher ideal. It is because of this woman. I want to belong here, with Sandrine. There is nowhere else in the world I would rather be, or die, for that matter.'

No one spoke. They all stared at Rolf. The silence brought embarrassment. He began to realise he should never have brought out what he really felt. They would think he was an effeminate fool. Talking of love, of Sandrine, and his commitment to her. He felt foolish.

Louis stared, open-mouthed. Claude however, stood up. He reached for Rolf and he planted a kiss on each cheek. 'I could almost think you are French. Only a Frenchman could speak in this way. To die for love. What more can a man ask for?'

'I don't intend to die. I intend to kill. I am one of you. Louis, is there no way you and I can learn to trust each other?'

Louis looked away. He stood up and gestured with an outstretched arm. 'I think you have all become crazy. All of you. We take in a German, a self-confessed Nazi. Everything then begins to go wrong. It doesn't take a lot of brains to realise what's happening. And you,' he turned to Rolf, wagging a finger, 'you don't fool me with your emotional speeches about love and belonging. I know you for who you are. You're a spy and I'll prove it.'

He stormed from the room leaving the others in silence.

Presently, Rolf said, 'I wish I could convince him. I can't do more than give you my word. I would die with you. Today Lucien and I found out that there is some kind of treachery afoot. The SB has inside knowledge. I don't know how, but I trust all of you, and yet somehow they know what we plan.'

'It may be some kind of recording device,' Claude said.

'But they couldn't have placed one here. They didn't know about this place. There was no time for them to place listening devices. No, I think one of us has made a mistake, let them know through an intermediary, and that's how they knew we wanted to kill Boucher.'

'They probably know we want to kill him anyway,' Sandrine said. 'It's common sense, after what he did to me.'

Rolf looked at her. He said nothing. They began to drink and after four bottles of wine and half a bottle of Calvados, they bade each other goodnight. Sandrine followed him to their bedroom.

They made love. Ending, cuddling in each other's embrace, Sandrine said, 'I don't understand how you could get Lucien out of there.'

'If you hadn't come in the car, I would have been dead. You saved my life.'

'No. You saved Lucien. We were just there at the right time. Did you mean what you said about me?'

'Of course. How do you French say it? Naturally. Yes that's right. I must learn how to speak your language like a real Frenchman if we are to be together.' He drew her close.

Sandrine turned her head away. 'I can't love you like you love me.'

'What do you mean?'

'I can't commit myself to you or anyone else.'

'I thought you already had?'

Sandrine sat up. 'You don't know what's happening. You don't understand.'

'Of course I do. Here, come to me. You just worry one of us will be killed. If that is what fate brings us, we must cope and go on. Losing you would shatter my life though.'

'Please, can we stop this? I can't listen to it anymore.'

Sandrine stood up and walked to the door. She turned. 'You think you've found love and people who accept you, don't you? Well, when the war finishes, they will hunt you down because you and I are on the wrong side. The Germans will win this war. They fight in the east, where they will take

Russia, and they'll invade the Rosbifs too. Once they own all of Europe, there will be no place to hide. You love me? Then get the hell out of here, with me or without me.'

The door slammed behind her. Rolf shook his head as he reached for a cigarette. Lying on his back, he blew the smoke into the air, a shifting blue column of peace, it seemed to him. If he was to make something of his relationship with Sandrine, it seemed it would require more work than he had realised. He had to soothe her anxieties, had to make her accept his love. That was all it would take. Extinguishing his smoke he lay on his side, and as his eyes closed he pictured the look on his father's face as he hung, swinging in the barn. The image would not go from his mind and he wished she lay beside him, to take it all away.

Chapter 9

"In politics stupidity is not a handicap."

Napoleon Bonaparte

1

Rolf awoke as if someone was shaking him. He became aware of Sandrine lying next to him, her face towards his. Her naked body and her soft, smooth skin aroused him. He began to stroke her back and he turned further towards her, studying her face. It was not her perfect features occupying his thoughts. He was studying her freckles. They spread across her nose and he wanted to touch them, he wanted to be inside them. Extending his neck, he reached forward and kissed her nose.

It wrinkled and she shook her head. Her eyes opened and he said, 'Sorry. I didn't mean to wake you.'

'Well,' she said, 'you have.'

She yawned and made to get up. He pulled her back with one long arm.

'Not so fast, young lady,' he said.

'What? Let me up.'

'We should make love today, not war.'

'I'm too hungry.'

'How can you be too hungry to make love? It's an impossibility, surely?'

'Stop it. We have plenty of time for that. Don't you think of anything else? Men. You're all the same.'

'You want the truth?'

'No. I don't want the truth. I want to get up and have some breakfast.'

She pushed his arm away and he leaned on his elbow, watching her.

She picked up her robe and as she swathed herself in it, he said, 'You know, you have perfect breasts.'

'You crazy German,' she said. 'Why don't we go and get some fresh bread and *petit pain*? There's a baker's down the road and it will put everyone into a good mood, God knows they need to be. I'm going to check on Lucien first.'

'Think he'll be alright?'

'The doctor said he'd lost a lot of blood but the bullet went clean through, so it's only a flesh wound.'

'It bled a lot.'

'If you'd pressed on it, it would have stopped.'

'I could have asked the soldiers to wait a moment while I did first aid, I suppose.'

'All the same, next time... Anyway, he would benefit from some breakfast.'

'He's a good man, you know. He tried to persuade me to leave him.'

'I know him and it doesn't surprise me. He comes from aristocratic stock. He would die for any of us.'

'Meaning humble farming stock like me, wouldn't?'

'Shut up and get that thing covered up. You look debauched.'

Rolf laughed. It was a soft, gentle laugh of contentment.

Being in her company was all he wanted now or forever. He shifted to sit on the edge of the bed, and stretched. Sandrine went out and crossed the hallway to where the doctor had tended to Lucien. As he dressed, he thought about the previous day. Every detail was embedded in his mind. He recalled how the SB and the soldiers were waiting for them. Boucher was either not there or else he knew to stay inside. Boucher could have no way to know they would come unless someone had tipped him off. But who? It had to be someone who knew their plans well enough to pinpoint the very time they planned to attack. It was no random security precaution, Rolf was certain.

Sandrine returned. She was smiling.

'Good news?' Rolf said.

'Yes. That Lucien. Strong as an ox. He asked for soup and wanted help to get up.'

'Yes. He's strong for a small man.'

She reached up and placed her arms around his neck. Their lips touched and she drew away. 'Let's go. It's a nice day for a walk. No rain.'

Rolf grabbed his overcoat and with pleasure walked down the roadway to the corner of the street, holding her hand and smiling. The smiles had become almost involuntary. A man dressed in a black overcoat and wearing a narrow-brimmed hat bumped his shoulder as they walked past.

'Pardon me,' Rolf said.

The man pulled at the brim of his hat and said nothing. The glimpse of his face set wheels in motion in Rolf's mind. He was sure he had seen that face before, but the recollection was elusive. Where could it have been?

Glancing over his shoulder, he saw the man stop at the end of the road, opposite the apartment block where the partisans were. He pulled a newspaper out of his coat pocket and leaning on the wall facing the apartment entrance, began to read. After a moment, he looked back at Rolf. Who was he?

'Come on,' Sandrine said. 'I'm starving.'

The patisserie was crowded when they entered. Five women were in the queue ahead of them and it took time before the proprietor could serve them. The smell of baking bread brought memories to Rolf of the bakers at home, the strudel, and the dark bread. They bought *petit pains* and a loaf of fresh bread, Sandrine, careful to count out her coupons, making sure she had a few left. It would be a week before the partisans could get more. There were no croissants or anything else but bread. The shelves were almost empty too by the time they left.

'Nothing is like it used to be,' Sandrine said—her face serious.

'No. Shortages everywhere, I suppose. It isn't much better in Germany, you know.'

She shrugged and they left, each with an armful of bread. They had many mouths to feed back at the apartment after all.

Reaching the corner, Rolf became aware of an uncomfortable feeling. It was as if there were prickles in the back of his neck. It felt like someone stabbed him repeatedly with a tiny pin. He stopped and shifting the bread to one arm, rubbed his neck.

'All right?'

'Yes, I just… I just…'

As a tidal wave breaks on a troubled shore, the realisation of where he had seen that man before came to him. It hit him with the power of a pile driver. How could he have been so stupid?

'I've seen that man who passed us before. So have you. I'm surprised you didn't recognise him too.'

'What man? I saw no one.'

'The man who bumped into me. He was one of the men in room thirty five.'

'Where? Rolf, you're imagining it. I never saw anyone like that.'

'Maybe you were too shocked to take in their faces, or maybe it was the blows to your head. One of your torturers from the Special Brigade is standing outside the apartment right now.'

They peered around the corner and saw the man. He was not reading now. He was signalling with the rolled up newspaper to three black cars. The vehicles drew up outside the apartment. Five men got out of each one.

'We have to warn them,' Rolf said.

'Yes, but how?'

'The telephone. You have the number?'

'I don't know the number. André never told me. What do we do?'

'The roof. I can get up on the roof next door and maybe get to them there.'

'It's too late. All we can do is watch.'

'You have your gun?' Rolf said.

'No. I left it behind. I wasn't expecting this.'

'I have mine. I can at least try.'

Rolf reached behind him and found the grip of his Walther. It was a police model, shorter and smaller than the repeating Luger.

'You'll be killed if you try to do anything. We have to get away. There is nothing we can do. Don't you understand? Don't leave me. Please don't leave me alone.'

She grasped his arm and pulled it to her, as if by embracing it she could force him to stay.

'Then come with me. I have to find out. I have to try. I didn't save Gerhard. I owe it to myself this time to try. Come.'

'I can't. It's certain death or capture. You're mad.'

'Wait here for me then. I'll go alone. Wait though. If they come up the street, run. I'll meet you at the Faison if you have to go.'

'Please Rolf…'

He pushed her hands aside and began walking down the street towards the apartment block. He didn't look back.

2

Clouds obliterated the moon and the thick black night bore heavily on all of them. Gerhard swore.

Rolf, lying beside him on the cold sad mud, turned to Johan. 'They're making the push tonight?'

'So they said,' Johan said.

'We can hardly see a few yards in front of us. How can we be expected to advance?'

'You're asking me?'

'Gerhard. What do you think?'

'I think we shut up and follow orders. We may have a chance of getting out of this alive then.'

'Always so serious, Gerhard,' Johan said.

Rolf said, 'I only asked, that's all. If they order us to go, we go. No choice is there?'

'Don't tell me, for the Fatherland. You two are about as intelligent as the French. The point is, we won't be ordered to die out there. It isn't like the First War. We are only here for tonight, then the fleshpots of Paris await. Our commanders know what is what,' Gerhard said.

'Are the enemy in large numbers?'

Johan said, 'How the fuck do I know? I only overheard the unteroffizier in conversation. What do I really know? Next time, I'll keep it to myself.'

'Good,' Gerhard said.

Behind them, squelching in the mud, their unteroffizier leaned towards his men. 'Ten minutes, then we advance.'

'Ten minutes then we advance.'

He repeated the order in a quiet, controlled voice all along the line and Rolf realised Johan had been right. He swallowed. He didn't like this war. There was something wrong with the entire set-up. Why fight against France or any country for that matter? What use was France to the ordinary German people? Didn't the reversal of the depression just require a more careful watch over domestic finance? Why fight and kill people? None of it made sense to him and this idea that Germans were superior to others just didn't ring true either.

Ten minutes.

Ten minutes in which to do what? Say a prayer? Maybe. But Rolf knew he wasn't doing God's work. He was doing Hitler's work and it was poles away from any religious process of which he had ever heard. Rolf glanced at Johan. He was smiling. He didn't care. He felt admiration for Johan. Salt of the earth, kind friendly and always joking. Johan was the kind of man you could depend upon.

A whistle blew behind them and Rolf stood up. The time had come. Kill or be killed. No other choice. Yet, even if he killed men, there was no justification for it, and as he ran forward all he could hear in his head was that damned mantra of Heine's. "They will burn people." It reverberated in his head. As he fired his first shot at a man standing, confused and alone, he knew Heine was right. They would burn people. The party machine did not care. They did not care about Rolf and it began to dawn upon Rolf as he parried a bayonet, as he threw a grenade, only Rolf cared about Rolf. It was a disgraceful way for a man of morals to behave, but he wanted to live. He wanted to experience what really mattered in life. He craved for it. Yet he did not know the face of it. It was a stranger to him, but he knew it for what it was. Love.

None of this matters; love is all, he thought as he ran up that hill, shouting, screaming and killing.

Chapter 10

"There are times when a battle decides everything, and there are times when the most insignificant thing can decide the outcome of a battle."

Napoleon Bonaparte

1

She's scared. I'm fucking scared too. She hasn't got a gun anyway. It would be stupid of her to follow. But if she loved me... Shut up you stupid brain. She's right. It's suicide. I don't want her to come to harm. I don't care about me. I've given up everything now. She'll be alright. Stay there, Sandrine. Stay there and be safe. Rolf will do the legwork. I am the man.

He took the stairs two at a time. Breathing hard as he reached the top, he realised the door was locked. Did he dare use his gun? Would he suffer if he wasted the rounds? No. The gun was for the SB only; he had no spare clips. Panting, he looked around. The carpet had ended on the floor below.

Stair-rods.

Of course, he muttered to himself.

Reaching the lower floor, he extracted a stair-rod from its brackets and chased up the remaining stairs. Inserting it into

181

the lock he strained as he twisted. The lock, a small, pale imitation of a German lock, gave way with a snap and he was out. Roofs were becoming a habit, he thought, as he raced along the flat roof towards the apartment block.

The door was unlocked. André planned it that way in case they needed to get out in an emergency. Next to the door was the metal bar André had hoped would let them lock it, behind them. If it ever came to that. If the Germans or the SB came. André seemed so confident when he took Rolf onto the roof. It was as if he refused to see his danger. But Rolf had known. Rolf was always suspicious. He knew his people and he knew Boucher. That knowledge burned in his mind right now. Boucher. The events of the night before had taught Rolf what to expect of the man. He was clever that one.

Rolf entered the stairwell and slowed.

The top floor was a store-place and he knew no one would be there anyway. There were no shots and no sounds of struggle. Either the others got away or they were already in the black cars. He opened a door. It was a small room, boxes littering the floor. He crossed to the tiny eaves-window and looked out.

He cursed because the street was not visible from there. He left and began descending the stairs. Silence. Silence everywhere. His booted feet making no sound, he crept down. The room in which only a few hours before he had made love to Sandrine, appeared in front of him. He heard no one. He looked in, seeing nothing of note. He turned to his right and peeped into the room where only an hour ago Lucien had lain. Empty.

Rolf descended to the next landing. The front door banged and he wondered whether everyone had left. He stopped. He smacked his forehead with his open hand. How could he be so stupid? Boucher was clever. He knew Sandrine and Rolf were in the apartment. He would have understood at once, the numbers did not fit. They were waiting below for him. Perhaps even on this floor. He backed away from the stairs. The cold hard surface of the door behind him touched his back. Still with his back to the door, he grasped the handle and depressed it. Rolf stepped back into the room and turned around.

The next thing of which he became aware, was a cold metallic object at the back of his head. Damn. Stupid. Of course, they were there. Boucher was running rings around him.

'Let the weapon fall to the floor.'

The voice was familiar.

Boucher.

Rolf let go of his lifeline. It fell to the floor by his feet with a dull thud. He swallowed. He was not scared now. He had no illusions. They would take him to the prefecture, torture him and then? Well, maybe the release that death brings. If they shot him it would not matter, as long as Sandrine was safe.

'Turn around, hands on your head.'

Rolf obeyed. Boucher sat there in a chair, facing him, his black suit immaculate, his hair greased and slicked back, as if it was a matter of obsessional tidiness. The man with the gun stepped back as Rolf turned. Rolf knew he could engage in conversation or he could act. But what could he do? He had to move fast. Let them shoot him. What did he care?

'You've led us quite a dance since you escaped with that whore.'

Rolf said nothing.

'Your friends are all below, waiting for you to join them. Every last one of them.'

'What are you going to do with me?' Rolf said.

He had no wish to know. He was thinking how glad he was that Sandrine had stayed in the street. She had been right all along. It was suicide to go back.

'Get him downstairs with the others,' Boucher said to the man with the gun.

Rolf moved fast. He had no plan. He had not even thought out what he was going to do, but he moved, and with lightning speed.

His right hand shot out, catching the gunman on the nose. It was not as hard a blow as he could deliver. It started from above, after all.

Boucher began to rise. Rolf's left foot jabbed out, catching him in the face. The gunman fired. Blind, inaccurate. Tears streaming down his face. Rolf had sidestepped. He ignored Boucher and laid into the gunman. Left hook, a right to the side of his head and he was down. Another kick. No time.

Boucher was shaking his head. It was a good kick, Rolf thought. He stepped forward onto his left leg. His right hand went back. Boucher had his hand inside his coat. Rolf's fist contacted Boucher's chin. This time it was no glancing blow. The man's head jerked back hard. It struck the back of the chair. It was enough.

Rolf knelt. He picked up his Walther. He ran out onto the landing. Footsteps from below and it began again. This time it was no trap. There were no men above. He leapt up the stairs, not looking back. Out onto the roof, he barred the door as Andre had shown him and in a minute, he was flying down the stairs of the next building and out; this time the back way, not the street entrance. He knew the place would be crawling with police or SB in moments. He could not go back to Sandrine along the street. They might get her.

A small yard at the back of the building held some dustbins. He ran and using one of them, he leapt onto the red brick wall and vaulted down the other side. Landing on both feet, he looked left then right and ran on. Breathing hard, he came out of the alleyway. A railing stood in front of him and the bread shop stood opposite. He looked to his right but Sandrine was not there. He ran the short distance to the corner but she was nowhere to be seen. He turned around and began walking as fast as he could along the road.

A woman pushing a perambulator stared at him. He continued striding to his left. The street opened out into a square. Grey and brown stone flags beneath his feet, he walked with unfaltering steps, head down, hoping no one would notice him, stepping over the tram-lines. He glanced to his right where two men in waistcoats and peaked caps, their striped shirtsleeves rolled up, were setting up a stall and a third pushed a barrow laden with vegetables. Fresh vegetables were scarce Rolf thought to himself, as he passed them and made for the other side of the square. In an hour, they would all be gone.

An old woman emerged from a grocer's to his left, and began swilling the grey flags in front of her shop. She had a kind, wrinkled face and she smiled at Rolf when he looked at her. He stopped and looked into a restaurant window opposite, waiting until she went back in. There was a smell of Paris mornings in the air. He could see the darkened, wet flagstones reflecting the morning light and he watched the mirror-image in the window before him, as sparrows descended and bathed in the brown pools. They hopped and flapped their

tiny wings. As Rolf set off again, they took off and he kept
watching them, envious of their flight and their freedom. He
heard no pursuit, but he had nowhere to go.

He kept walking, a deep and bitter emptiness in his
heart. Walking: it was all he could do. He dared not settle,
and by early afternoon he had slowed to a stroll for hours,
always in the smallest streets, narrowest alleyways, avoiding
main streets and boulevards, in case anyone might notice
him. His feet became sore and he reflected how that was
nothing when compared to the pain he felt, in case he would
not see her again.

Rolf stopped once and ate in a tiny café. Bread and
sausage with wine and water. When it came to pay, he had
no coupons and the proprietor shook her head muttering, but
caused no trouble. When he left, he had still not formulated a
plan, all he had done was ruminate, fretting over Sandrine.
Where had she gone?

2

It began to rain as he rounded the corner into the cobbled
street. The stones were grey and shimmering in the streetlight's eerie glow. He shivered, but it was more a nervous
reaction than a feeling of cold. He had walked the city streets
all day, not daring to stop or speak to anyone, and now he
was hungry again. He was tired too, but he shrugged off that
feeling as he had shrugged off Boucher's attempt to take
him.

If Boucher reacted the way Rolf guessed he would, he would
find out all there was to know about Rolf and Sandrine's
escape and then the new-made friends they had shared in his

rescue would be in danger. He knew this, but at first he doubted he had time to warn anyone, let alone salvage himself. But the partisans, they had a rule: if you are caught, don't say anything for twenty-four hours. He hoped it would give him time to find Zedé; he had no idea how to find anyone else. Manouchian could have been on the moon for all he knew.

Damp and bedraggled as he was, Rolf was sure he was in the right street. He had only been there once, so he had made his way to the bar where he and Sandrine picked up the old man. He worked out where to go, despite the fact he had been a little drunk when last he was there. A ginger tomcat skittered away as he mounted the steps. He hammered on the door with his fist—there was no knocker. The rain began in earnest, turning the cobbled street into a series of shiny puddles in moments. Soaked and irritable, he continued to bang on the door.

No answer. Rolf was about to give up, sat on the stone steps beneath the doorway and took his head in his hands. It was hopeless. He had lost Sandrine. Zedé was not there and he was soaking wet. He cursed his ill luck. He bemoaned the ill fortune dogging them since the rescue. Then he became aware of a figure in front of him. Looking up, he saw Zedé, staring at him, umbrella aloft, black coat and lapel-flower, now drooping.

'You look soaked,' Zedé said. 'Has something happened?'

'I… I need to go in.'

'Of course my boy,' he said.

Key in hand, he advanced, sidling past Rolf, and opened the door. Inside, he shook his umbrella and looked at Rolf, from head to toe.

'I thought you were one person I would never see again.

What has happened?'

'SB. They came and arrested the entire group I was with. I escaped, but I've lost Sandrine.'

'Lost her?'

'Yes. I went back and she was gone by the time I escaped.'

'They took her friends?'

'Yes. They all know about you, or at least Gautier does. I came to warn you.'

'Warn me? It is very generous, but unnecessary. I don't care if they do come. I don't know anything they would find useful and I have nothing to lose but an old and worn, tattered life. A lonely existence. If they end it so much the better. They have all gone before, you see. All that will happen is that I will join them.'

'We have to get away. Surely you understand that?'

'You have to get away. I will stay. Don't tell me where you are going. I don't want to know. I have some apple brandy upstairs. You look like you need a drink.'

Zedé began climbing the stairs and glanced over his shoulder at Rolf, who followed. 'How soon will they come?'

'I don't know. Maybe in the morning. The others won't talk for a day or so. They were arrested this morning.'

'Then you can stay here tonight?'

'I don't know. There was a restaurant where we hid and a man who sheltered us. I suppose I need to warn them. It's all a disaster. I don't understand how they found us. It happened twice.'

'Twice, you say?'

'Beyond bad luck. They even knew about an attempt to kill Boucher. They were there in force.'

'A traitor?'

'They all thought so. I didn't believe it until now. There

was no one who I could imagine…'

Rolf stopped mid-sentence. A doubt came to him. He pushed it away as soon as it came and he looked up at Zedé who stood, bottle in hand, above him as he sat on the couch. Zedé passed a small glass to Rolf, and filled it with brownish clear liquor.

He said, 'You know, the way to find a weakness is to look carefully at everything. The traitor would be safe from arrest. Sometimes they arrest everyone and later let their man out. Other times you need to examine who was not caught to realise why they remain at liberty.'

'It wasn't me, was it? I wouldn't be here now if it was. I'm on the run.'

'No. I didn't mean you. Was there anyone else who they never caught?'

'Only Sandrine, but it can't be her. They tortured her. I got her out of there, you know the story.'

'Let us be objective here.' Zedé sat down beside Rolf. He put a hand on Rolf's shoulder. 'Consider this. No one has ever escaped from the prefecture since the Germans came. No one.'

'So?'

'Think about it. Was it not quite easy to get out? Do you not think they could have stopped you if they had wanted to?'

'You're insane. I…'

'You said yourself, this man Boucher is clever. Is he clever enough to let you get away and lead them to the partisans?'

'We weren't followed if that's what you mean.'

'They didn't need to follow you. They allowed Sandrine to go. They let her leave with you and they made it look good, but she was the Trojan horse, the sixpence in the

189

pudding, as the Rosbifs say.'

Rolf stood up. 'No. No. You're wrong. It's ridiculous. I saw what they did to her.'

'What did they do? A few judicious bruises here and there, a few small burns. Maybe she cracked; maybe the pain was too much. Then they turned her and now you are here.'

'It can't be,' Rolf said his voice barely audible.

He sat down again. He emptied his glass and the raw spirit burned his throat, though it was welcome. He shivered. She loved him. He knew that. His ears rang to the sound of her moans when he made love to her. Her smile as he caressed her. No. She loved him. Then it all came back to him at once. It was her suggestion they go to the bar after Ritter's death. It was she who dragged him out to the baker's and then she escaped. Perhaps she made a deal with Boucher to let Rolf live. Perhaps she was Boucher's lover? No. Impossible. They must have hurt her so much. They must have brought her to the edge and she had no choice.

'More Calvados, Rolf.' Zedé filled Rolf's glass, then his own. 'Pity. She was a beautiful girl. I wouldn't have thought it to be honest, but it seems obvious to me now as an outsider.'

Rolf said nothing, he stared at the floor. There had to be an explanation, it must be some kind of mistake. Zedé put a hand on Rolf's shoulder again.

He said, 'Look, a lot of good people are giving their lives in this war; on both sides. If this girl did betray you and the group she belonged to, then God's justice will pursue her. You must forget about her. I feel for you. I know how it feels to love and lose.'

'It can't be true. It just can't.'

'If time is short, maybe you need to go and warn these

friends of yours tonight. I will make preparations for the arrival of this Boucher. I need to compose myself and say goodbye to my friends.'

He gestured the walls, hung with photographs, his memories.

As Rolf descended the steps, he still had doubts. If Sandrine was the informer, they might be waiting for him at the Bon Faison.

Chapter 11

"As for me, to love you alone, to make you happy, to do nothing which would contradict your wishes, this is my destiny and the meaning of my life."

Napoleon Bonaparte

1

After two more hours of walking, still wet and now cold, Rolf found his way to Rue Pecquay where the Bon Faison stood. The tiny side street off Rue Rambuteau was empty, and though it was evening some customers would have been normal. He stood on the street corner looking up and down. A man riding a bicycle, with a basket-holder in front, passed by. A couple in raincoats, she with a beret, he with a hat, both sheltering under a black umbrella. No sign of the Special Brigade. The glazed door of the restaurant stood shut and a hanging sign said "Fermé" indicated the premises were closed. He knocked, but there was no answer so he walked further down the lane to the corner of the road where Josef lived. He stopped there and waited. He could see the whole lane beneath the archway and the streetlight outside where the apartment stood. He ducked into a doorway and still he waited.

Half an hour passed and the door of Josef's apartment opened. Rolf looked up and relief flooded him. She was there. He had misjudged her. How could he be so stupid? One step towards her, and he drew back again.

She was not alone.

Following her through the door a tall man appeared. He wore a dark overcoat and a hat. His face seemed familiar, Rolf recognised him for the man who bumped into him that morning. He could see Josef behind, standing on the steps. His face was bruised and battered. Rolf noted how he held onto the small handrail at the top of the steps. He swayed, and Sandrine turned towards him, stretching out a hand. The old man spat in her direction, bloodstained spittle, joining the murky rainwater at Sandrine's feet.

The tall man took Sandrine by the arm in a rough grip and pushed her along the street, towards the doorway where Rolf stood. Flattening himself against the inset wall, Rolf kept still, hoping they did not see him.

He heard the man say, 'A little special treatment for you in room thirty five. Thought you had it good before? Just wait.' He chuckled. 'Maybe you will join your friends now, maybe not.'

They were level with Rolf and he could see a look of hopelessness in his lover's face. He drew his gun. The grip of the Walther felt firm and warm to his hand. It seemed a simple matter to step out behind them. No thought. No mercy and no regret.

Rolf placed the tip of the barrel to the left of the man's back and fired. Point blank. Close-up death. Rolf knew it was a coward's play, but he took no chances. He had ceased to care in that moment. The violence and hatred in his life had culminated today in one little flexion of his index finger and he remained unperturbed.

The man fell as if crushed by a falling building and Rolf reached forward to Sandrine. She jumped aside and stood, shock registering on her face, before recognition came.

'You… You,' was all she said.

Tears streamed down her cheeks mixing with the raindrops and Rolf took her in his arms.

'We have to run.'

'They made me bring them here. They forced me. I had no other choice. You have to believe me.'

'I believe you. Now we go. Talk later.'

He grabbed her hand and guided her, walking fast at first, then a jog and finally they ran. Within a hundred yards, she pulled him to a stop and removed her shoes. Then they continued. Rolf in front, Sandrine, still clutching his hand and following behind.

On they ran, no specific place, no designated direction. Turning left or right in random patterns they avoided big streets, avoided people they saw, just on and on. In Rolf's mind as they ran, a simple thought repeated itself. She was safe now and he did not care what happened next, he would protect her.

2

The proprietor showed them their room. He asked no questions. Fat and friendly, he dragged his portly figure up the narrow staircase. He smiled as he opened the door, his balding head, with hair greasy and unkempt, nodding as he gestured them inside.

'The best room in the house,' he mumbled.

They walked in and Rolf gave the man fifty centimes. He turned, placing it in his waistcoat pocket and left Rolf looking at the room. Rolf put down the bag they had bought from a small shop on their way. The empty canvas sagged with emptiness on the floorboards and Rolf stood at the foot of the window. Sandrine was sitting on the bed. She unbuttoned her coat and it fell onto the bedcovers around her. Rolf noticed the worn armoire with its mirror, the new chest of drawers, and the bedside table. He looked out of the window. The little square below was black, not a light showing in the blackout, and he closed the curtains, creating a noise like mice running along a pipe.

'I'm sorry we are together in a place like this.'

'He thinks I'm a whore.'

'Do you feel like a whore?'

'No. I've always been a good girl. I am a good girl aren't I?'

'Yes. Good. We are in trouble.'

'Yes.'

'Will we always be together?' he said.

She shifted on the bed and dropped her shoes onto the floorboards below. Sandrine leaned back and lay down. 'Always is too long. We are together now. It is enough for now.'

'You know I love you.'

'Yes. I know you love me.'

'And you?'

'Yes, I love you.'

'Then we will be together always.'

'Maybe.'

'What do we do now?'

'Now? I don't know. We must go far away.'

He stood looking at her and she lay quiet and still, staring at the ceiling. Rolf looked up at it too. It had a wide crack the whole length, descending along the far wall. A sound of dripping water interjected and Rolf shivered.

'But you do love me?' he said.

'Love you? Yes. I love you.'

'Then tomorrow we find a way out of this.'

'Yes. Out of it. Where?'

'Switzerland?' he said.

'No. England. Many of our people went there after the Maginot line. If they hunt us here now, the coast may be easier. There is a ratline in Dieppe.'

'You know this?'

'I've heard of it.'

'You don't know though?'

'No. I don't know. I've heard of it.'

'Who does know?'

'Tomorrow, we lay plans. Now we sleep. Come to bed.'

'You told them about Joseph?'

'I had no choice. They threatened to shoot André and the others. What could I do?'

'Zedé thought you sold out the others. He said it was the reason you escaped every time.'

'You believe him? You think I would?'

'I don't believe him.'

'Come to bed.'

'You'd never betray me, would you?'

'I'd never betray you. I want to keep you safe. I want you. Come to bed.'

Chapter 12

"*The only conquests which are permanent and leave no regrets are our conquests over ourselves.*"

Napoleon Bonaparte

1

A summer sky of blue and a golden sun above them, they lay on their bellies on the hilltop looking down at the clearing. The breeze rippled the golden grass and a crow cawed its raucous cant, high above. Rolf was sweating, not from the hot sunshine, but from the anxious trek up the hill. They lay hidden behind a boulder, which broke the skyline enough for Uncle Reinhardt to feel they would be invisible to the quarry below. The old man placed a hand on the boy's shoulder.

He whispered, 'Quite still now. Wait until they come out into the clearing.'

Reinhardt was a rotund fellow, balding and breathless. Rolf knew him now. He trusted him despite only living in his home for a year. Reinhardt was the only man he knew well, apart from his father, and living on his farm with Aunt Elsa taught him there were men who did not drink and who treated others well. Today, they were hunting. It was a privilege. Deer hunting took days at a time and Reinhardt had given up two whole days to be here, lying beside the lad, instructing him in the hunt.

Below them, three does and a stag entered the yellow meadow below. They began to graze and the stag followed, raising his antlered head often, sniffing the air, looking around in case of danger.

Reinhardt whispered, 'Wait until you have a certain shot. He must turn sideways on. Behind the shoulder. Yes?'

Rolf nodded and drew a bead on the stag. He sighted the chest. He could see with the eyes of a youth, sharp and clear.

'When you have the shot, take it. It has to be clean. Through the heart. If you miss, he dies in agony. You can do this.'

'He's beautiful.'

'Yes. We should honour him by doing this right.'

Rolf put down his rifle. He looked at his mentor. 'I can't do this.'

'Yes you can. A clean kill. It is honourable to kill for food.'

'I can't. He's proud and beautiful. I'm sorry; you think I'm stupid, a fool.'

Reinhardt looked long at the boy. A tear crept into the corner of his eyes. 'You know, I think you are right. One of God's creatures, eh?'

'I'm sorry.'

'Yes, you are sorry. You apologise for being a hero. Only a hero would refuse to kill a noble creature like that. Let's go and eat that rabbit. He'll cook nicely and we'll eat him and praise his flesh and his life. I understand.'

They stood up. The deer scattered below them in the

golden field. A sense of relief came over Rolf. It was as if a great pressure had been lifted, as if his inability to kill the stag came to him like being let out of a confined space. He had felt imprisoned by what he imagined his uncle expected of him and now he was free.

'Uncle Reinhardt?'

'Yes, my little friend?'

'You're not angry with me?'

'No. We should all interpret God's law in our own way. If killing that proud and noble beast is your way of living in Christ's shadow, then that is good. Me? I'm a hunter by nature. I worship the creatures I kill and I eat them too. It is how I can live with myself. I would never kill another man, but that is God's law, is it not?'

'I think my father would not have cared. He would have beaten me for not shooting.'

'Max was a difficult man. When he was sober, he was good. Well, it is all behind you now. We, you and I, need to look ahead. We need to peer into the misty future and understand that God wants us to fight evil wherever it raises its ugly head. If not killing that beast is your way of being closer to God, well, I understand. We haven't wasted the last two days, it has all brought us closer together, like comrades in a war. We stand together, we fight side by side, and we triumph.'

The wooded hill was green and yellow, low hazel bushes and pine trees making their progress hard going. They crossed a stream and Rolf made an awkward step, placing his boot into the cold, clear waters. He cursed, and Reinhardt scolded him for the language, but they laughed at his wet socks, and later at their camp, they built the fire together in the gathering gloom of dusk.

'See, Rolf, this is how you spit-roast. High up, so the beast does not burn.'

'Uncle?'

'Yes, Rolf?'

'You knew my father well?'

'Yes, I knew Max well.'

'He was a bad man. I hated him.'

'It is for God to judge him, not us. We hunted together, like you and me. We drank wine together and we laughed. We laughed sometimes until we could not breathe. He was a funny man sometimes, your father.'

'He killed my mother.'

'He became mad. The Max I knew was not so bad as everyone thinks. He helped me often when I needed him. How can we judge another when all we have in our memories is good?'

'He killed my mother.'

'You think I don't know this?'

'I…'

'Look, there were qualities in your father that were good. The end was bad. Don't just see him that way. People are complex. No one else does, but I miss him, though I think he was a foolish, drunken violent man in the end. He was not always so. It is never a good thing to hate anyone. Remember that. One day, someone you love will betray you. It doesn't mean they don't love you. It is a matter of priorities. Some people can't help but be weak.'

'It's cooked?'

'Yes, my boy. It is cooked and we will eat. Just remember this rabbit had a life; we took it. We should honour the creature as we eat its flesh. Now eat. Be at peace.'

Rolf found sleep elusive that night. Visions of his father,

swinging from the rope, crept into his mind. Whenever he closed his eyes, the black shoes swung to and fro.

2

The autumn sky was overcast. The purple clouds held rain and it seemed to Rolf they would burst at any time. They rode past rosehip and gorse bushes and elm trees and once in a while, they stopped, examining the flat, bare landscape around them, hoping the rain would not come. Neither of them wore protection from it. The sun had shone when they set out, but as the clouds had come, the world seemed darkened, and Rolf reflected how it mirrored his thoughts.

They stopped at a roadside café. They felt cold and damp like the café. Inside, the floorboards squeaked as they entered and the three tables looked bare, brown and unhappy. The proprietor matched the surroundings and although they obtained bread, neither felt satisfied.

'You have wine?'

'Early for wine?'

The owner of the café was a short, plump woman in a lilac flowery dress, her protuberant gut swinging as she walked. Her backside did the same. She wiped away a wisp of dry, grey hair and stood on one leg then the other, waiting for a response.

Rolf and Sandrine looked at each other. The smiles crept up unawares, involuntary to both their faces.

'But you have wine?' he said.

'Yes.'

'Please,' Sandrine said, 'we have been traveling since early morning. A little wine would be very welcome. Oh, and more bread.

The proprietor said, 'And sausages?'

'If you please,' Sandrine smiled as she spoke.

The woman stomped away, across the noisy floorboards and they shared another smile.

'You will need to pay, you know.' she said.

'Yes, of course.'

'I have only twenty francs and no coupons.'

'I have plenty of Deutsche marks. The bicycles only cost ten each.'

'They robbed you. Twenty francs to the mark. They robbed you.'

'I don't mind being robbed. As long as I'm with you…'

'You talk such rubbish. You are very sentimental for a German.'

'Some Germans are very sentimental. Heine…'

'Oh, shut up now. We won't get to Dieppe for half a day and then I don't know clearly where to make contact.'

'We will have a fine life together in England.'

'Yes, a fine life.'

She smiled and the woman came with the bread and sausages.

'Bon appetite,' she said and creaked her way out to the back kitchen.

Rolf said, 'I wish we could stay in France. I don't know England. I don't think they will welcome me or trust me after Dunkirk.'

Sandrine stared into the distance. Her face was serious. 'We don't need to consider it now,' she said. 'Worry about it when we get there, eh?'

'We will have a good life and many children—after the war ends; if it ever ends,' Rolf said.

'It will end, but maybe the Germans will win. All of Europe will suffer when they do, you know.'

'No. They can't win. You say all the time they are my people but always I deny it. They are my people, but the war is not because of the people. It is because of politics and greed for land we have no real use for. Ordinary German people are kind, hospitable and smile a lot. Since Hitler came to power, it has all changed and no one smiles. I don't want to go back there. Since I met you, I have always wanted to be French.'

'You have a sister there, don't you?'

'She can take care of herself. She will marry a rich farmer and be happy. She doesn't need me now, she never has.'

'Never?'

'Almost never. There was one time, but history is about the past and the past is best forgotten sometimes.'

She reached forward for his hand. Grasping it, she said, 'I love you. I would never let them harm you.'

'Who? The British?'

'No. Anyone. I love you.'

He drank the tart red wine and putting his glass down, said, 'I wish they had a good wine. A Bergerac would be nice.'

'You know nothing about wine. Bergerac is not especially good. You ordered a bottle of it in that restaurant the first time I saw you.'

'You said I had to drink it. You said it was good enough for a German.'

'I said that?'

'Yes.'

'Then it was true.'

Sandrine raised her glass. 'Then I salute you as an adopted

Frenchman. I make you French for a day.'

They both laughed and Rolf looked at his watch. 'We don't have half a day left. It's four o'clock. Do you think they have rooms here?'

'We can ask. She can see how I love you and I'm sure she will give us a room.'

When they asked, the woman showed them to a small room, upstairs, the wide window overlooking stubble fields and green hazel bushes, stretching for miles. The rain did not come but they were happy to be together and the shelter of the tiny café was a shelter from Germany and France, for it put them together, and that was good.

They made love as soon as the owner disappeared and then lay with the curtains and window open looking out at the fields and the trees. She smoked and he ran his fingers over her, as they lay like spoons in a drawer, she facing the open window, he behind her. And all the while, he touched and caressed her as if he obtained strength and resilience from the contact, though she said nothing, only stared at the darkening landscape and smoked.

Chapter 13

"Death is nothing, but to live defeated and inglorious is to die daily."

Napoleon Bonaparte

1

In the morning, early, they made love again, but she cried afterwards. Rolf lay on his side, propped on his elbow and reached towards her. He brushed aside a tear that rambled down her cheek.

He said, 'What's wrong?'

'Nothing.'

'Nothing? We make love and you cry about it? Tell me what's wrong.'

'No.'

'Tell me.'

'It's nothing.'

'Nothing won't shed tears. Tell me. I need to know.'

'It's just… I don't want this to end.' She sat up and took a cigarette out of the blue pack on the bedside table. 'I'm being foolish.' She placed it in the corner of her mouth.

'You didn't betray André's group did you?'

'No. Of course not. Why would you think that?'

'Just…'

'So now you love me and you think I'm a traitor?' She took the cigarette out of her mouth and spoke, fast and loud, waving it as she held it between her fingers. 'You think I could do that for no reason? What possible reason could I have? Ask yourself. It could have been any of a hundred unlucky events.'

'What's wrong? Last night…'

Sandrine stood up. She waved her hand at him again. The agitation in her seemed to Rolf to be born of anger and something more.

'It's not fair. You can't blame me.' She began to pace, her hands still waving about. 'You must have heard what the man said to me before you shot him. He was taking me back to room thirty-five. I'm no traitor.'

'But you betrayed Josef.'

'Yes. I had no choice.' She stopped and stood looking down at him. 'They were going to shoot one of the group every hour until I talked. You must understand. Anyway, Josef is not a partisan and they knew that. They asked him questions about you and then left him.'

'Let's not argue. I love you. I don't care about anything else.'

Sandrine sat down on the bed, facing the window. Rolf laughed.

'What?'

'You. Naked, waving a cigarette at me. It looked funny.'

'Bastard.'

He reached out a hand and caressed her back. 'I wasn't laughing at you. Maybe with you, but not making fun of you. I do love you, you know that.'

She turned, and placing her hands either side of his face,

craned her neck to kiss him on the lips.

'I know it. I know everything. I don't mind anymore, but let's keep this moment. Let's stay here forever and the war and the Special Brigade will go away and leave us alone.'

This time, they held each other. There was no sex, only warmth.

2

They paid the proprietor and mounted their bicycles. The woman, still in her lilac dress, produced a brown paper bag, and handed it to Rolf. It was the first time he had seen her smile. The change in her face seemed to erase years from it.

'Here. Some bread and wine.'

'You are very kind. I can pay you?'

'No. I am pleased to help a young runaway couple. And you, not even French. We French people believe in romance; you didn't know that?'

'You are very kind,' Rolf said again. He placed the bag on the parcel-holder behind his saddle, snapping the spring-loaded bracket over it.

'It is only a little food for when you stop. I hope God protects you and whoever is chasing you never finds you.'

'Thank you,' Sandrine said and she too smiled, though Rolf thought it seemed half-hearted as if something remained hidden inside her.

The rain clouds from the previous evening had dispersed and left a clear blue sky, though the sun remained low on the horizon behind them as they cycled north on the straight road towards Dieppe. Long shadows from lines of poplar trees intersected the road in places and they rode past single storey buildings and farms. No one seemed to be about and Rolf was relieved. He felt as if there was at last, some clarity in his life. It was as if he emerged from a mist to find the world refreshed, and when they stopped to eat and drink he took Sandrine in his arms. The feeling remained one of hope and relief.

Late in the afternoon, they entered Dieppe. There were bombed-out buildings in the outskirts, empty ruins lining the road. A bakery stood, the roof caved in and bullet craters in the walls. The massive ovens lay on their sides like huge, empty shells from which the occupants had long since emerged, their homes discarded and futile in a world where such destruction was now commonplace.

Dieppe was a depressing place for Rolf. He understood now what his people had done to every coastal town in France. Destroyed, taken over and no hint of re-building anywhere as if the townspeople accepted there was no point to it. They knew perhaps, there was to be more to come.

The market square was empty and only one café remained open. They parked their bicycles and sat outside. A waiter came wearing a striped apron and a white shirt. He stood in front of them, silent at first, then enquiring what they wanted. Rolf said nothing, he knew his accent would ostracise him and he left Sandrine to order bread and sardines and a white wine imported from the south. She stood up.

'I need the toilet,' she said, and entered the café.

When she returned, she said, 'They have no telephone here.'

They ate. Wiping her mouth with her white napkin, she said, 'I have to telephone to make contact. There was a hotel further up. Maybe they have a telephone.'

'I'll come with you,' Rolf said.

'No. You stay. Finish the wine, I won't take long.'

'What's wrong?'

'Nothing.'

'You're doing it again.'

'No. Not again.'

'What then?'

'I'd better go'.

'I'll come too.'

'No. They will be looking for us together. Let's not take any more risks than we have to.'

Rolf reached out and grasped her hand. Looking up, he said, 'I will always love you whatever happens, you understand that?'

'Yes, I do know that. I'll be back.'

'Naturally,' he said, picking up his glass and sipping the sharp white wine.

He watched as she mounted her ride. She began peddling and glanced over her shoulder. He smiled and waved. Her face seemed serious.

He placed his foot on her chair and sank back into his own. Rolf poured more wine as the waiter approached.

'Pity,' he said. 'The beautiful young woman has gone. Has she left you?'

'Only for a moment. She has gone to telephone from the hotel.'

'But why?'

'She said you have no telephone.'

'But of course we have a telephone. The lines do not always function, but she saw the telephone.'

The waiter shrugged and began walking into the café.

'One moment, please,' Rolf called to him.

'Monsieur?'

'If we had to leave this café quickly, where would we go to?'

'Quickly?'

'If people were hunting us.'

The waiter shrugged. 'I'm sure I do not know. If I could escape this place I would do so myself.' He smiled.

Rolf drummed his fingers on the paper tablecloth. He looked at his watch then decided if she did not return in half an hour, he would walk up the road to the hotel. He began to think how it had been making love, the previous night. He felt his arousal and smiled.

'Monsieur,' it was the waiter.

'Yes?'

'I'm sorry if I seemed unhelpful. I have a friend who has a boat. Is it England you want to go to?'

'Why?'

'It is possible to travel, but you will have to row. You and the lady will need to be strong. There are patrol boats but my friend says he knows when they come and he can help you. You have money?'

'I have seventy Deutsche marks. That is all.'

'Offer him fifty. Since the franc was devalued, fifty is as good as a thousand to him.'

'Where is he?'

'When your young lady returns I will take you.'

'You are very kind. She may have another way to go, but I can tell her when she returns.'

'It is as you wish. You want more wine?'

'That would be very good,' Rolf said.

With the second bottle opened, Rolf began to enjoy it. He wondered if it was the sort of wine that the more of it you drank, the better it seemed. He felt good and he looked at his watch. She had been gone twenty-five minutes. He became worried, wondering when she might return.

He was draining his second glass from the second bottle, when events transpired he would never forget.

Chapter 14

"Never awake me when you have good news to announce, because with good news nothing presses; but when you have bad news, arouse me immediately, for then there is not an instant to be lost."

Napoleon Bonaparte

1

At first, Rolf wondered whether he imagined it. A glint from some metallic surface, reflecting the distant sunlight. He listened then took a mouthful of wine. The sound of booted feet on concrete. He was sure of it. From where he sat on the edge of the square, he could see across the wrought iron railings into the park, around which stood elm trees and small dark-green herbaceous bushes. In the centre a path cut across, and to his right stood a statue of a man on a rearing horse, armed and waving a sword. Some shops and cafés stood opposite and far to the left was a bread shop, closed like the rest.

He had felt as if he were the only occupant of the square, but now he knew he was not. Looking down at his glass, he used his peripheral vision and there it was again. A movement quick and ephemeral but he knew what was happening. They were surrounding him, as quietly as any large group of jack-booted soldiers could expect to do.

Rolf stood up. He drained his glass and acting unsteady, walked towards the café entrance.

'Monsieur?' the waiter said.

Once inside, Rolf turned towards the man and said, 'Is there another way out of here? The square is crawling with Milice or German soldiers.'

'Soldiers? But no…'

'Soldiers, but yes.'

'If they catch me they will think you hid me. Now, any other way out of here?'

'Please, what can I do?'

'In five minutes this place will be full of soldiers or Milice or whoever they have sent. I have to get away.'

'Through the back there is a door to the cellar. There is a hatch for deliveries. Climb up there. Turn left and the alley ends in a hill. Go up and then down. Along the beach, there is a rock with a cave. It is a long way. Stay there and I will find you. Hurry.'

Rolf walked to the entrance of the café. He looked out. Across the railings, beyond the tall elm trees, he saw, or he thought he could see, a black car. A flash of auburn hair, her silk scarf, and her brown coat. Sandrine sat there in the black car, and Rolf began to wonder if he could get across the railings and the parkland to rescue her. He held no fear for himself. He felt behind his back for the Walther. Extracting it he checked the clip and pushed off the safety with his thumb. He stooped, ready to run.

Then he stopped. It all made sense. He saw Sandrine get out of the car. He saw Boucher get out of the driver's side.

Boucher offered her a cigarette and she took it. He smiled and spoke to her. She shook her head and pointed. Had she been able to see him in the dark of the café she would have been indicating straight at him.

Rolf ran. The Devil himself could have been after him, but he could not have mustered better speed. As he descended the cellar stairs and groped in the dark, finding his way to the hatch, he realised he had been a fool. He knew that all his stupid faith in the woman had been misplaced. Feelings of love and feelings of hatred mixed in equal proportion in his mind, just like they had after his father's death, as he opened the hatch and clambered out into the cobbled alley. He ran.

No. It can't be. It must be some misunderstanding. She loves me. She's the one. I've been such a fool. But she said she loved me. She betrayed us all. More than once. But she loved me. She condemned Andre and the others to torture and death. Now she betrays me too. I trusted her love. I felt her love. If I could have got in a shot, I could have evened the score. Damn this bloody sand. Damn this life too. I love her. I really loved her and the bitch sold me out. I must be wrong. Maybe Zedé was right. Maybe she was a traitor even before the escape. Impossible. I loved her. Had it been so simple? Gerhard gave his life for nothing. For Boucher. They both deserve to die. No time now. Shit, I hate this bloody war.

All the while, he ran. He thought, he hated and swore revenge. Impossible now. Now was a time to find a way out. A mile down the beach the dark cave orifice loomed to his left, and he entered. In the gloom, he bumped into a tall stalagmite, bruising his knee, but he felt his way as far as he could, until he stood in the utter blackness and freezing underworld, like Cerberus, ready to kill anyone who entered.

The rock beneath his feet felt cold and damp, even through the thick leather soles of his boots, but there was cover from the craggy, brown rock surface beside which he stood. He crouched behind a boulder and put his gun away. He peered around the corner of his rock and waited. There was a sound of water dripping to his left and a smell of damp and fish filled his nostrils.

Could I be wrong? No. I saw her with him. She betrayed me. She betrayed everyone. Dear Christ in heaven. I loved her.

He felt more pain now than any time he could recall. It burned within him, but like the feelings for his father he pushed it down, down deep in his mind, to fester, and emerge another time. This was what he was good at, he reasoned. He was able to tolerate and dissemble, hide and inter those feelings and he would not allow them to colour his thoughts, not now when he needed every ounce of concentration. Then, there it was again.

I loved her. I know she loved me. Maybe she only loved me for a while, for a moment, for one tiny glimpse of my soul. I felt her love. I hate her. No. I love her. Does it matter? I'm not one of the French. But she betrayed them all, her people, her heritage. But I love her still. God! What are you doing to my heart, my soul?

Time passed. An hour after entering the cave, he noticed water lapping at the ankles of his boots. He shifted position onto a higher rocky ledge. He watched the cave entrance. Water lapped the rocks. Cold came but he ignored it. It was not that he had his love to keep him warm; it was more his burning anger sustaining him. No one came. It remained as silent as the sunken hull of a wreck at sea. He wondered whether he too, might become like that, the water rising until he, struggling to stay afloat, would sink and become sucked away in this green and salty world of death. Knee deep in water, he decided it was better to meet the searching Milice than to drown in a frigid black cave, so he waded out into the deepening waves until he stood, like a guardian, by the stalagmite at the entrance.

'Monsieur. You are there?'

The voice came faint, as if from a distance, and it was low enough for Rolf not to jump. He looked around. Nothing.

'Monsieur?'

'Here. I am here,' Rolf said.

He waited and presently the silhouette of the waiter appeared out of nowhere, ghost-like and vague.

'Monsieur. Here. Quickly.'

The man gestured for Rolf to emerge and as he came out, he noticed the waiter was not alone. The man with him, in Rolf's eyes, seemed huge. A true bear of a man; it would not have surprised Rolf if the man had growled. At least six feet six tall, his hunched shoulders and broad chest made him appear gargantuan.

'I don't know your name.'

'It is perhaps better you do not,' the waiter said. 'This is Robert. He is the man with the boat.'

'You don't mind me knowing his name then?'

'Does it look like it troubles him?'

'Maybe not.'

Robert spoke, his voice deep and gruff, 'Why are they after you?'

'I'm a deserter and I was with an MOI FTP group. That girl I was with betrayed me.'

The words came out of his mouth and stabbed him in the heart as he spoke them. In his head, he could feel the blood cascading down his chest. She had betrayed him.

Boucher of all people. Perhaps, as he once thought, they might be lovers. But no. He knew how, when he made love to Sandrine, he had meant something to her, but what was the point of this chase if she was always going to betray him to Boucher? They could have taken him anytime, even in Paris. But he also knew she had never been out of sight: she had no chance to leave messages or make telephone calls. She had to wait until she could ring Boucher. And he had come.

Robert grunted. 'You could be a Milice spy. Plenty of them nowadays.'

'This man saw they were after me. You can help?'

'I can help. You have money? Deutsche marks?'

'Yes. Fifty.'

'I don't know. It's not enough.'

'All I have.'

'You want to take your chances with the place crawling with Milice and policemen? Eh? Go back to Dieppe then.'

'You have a boat or not?'

'I have several boats. If you want to go across the water, you will have to row. The patrol boats hear everything and then they come.'

'You'll take me?'

'You think my life and yours is only worth fifty marks?'

'It's all I have. It's a lot of money to you.'

The waiter grabbed at the giant's arm. 'Robert, you can take him. You know the tide and the patrol boats. Come on.'

The man mumbled assent and then began walking across the sand, away from the port.

'Your boat is here?'

'Along the beach. I have it hidden.'

'Far?'

'No. Not far.'

They trudged and the waiter tapped him on the shoulder.

'I must go now.'

'Go?'

'Yes. If they search and find no one, they will suspect me of helping.'

'Yes. I understand. You've been very kind. I wish I could thank you.'

'My reward is to see you safely away.'

Rolf shook the man's hand. The waiter's forehead glistened; his hand too was cold and sweaty. Rolf felt he could hardly blame him. Who could tell what awaited him at the café? He departed across the damp, dark sand towards Dieppe. Had he not been so confused in his emotions, Rolf would have embraced the fellow, but now he was gone, fading into the dark, windswept night.

2

They trudged almost half-a-mile along the soft, wet sand, Robert in front and Rolf behind. Twenty minutes from the cave, an inlet appeared where a stream flowed down from a hill above and the descending water scored and cut the sand. Rolf could hear the trickling of the stream as it flowed to the sea and he followed Robert as he turned up towards the tree line through the grass covering the dunes. Fifty yards from the inlet, Robert stopped and indicated some low shrubs.

'Here,' he said.

Together they pulled branches and shrubs away and Rolf saw the boat, hidden, invisible to the passing eyes of patrol boats or walkers on the sands below.

The two of them heaving the boat towards the break-line,

Rolf stumbled often in the sand, but the massive bear-like quality of his companion kept the boat moving.

Robert looked at his wristwatch. 'Eight o'clock. We wait now. A patrol boat passes by in forty minutes and takes another forty minutes to come back. If we row hard, we have time to get beyond them. No lights and they won't see us.'

'They can't see us on the beach?'

'In the dark?'

'All right. I understand. I'm not used to boats.'

'If you vomit in my boat, you can clear it up before you get out.'

Robert did not smile. He was humourless and solid as an oak. They waited. Still Rolf ruminated over Sandrine. The thoughts burned him and nagged at him until he could contain them no longer.

'You know, that woman. I thought I loved her and she betrayed me to the Special Brigade. You know—the police.'

'You can't trust women. All of them, the same.'

'I trusted her.'

'Then you are a fool. I trust no one.'

There was silence then and Rolf, standing by the boat, shifted from one foot to another and realised he felt sleepy. It had been a long day. He wondered whether the tiredness was, at least in part, due to his grief over Sandrine. He shook his head and tried to stay awake despite the fact he was in damp sand and leaning on the cold gunwales of a rowing boat, his feet soaking in wet boots.

Robert did not speak and the only sound was the faint lapping of the waves on the sand. The salty smell of the seashore tickled Rolf's nostrils but nothing distracted his tortured mind from thoughts of the woman he knew, deep inside, he still loved. When he analysed it, it seemed clear.

His anger left him; all that remained was unhappiness. The trouble was, he still loved Sandrine, whether she had betrayed him or anyone. He knew his feelings for her remained and the bitterness of that realisation was immense.

Far off in the night, crossing from left to right a light appeared. Robert pulled Rolf down and they crouched behind the gunwales, waiting. The patrol boat departed, without betraying any interest and Robert began pushing the boat out into the black waves until he signalled Rolf to climb in.

'Get in the front. I'll row first.'

Obeying, Rolf settled himself in the prow and watched as Robert set the oars into the rowlocks and began pulling at the oars. He made deep strokes, deeper than Rolf had ever used rowing on the lakes at home. It was not the same technique and he watched with care, since he knew he would have to take his turn once the bear had finished. An hour and a half passed.

Robert stopped rowing. 'You can pay me now. Then we part company quickly once we are across.'

'How long will it take?'

'The money.'

Rolf reached to his back pocket. He extracted his wallet. Counting, he drew out fifty marks and passed it toward the big man. Robert took it and then counted it, before placing it in his trouser pocket.

'So, how long?' Rolf said.

'If I'm rowing, eight hours. If you slow us down, maybe twelve.'

'Not so long then.'

'Your hands will look like raw steak by the time we arrive. Nothing to smile about.'

'You have a family?'

'You don't need to know.'

Rolf shut up. His companion was not a man to pester with questions and he understood that now. He had paid him; there was a job to do, that was all.

By midnight, Robert asked Rolf to take over. Rolf stood up. The unsteadiness of the pitching boat made him sit again, but he stood once more and made his unsteady way towards Robert, clutching at the gunwales as the boat rolled in the waves. Robert made to pass him. Rolf turned his back to sit.

Then he realised his foolishness. The blow hit him hard. Stars came to him but not from the sky above. A hard, muscular arm encircled his throat from behind. Swaying in the wave-rocked boat, he began to choke.

Chapter 15

"Glory is fleeting, but obscurity is forever."

Napoleon Bonaparte

1

Summer was Rolf's favourite time. The hayloft was his favourite haunt, the one place where solitude and reflection came to him. It was also the only environment in which he allowed himself to think—hard and deep. He stood and looked out of the hatchway from the platform high above the stable floor and sighed. The golden, rolling fields spread before him toward the river, which in summer flowed blue, fast and clear through the farmlands below. Boulders stood out in the centre of it and hazel trees lined the banks, the green of their leaves standing out in a stark contrast against the backdrop of the yellow cornfields behind. Beyond the river, dry stone walls made rectangles, in which the golden corn leant in the breeze as the wind whispered past, creating patterns that drew the eye.

Rolf stared at the passing clouds above. He imagined an elephant, then a large rat, then nothing at all. For once, he did not brood, nor did he want to shout and scream. Today was the first weekend of the summer leave from University, the first visit to the farm since Christmas, and his homecoming was all he had hoped.

'What are you thinking about?' Annika said, climbing up the ladder to join him.

'Thinking? I was reminiscing.'

'What about?'

'We used to sit here together all those years ago. Remember how I held you?'

'Yes. I needed you.'

'Needed? Not need?'

'I've grown up a lot since those days. I am strong now. You still have the book?'

'Yes. I could read from it now, if you wish.'

'No. Not now.'

'It's all right. I don't mind you know.'

'What?'

'I don't mind you not needing me anymore.'

She stood close and took his hand. They embraced and then sat down in the warm, soft hay, the scent of it filling their nostrils.

She said, 'What do you philosophers do?'

'Philosophers? We dream and we show the way. We teach systems of thinking to people who are blind to the true values of the world.'

'Rubbish. You are all dreamers, that's true, but that is as far as it goes. Philosophy never put bread on the table, never paid any bills. You need to be more practical.'

Annika was smiling as she spoke and Rolf pushed her by the shoulder, realising her humour. She lay on her back giggling.

'You,' he said.

'Will you really be a teacher here in Dortmund?'

'If there is a job. Maybe I'll stay in Berlin for a while then move here when a job comes up.'

'How is Berlin?'

'Bad,' his face darkened.

'How so?' she said and sat up.

'Everywhere you look shops are shut, brown-shirts and SA soldiers arrest people who are never seen again. All Jews have restrictions and those who haven't been forced to emigrate can only go to shops between three and five o'clock. I saw one man set a synagogue alight outside the city. There is a lot of violence on the streets.'

'Mainly Jews, isn't it?

'Yes, but no one who opposes the party is safe. They execute some.'

'But you are safe?'

'Yes, I am safe.'

'I am glad I don't have to go there.'

'Yes. I would worry about you all the time. We are Catholics and they don't like Catholics. I don't tell anyone and never talk about religion. I still go to church but try to make sure no one sees me.'

'They aren't against us. Most of them are Lutherans anyway. They aren't closing churches and priests have not been threatened. I read about it in the V. B.'

'I don't believe anything I read in newspapers anymore. Propaganda all of them. Censorship and book banning. It's shit. But I'm home now for three whole weeks, and I don't have to think about it anymore. Aunt Elsa said she'd make me bratwurst with potato rösti.'

'You look thin. She said she would fatten you up like one of the pigs.'

She laughed and the gloomy talk of Berlin flew away as

they tussled in the hay, like old times. They continued to laugh and talk all afternoon and when they came in, it was to say grace and enjoy a family meal.

For Rolf, it was a day he would often revisit in his mind. A day when all the troubles he had witnessed during the last year dissipated, floating away like so much hay in the wind.

2

Rolf clawed and bit. It was futile. He had about as much chance of loosening Robert's grip as he had of flying away into the sky. There was a bursting feeling in his head. It felt as if all the blood of his limbs was being squeezed into it. He felt the strain on his neck. He thought Robert's tree-trunk like arm would rip his head from his shoulders. More golden stars flew in front of his eyes. He reached behind him. The Walther PP came to his hand. Robert shook him as a terrier shakes a rat. Rolf's grip on his gun did not loosen. His only doubt was whether he could get in a shot before he lost consciousness. Already his arms felt weak and limp. He flipped the safety. He cocked the gun and keeping his hand behind him, he felt the barrel-tip on the soft stomach of his assailant. He fired. Not once, but three shots, then a fourth. On the first shot, nothing happened. By the time the fourth shot rang out across the black sea, the pressure around his throat began to slacken. He gasped. Deep lungsful of air came. Robert fell backwards, across the rowing plank and Rolf fell forwards. He still had enough presence of mind to grab for the oars, reaching out of the boat for one of them as it began to slip away into the swell.

He crawled on all fours. Vomit came and he slumped

down on the boards beneath him. It was minutes before he could stand. He examined Robert. The pulseless hulk that had once been a man lay flopped onto its side across the rowing plank. He had been huge. Rolf was a big man too, but still gasping, his head bursting, he had not the strength to shift the corpse over the gunwale. Sitting down next to the dead Frenchman he took his head in his hands, his throat sore and swollen, breath rasping.

More time passed and he felt recovered enough to lighten the boat. He took hold of Robert's right leg and bending it at the knee, managed to shove it onto the gunwale. He pushed and shoved. He used all his strength and the hulk began to turn, following the leg. He braced the corpse with his knee so as not to lose the ground he had made. Next, he took hold of the right arm and shoved that too, over the side. He rolled the body over, though it took all the strength he had. Rolf strained and grunted and the procedure took many minutes. Robert's corpse greeted the waves with no audible sound and disappeared in seconds.

Shit, shit, shit. Fucking monster. No wonder he didn't care if I knew his name. He was going to kill me all the time. I didn't even retrieve my money. Why didn't I think? I don't know which direction to row. I don't even know how far it is. Shit.

He sat like this for what seemed an age with his head in his hands, the only sound in his ears the lapping waves on the sides of the drifting boat. Presently, he looked around. No lights, nothing. Deep bootblack night as far as he could see. He looked up and saw the moon, obscured in part, by pale grey clouds. Stars winked at him here and there and he wished he understood them, wished he could steer by them, but he had never learned how.

Think Rolf. Think.

He looked at his watch. Two in the morning. It had been nine o'clock when they left. The moon had been behind them as they rowed. Now it was off to his left. North had to be at right angles to the path of the moon. If it was not, he would be rowing back to France. No. He was sure he was right. He picked up both oars and placed them in the rowlocks. Grasping each, he began to row, keeping the moon to his right and hoping he had not become stupid despite the thumping headache that banged inside his skull.

Part 3

Chapter 1

"*A pessimist sees the difficulty in every opportunity; an optimist sees the opportunity in every difficulty.*"

Winston Churchill

1

Darkness surrounded the little boat as Rolf rowed. Occasional clouds exposed the moon in its bright fullness and then he could see the silver light reflected off the black waves as far as his eyes could see. There was no other light, no land and especially no sounds of patrol boats. When the clouds obscured the moon, he sank into gloom. He was not happy.

Deep inside, losing Sandrine gnawed at him until he was raw. He could not explain what he had seen across the square in Dieppe any other way. There could be no other explanation for why she had been in that car with Boucher. He was tempted to hate her. She had betrayed him. It seemed strange to him, because thinking of her did not bring hatred, or any desire for revenge, nor did he even wish harm to her. The thoughts brought only a deep, cavernous emptiness. He knew he loved her and the depths of that love scored a fathomless trench in his soul.

His hands ached at first, so he stopped and wrapped the oars with strips ripped from a brown rag he found in the stern. He hoped it would delay the inevitable blistering. His hands had become soft after years of being away from farm work, he was well aware of that.

Rolf pulled on the oars. He had rowed on lakes many times, but he had never been at sea in a small boat. Before he killed him, Rolf had watched as Robert rowed. The oars dipped deep in short strokes and although he missed sometimes when the swell lifted the boat high in the water, Rolf believed he was managing. The only sounds in his ears were the waves and the squeak of the rowlocks. There was nothing to see and all he had to guide him was the moon. Keeping it to his right, he felt sure he would be heading north.

At one point, a seagull landed on the stern board. It stood awkward and shy, but looking at him. It cocked its head to the side as if eyeing its dinner and the presence began to irritate him. He tried to shoo it away and waved his right hand. Almost losing an oar, he cursed and gave up. He picked up the oar where it had stopped in the rowlock because of the rag binding.

Dawn came and he seemed no closer to land. Whenever he looked over his shoulder nothing but mist greeted his gaze. Another seagull came and the first flapped its wings to see off the intruder. Rolf now felt stupid. If there were seagulls there had to be land nearby. An hour later and his grey companions left. They took off in the direction in which he was rowing and it provided a small measure of reassurance. His back ached and his neck had stiffened during the night. He inspected his hands in the faint dawn light. The left palm was one huge blister, the skin broken and raw. The right was not much better, and every time he pulled at the oars the stinging pain became more severe. He wondered whether he should have applied the rags to his hands not the oars, but this was all new to him and he felt like a man thrust into some strange sports match, desperate to win, but handicapped by ignorance of the rules.

Still he rowed, licking his dry and cracking lips. There was nothing to drink in the boat, but it came as no surprise; Robert had not intended to be out very long. He would have disposed of Rolf's body as soon as an opportunity came and then rowed home.

A faint sound came to his ears. It sounded at first like a large insect buzzing far away. It became louder and he shipped his oars and waited. It had to be an engine, but whose it might be, he could not guess. The white mist hung on the grey sea and the sunrise remained shrouded in cloud. He scanned the horizon. Nothing. Rolf waited but the sound came close then began to fade, and he was alone again. There was no moon to guide him now, but he estimated where the sun was rising from a faint glow on the horizon and it guided him north again. More pain, more doubt. He thought the doubt was his greatest enemy. He could put up with pain.

The shore came faster than he realised. The first sign of it was the scraping of the hull on shingle. The boat turned sideways and the waves rocked it as Rolf jumped out, into a foot of seawater. He plodded ashore and stood looking around. Still the same monotonous vista of white mist. The sound of the waves, their tiny crashes on the cold grey shingle seemed soft and lonely to his ears.

Rolf removed his boots and wrung out his socks. Replacing his boots he stood up, wondering where to go. He dragged his feet across the pebbles and walked perhaps fifty yards, coming to a flat grassy place but he saw no houses. There was no one to ask. He trudged inland then turned to his right, wondering whether he might find a house or a road. He needed to speak to someone in authority; he knew that. There would be procedures, forms to fill and then what? Would they lock him up?

And now he was alone. He pondered as he walked. He wondered where Sandrine was at that moment. Was she lying in Boucher's arms? Was she a prisoner in the prefecture, or even being interrogated in room thirty-five? He knew she had turned him over to Boucher, or tried to at least, but with his escape, she might have incurred Boucher's displeasure to such a degree the man would turn on her. He had no answers and by the time he had walked half a mile or so, he reached into his pockets. He wanted to assess his resources.

There was a damp twenty-mark note in his right hand pocket and some French change. Twenty marks would not take him far but he was thirsty and hungry. At least it would buy a meal.

A gust of wind brushed his face, and as it continued he could see the mist easing in front of him. A dark, dull shape appeared. A house. Then another and another. There was a roadway beneath his feet and he followed it. He sweated and felt his heart beating. He did not even know where he was. Following the road, he came into a small town. The buildings had red-tiled roofs and smooth, white, rendered walls. A car stood parked outside one of them and he was tempted to take it. He knew how to start it, but the thought of beginning his time in England with a crime seemed anathema to him so he kept walking.

He came to an empty cobbled square. To the right was a low wall and he could see a harbour beyond. The street opposite the wall held shops, though none of them seemed to be open. Crossing the cobbled roadway, he sat on the wall and checked his watch. Seven-thirty. Of course, no shops would be open. He had to wait. Rolf knew they would not take Deutsche marks. He would have to find a bank or a post-office, before he could buy food. He waited.

2

Seagulls, some grey, some white and black soared high above, and their plaintive cry filled the sky. The sun had at last risen high enough over grey banks of cloud to peep through, casting pink and purple colours across the far horizon, and all the time he could hear the soft and gentle waves that nudged the little harbour at his back. A fifty-something woman walked in his direction. She was exercising a poodle. Rolf watched as she approached. She wore a wide-brimmed, greenish tweed hat and a matching suit. In her right hand she held a walking cane, and in her left the dog's lead. They came close enough for the dog to sniff at him. Rolf sat still as the dog cocked its leg, ready to urinate on his left leg. He stood up and shoved the beast away with his foot.

'Naughty boy, Dougal,' the woman said, smiling, though her accent seemed strange to him. It was not at all like the typical English of the movies he had seen, like Claude Rains in Casablanca. English people in those films had a particular lilt he could not detect in this lady.

She smiled at Rolf, apologetic, but continued her walk, on down the roadway towards the beach where he had landed only two hours before. Another woman of similar age, wearing a white apron, came out of a grocer's shop opposite. She looked up at him as she bent to some wooden crates filled with turnips that rested, tipped at an angle to display their contents, against the shop-front. There was a quizzical expression on her face. She smiled, and Rolf despite his feelings, smiled back. She turned and re-entered her shop. His palms ached and stung, raw and worn where he held them in his overcoat pockets. Presently, more people walked or cycled past. No one took any notice of him.

Rolf wanted to tell them, tell anyone, who he was.

I'm a deserter from the German army. I fought with French partisans and now I'm here. I need your help.

A Post Office stood further down the road with a large red post-box outside. When he saw the plump post-mistress change the sign from "closed" to "open", then pick up a bundle of newspapers on her doorstep, he got up and approached. There was a tearoom next door and he glanced through the window, catching the eye of an old man, who sat sipping tea from a pink china cup, a cake of some kind in his other hand. The pink teapot seemed incongruous: Rolf had never used bone china in his life. He opened the door to the post-office and walked in, the doorbell ringing a cheery little chime as he did so.

He looked around. There was a newspaper stand to his right; the counter ahead seemed cluttered with leaflets and a box with a slit, for donations, labelled "War Orphans" sat next to the grille that separated the customers from the staff. To the left was a bench, polished smooth by English buttocks. Perhaps they all wore tweed like the lady with the poodle.

'Yes, my love?' The post-mistress said.

She was small and round, with gold-rimmed spectacles and she wore a woollen cardigan over a white, lacy blouse and a skirt of blue wool. Her permanent-waved, mousey brown hair and her wrinkled smile gave her an air of friendliness and calm. If there was one thing Rolf needed now, it was some sign he was not the pariah he expected the English to make him.

In his best English he said, 'Excuse me Madame. I need to change some money.'

'Money? What, foreign?'

'I have only German franks left. Could you perhaps change them for English pounds?'

'Change German money?' She looked him up and down.

'Yes,' he said, bowing slightly before realising his mistake.

'German are you?'

'Swiss. I am on holiday.'

She looked him up and down.

'I need to get permission to change German money,' she said.

'Oh. Will it take long?'

'Take a seat over there, my love, and I'll phone the bank but they don't open till half-past. Won't be a minute, my love.'

Rolf sat down. He was sick of sitting down. He had been rowing all night and all he wanted now was a hot meal and something to drink. The woman was gone a long time it seemed to Rolf. He looked beyond the counter as he waited. Brown wooden shelves covered the wall either side of a solid wooden door, but they were empty. Opposite him, on the wall, was a poster announcing a "Newspaper Drive" at a local church hall. He wondered what that might be.

He looked at his watch. Nine twenty-five. He undid his shirt-collar button. The swelling in his throat was becoming uncomfortable. Under his breath, he cursed Robert. Nothing but a killer and a thief. Silence surrounded him. There was no sign of the post-mistress, so he stood up and walked to the door. He wanted air and opening it, he stepped outside.

A man in a round, grey metal hat stood to his right. The helmet bore the letters "S.C. POLICE" and in his hands, he grasped a .303 rifle. As Rolf turned, another rifle barrel pressed hard against his back.

'Now, we don't want any trouble, do we?' said the first man.

He was about fifty years old and his grey hair poked out from beneath his bowl-shaped helmet as if it wanted to escape. He wore a brown battledress uniform with black boots. At his waist was a mustard-yellow webbing belt, the brasses polished to a bright almost white shine.

Rolf put his hands up.

'Am I under arrest?'

'What's all this about German money, then?'

'I have a gun.'

'What?'

'In my belt at the back. You may need to take it.'

The man behind Rolf slung his rifle over his shoulder and searched behind Rolf's back, with clumsy, shaking hands.

'Bloody hell. It's true,' the man said, pulling the Walther from Rolf's belt. He could scarcely have been twenty, Rolf thought.

'I am a French partisan. I escaped from Dieppe by boat. You will question me? This is so?'

'Too bloody right mate,' the older man said.

They marched him two hundred yards further up the road and turned left into a small narrow street where a blue sign hung outside, above a wooden door, like a bar in a Paris

236

alley. "Police Station", the sign read. They marshalled Rolf inside and then downstairs into a basement where there were two cells. Both were empty and as the door clanged shut behind him, Rolf said, 'I am very hungry. I rowed all the way from France during the night. Can I have something to eat and drink?'

The younger man, who had locked the door, said, 'Ere Jimmy, he wants something to eat. Only just put him in the cell, and the Kraut wants something to eat. Well he can, if he's got bloody coupons, that's what I think. Got any fucking coupons mate?'

'Please. I am your prisoner. At least something to drink.'

'Not having you piss all the time in our cells. It's me has to empty the pot. Bloody krauts. You can wait till Captain Jones gets here.'

'Even a cup of your famous English tea?'

'Eh?'

'A cup of tea. Please, I've been rowing all night.'

'Jimmy? Can I give him a cuppa?'

'Call me sergeant will you and stop bloody well shouting. Yes. Make the bastard a cup of tea. I'm on the phone.'

The hot, sweet brew in its enamelled blue and white tin mug disappeared in a minute and Rolf asked for more. After a second mug of sugary tea, he sat on the low bunk. Exhaustion took him. He lay down, covering himself in the grey, rough wool blanket, and drifted off into a dreamless, deep sleep.

Chapter 2

"It is my belief, you cannot deal with the most serious things in the world unless you understand the most amusing."

Winston Churchill

1

Something about the office in which he found himself, reminded Rolf of room thirty-five in the Paris prefecture. He puzzled over it for a moment then realised it was the long bench on which he was sitting. There was no rail for the handcuffs behind him and that relieved him to a degree. It was early afternoon and little light came in through the wide window above the desk opposite him. It had rained all day and now the December sky was grey and morose, dropping sleet on the passers-by below. His hands itched and he rubbed the palms where the new skin had formed, bright red and thin.

At the desk opposite sat a young woman. Rolf thought she was his own age, in her late twenties or early thirties. He imagined her lips close to his, and how it would feel to touch her. Sandrine intervened. She always did these days. Guilt came then. He did not want to acknowledge the thoughts passing through his mind at times and he shifted, restless, on the bench.

She looked up then. Her blonde hair, cut in a 'bob', swayed as she did so and she put down her nail file. The typewriter in front of her had remained silent and so had the black resin telephone by its side, ever since Rolf entered.

She said, 'You alright?'

'Yes. Thank you.'

'Cup of tea?'

'That would be fine,' Rolf lied.

He felt as though should he drink any more of this damned British tea it would come out of his ears. Where was the coffee? No one ever offered coffee in these government offices. It was like being in France again. Chicory or tea, not coffee; tea and scones. Fish and chips. Even the sausages made him feel nauseated and homesick. But there was nothing now to go home to. Reading the newspapers and peering between the lines, told him how people suffered on both sides of the Channel. He knew stringencies were not confined to the French and British and he often thought about his sister, wondering how she fared in the farmlands of his home.

This time, tea arrived in a white and blue china cup with a saucer. Rolf smiled and thanked the secretary. He smiled to himself too when he realised he must be seeing someone more important than the rest of the military administration who had interviewed him so far. Only an important man would serve tea with a cup and saucer instead of a mug. He watched the girl filing her nails as he sipped from the china cup.

Outside, lightning flashed, illuminating the office as if all the lights had come on at once. Rolf waited, and then a peal of thunder came. He had counted to fourteen so he thought it must have been two miles away. The memory of his uncle teaching him how to estimate how far away a storm was provoked nostalgia, and he tried hard to shift his thoughts.

The buzzer on the desk came to life. Pressing a button, the girl said, 'Sir?'

A distorted, tinny English voice said, 'Send him in, will you, Sarah.'

Sarah looked up at Rolf and said, 'Major Foy will see you now.'

When Rolf opened the door, he took in the office beyond, in a glance. It was no more than three yards square and contained a desk, a bookcase, with a filing cabinet in the corner. The window had no shutters and no sill and overlooked Baker Street in central London. On the bookcase stood a carved African figure and on the far wall, two crossed native spears peeped out from under a white and brown hide-clad shield. On the wall to the left was a framed photograph of two young men wearing climbing boots and breeks standing next to each other, highlighted against a mountain. Underneath was a plaque with the words "Kilimanjaro 1934".

The man behind the desk stood up when Rolf entered. He was of a similar height to Rolf but thin and angular. He wore a short moustache and his clothing was military. Rolf did not know the uniform; he had not become familiar with British military gear, but he guessed it was army rather than naval.

The man reached out a thin, long-fingered hand across the desk and Rolf stepped forward and shook it. The hand was firm, bony, and dry.

'Patrick Foy,' the man said.

'I am Rolf Schmidt. You of course know about me.' Rolf bowed and clicked his heels.

'Have a seat, would you?' Foy said, indicating the chair in front of the desk.

Rolf sat down and said nothing.

Foy opened a file on the desk and thumbed through the first few pages, then looked up at Rolf.

'They've been treating you well?'

'Yes. Well.'

'Good. Good,' Foy had a deep masculine voice. He looked again at the file. 'Well, I've some good news for you.'

'You have?'

'Yes, your story checks out, actually.'

'It does?' Relief swept over Rolf.

'Seems this fellow Zeddy...'

'Zedé,'

'Anyway, he's known to some of our resistance groups. So is Manouchian. We've made some enquiries and your story seems to fit. This Zeyday fellow vouched for you. It wasn't easy to get the information, that's why it's taken time.'

'Zedé is alive?'

'Suppose he must be. The file says he said to tell you to enjoy Bogart now, at last.'

Rolf smiled.

'Joke?'

'No. He knows my taste in films that is all. So they didn't get him?'

'Seems so. Don't know anything about it really. All we asked for was corroboration of your story.'

'Corrober...'

'Confirmation. We don't now consider you a spy. If we had been unable to find out who you are, you might have been shot for a spy. You know that?'

'Everyone wants to shoot me.'

'Eh?'

'Everyone wants to shoot me. First my own soldiers, for deserting. Next the French Special Brigade, then the partisans, now the British. Everyone.'

'Well I don't want to shoot you. I want to train you.'

'You mean?'

'Train you. We may have a job for you.'

'I don't understand.'

'This fellow Boucher.'

'Boucher?'

'Yes, he is very close to finding one of our agents. The partisans are all fighting each other and we can't get anyone to agree to our suggestion.'

Rolf said nothing. He could guess what that suggestion must have been.

'I've read your story. We need someone resourceful, who can impersonate a German officer without being noticed.'

'You need an actor then. I'm not the right man for this.'

'You understand what we're asking? We need someone familiar with Boucher, who won't remove the wrong obstacle.'

'You want him dead. I know that much. Manouchian tried and failed. My group had no success on two attempts. You think this will be any easier? You would be sending me to my death.'

'The alternative is to be interned in Scotland. We can't have German soldiers wandering about in our streets. You understand?'

'But you know I'm a deserter and a fighter for the French.'

'All the same.'

'Can I think about it?'

'Yes. You can evaluate the missed opportunity on your way to Aberdeen.'

'What do you want?'

'Heard of SOE?'

'No.'

'It's a clandestine operation to train men and women who will go to France, Italy even Germany and Poland to make life difficult for the Reich.'

'Why do you always talk around subjects? Tell me what you mean. Spies? Assassins? I don't understand you English. Never straight.'

'I'll spell it out for you. We want to train you until the risk of you being detected is minimal, and then drop you in France so you can kill Boucher. At the moment, we hope to dress you as a Heer colonel. We're just waiting for the uniform to be made. Boucher will open the door to you and you kill him.'

'But it's what we tried last time. Dressed as Milice.'

'This will be more authentic. You will have back-up too.'

Rolf shook his head. He felt like a man on a slippery mud-bank. There was no place to go and digging his heels in would serve no purpose, he was there for the whole dirty ride. Besides, he too wanted Boucher dead.

2

It was raining again. Since Rolf had run ashore on the shingle beach, it had rained every day. Sometimes it snowed, and over the winter sleet had jabbed at his face too. The misty, wet climate did nothing for his morale though he knew he was better off here than in France or Germany. At night, he read his psalm book; he prayed for Sandrine too. In his prayers, he begged for her safety and he understood he loved her still. He knew he should have hated her, but he also knew how loyalties could become confused. Had he not been disloyal to his own convictions when he joined the Nazi Party? He reasoned that whether she had betrayed him to Boucher or not, it would not have been because she wanted him dead. There was some missing piece in the jigsaw, some undefined thing of which he remained ignorant. If the war ever ended, he swore he would find her, to find out.

He climbed the steps of the barrack hut and the planks creaked beneath his feet. Ringway, near Manchester, was not his idea of comfortable accommodation , but he had already experienced his share of stately homes, where they had taught him trade craft, explosives and even made him brush up on hand to hand combat. Apart from explosives, he flew through the training. He knew most of it already. Now the final leg was learning to jump out of an aeroplane without breaking his neck. Parachuting seemed to Rolf, to be the only thing in the training that frightened him. He even disliked the word "parachute". To Rolf it was as comfortable on the tongue as a pistol barrel.

He ducked as he entered, out of habit. He still had a scab on his forehead from the drunken night the previous week-end, when he and some of the others returned from the mess. Marco, alone in the hut, lay on his bunk, but sat up as Rolf entered. He was younger than Rolf, short and squat, with greasy black hair and a clean-shaven, open face. Their training had coincided over the explosives course and now they shared the parachute course.

'Hey, Gerry. How are you doing?'

'Fine. I had a good jump.'

'How many jumps you do now?'

'Two. They cancelled the second one today. Too much wind.'

Rolf began taking off his overcoat.

'Always too much wind. This a windy place.'

'Yes.'

'Not like home.'

'So you keep telling me, Marco.'

'My village is up in the mountains. It is a fine place. You like my village. Maybe you go there one day.'

'Yes.'

'You like it. No. You love it. The girls are beautiful. Not… How you say? Angry, like women here.'

'No?'

'Why you so quiet today? You no want to talk to your good friend Marco?'

'No.'

'I tell you about my village. It was a quiet summer day. The Germans, they came. They shoot the priest. He was a good priest that one. Always have time for people. They say he hide some Jewish feller. Then they shoot him. Pouf! Just like that.'

'I'm sorry.'

'You sorry? When they finish shoot the priest they take all of the young men to the army. So I find myself in Il Duce's army. It was so bad, I leave in the end.'

'You've told me.'

'Why you here? You leave the army and now you join the other side. You tell me why this time.'

'No.'

Marco raised both hands, palms up. 'No one can understand you, you Sauerkraut sonofabitch. Soon they send me home and I not meet any more friendly German sonsabitches. I kill them instead.'

'Sending you home?'

'Yes. They drop me near my village and I do bad things for the German troops. Maybe you don't like that?'

'Of course I like that. I'm here aren't I?'

'Yeah, but you don't like to talk. We are brothers in arms and you never, never talk to me. All you do is drink beer. Beer all the bloody time. No talking, just drinking. I can't wait.'

'Wait?'

'To go home. People there are nice. When they drop you?'

'Next week.'

'How many more drops before then?'

'Two more. Then I'm ready.'

'They drop you in Germany? Where they drop you?'

'I can't tell you that. It could be anywhere.'

'See? You never tell me any things at all. Like you don't trust me. I tell you, silence is for the grave. We not dead yet. We should talk.'

'No. No talking about missions.'

'I don't like this bloody war. It makes enemies of friends and friends out of enemies. I say a prayer for you anyway.'

'Marco, I wish you luck when you return home. I hope you do well and have a fine war. You should not have told me about where they drop you because I could be captured and they can find out things.'

'You scared?'

'No.'

'Me? I'm plenty scared. I don't like to fly. No Italians is meant to fly. If we was supposed to fly, we would have wings. At least you are a Catholic like me, and you can pray.'

'Marco?'

'Yeah?'

'Shut up. I love you, but shut up now.'

'You always so closed, my friend. We are both plenty scared. Talking is good. Make us brave'

'Shut up. I need to sleep. I have another jump in the morning.'

'Ok. I shut up.'

Rolf lay down on his bunk. The last thing in his mind as sleep came, was an image of Sandrine's naked back on the bed next to him, in the little café bedroom on the way to Dieppe.

Chapter 3

"Many fine things can be done in a day if you don't always make that day tomorrow."

Winston Churchill

1

The Albemarle banked in a steep descent and Rolf felt nauseated. He hated flying and now, to cap it all, they were making him jump. There was reassurance in the thought that Marco had felt the same, but now he was scared, just plain scared. He sweated even though it was cold and he drew the overcoat collar up to cover the nape of his neck. They had briefed him well. SOE had even planned for some partisans to meet him, but they gave him a failsafe plan in case it went wrong. He wanted to empty his bladder but he knew it was too late. Minutes to go, he stood up and stretched his aching muscles. The plane banked again, then coming round, it pitched him to the floor of the fuselage among the rough wooden boards and to the laughter of the flight sergeant whose name he could not remember.

'How many jumps you done mate?'

He was from London and his strong accent sounded friendly to Rolf.

'Four.'

'Why you're a ruddy expert then. Don't worry, we know what we're doing. You ain't the first. We dropped a bloke last week, matter of fact. Saw him come down in a field, not that we waited.'

'He was all right?'

'All right? Course he was. We train yer good, mate. You'll be fine.'

The red light flashed over the hatch and the flight sergeant stood up, bracing himself and holding onto a strap attached to the wood frame above his head.

'Almost time,' he said.

Rolf got to his feet and made his way to the hatch, as the man opened it. He clipped the webbing strap from his chute to the rail above his head. The inrush of air froze his cheeks and he stepped back. He felt a hand between his shoulder blades.

'All right, don't be nervous. Stand at the mark and I'll let you know when the light goes green. All right?'

Rolf gave a thumb's up as they had taught him. If the chute failed to open... It would open. The men here were experienced. It would open. They wanted him to succeed. The thought reassured him for the next thirty seconds before he felt himself pitched out of the aircraft by the firm hand of the cockney flight sergeant.

His first sensation was nothing but cold wind on his cheeks, despite his goggles. He held his arms crossed across his chest and kept his feet together, knees bent a little as they had instructed him. Once clearly out, he opened his arms and parted his legs. He could see nothing below. Then the jerk of the chute opening. The harness pulled on his inner thighs. It strangled his testicles for a moment then the pressure reduced. He swallowed. His next sensation was of dropping. No. More like sailing fast towards the ground. He grasped the toggles. The round army chute was impossible to steer and he could only guess where he would land.

Then he was down. His feet together, he bent his knees and he rolled on impact. Despite all they had told him, it was still like jumping out of the hayloft at home. Like leaping nine or ten feet onto a grassy surface. Rolf lay on his back at first as the wind took his chute. It dragged him a few yards then the breeze calmed and he lay still. His left ankle ached but he knew he had not broken anything, for he could stand as he gathered in the billowing white of his parachute, before he hit the buckle on the front of his belt and released himself from further entanglement. He gathered in the chute, stowed it in its bag and left it there, in the centre of the field in which he landed.

He waited. There was no one around. He could see the poplars lining the western side of the field, and to his right a low stone wall. But no one came. No one met him. He sat down. He had detailed instructions and remained calm. He checked his watch, the same Swiss timepiece he had carried all the way from home. He waited five minutes then made a beeline to the trees. Of course, he had no idea where he might be, but he knew the approximate area and he knew the direction to take even if he was alone. He headed east. He was going to Paris, to fulfil his mission. To vent his anger and achieve revenge.

Boucher.

2

The soft turf squelched underfoot as he made his way to the poplar trees, leaning black and tall in the breeze. The sky was clear, and when he looked up he could identify Orion's Belt and the Great Plough high up and far away. His rucksack chafed on his shoulders and his left ankle felt sore, but he remained determined, his focus honed in upon the task ahead. Beyond the trees, he climbed a low wall and stood in a stony rough lane. He looked sideways, one way then the other. He struck out in the direction of the Paris road, though he puzzled over the absence of the partisans. Without them, he doubted whether he could accomplish his task, but he knew he would try, whatever happened. Boucher was doomed in Rolf's head, a dead man. Nothing would stop him now.

A constant thought was that he might see Sandrine again. He knew it was foolish, but somehow he clung to that hope as if he clung to the bank of some deep river threatening to sweep him away. His mission was like that to him. It was a maelstrom absorbing him, dragging him in whether it exposed him to danger or not. SOE did not care about him, he was aware of that. They cared about their agent whose identity might be at risk if Boucher lived. It seemed a just cause to Rolf and he did not mind risking his life for it. Without Sandrine, he was nothing.

He walked for an hour and arrived at a crossroad where he headed north until he came to Montfort-l'Amaury. The signpost put him right and he knew now he was in the Yvelines department. Paris was a short morning's walk away to the east. Rolf realised, as his commander had told him, he needed to find somewhere to hide until the afternoon, but he saw no one and the houses and farms seemed somehow inhospitable. By six in the morning, he reached the outskirts of Paris. Now he needed a place to wait until he could contact the FTP, his liaison with the French underground.

He walked into Versailles along the Avenue de Paris, the railway line to his right but no hotel or even a café appeared. By nine o'clock the streets were becoming busy and cyclists overtook him from time to time. No one spared him a second glance and that gave him comfort. He had no desire to be conspicuous. The trick of tradecraft they had told him, was to be ordinary: so ordinary, one became invisible.

Reaching Saint-Denis, he found a small hotel, in Gabriel-Péri, called Hotel Sovereign, an English-sounding name for which even the proprietor could not come up with an explanation. The elderly owner stood behind a counter in the room that served as a foyer and looked Rolf up and down.

'You are here because?'

'I am here.'

'No. I mean why are you here?'

'Because it seems a nice hotel.'

'We don't get many Germans out of uniform.'

'I was wounded and they let me go. I've just come out of hospital and need a place to enjoy my convalescence.'

'Then our hotel will be the good place for you. We have a room on the ground floor. No stairs.'

'A fine room I'm sure. The hotel is busy?'

'No. Only one other. I am Henri Lusard, this is my hotel.'

He sounded proud. Rolf bowed his head and signed the register in the name of Johan Bachofen. The name was a private joke of the cryptographer's who made his passport, knowing that the German philosopher's name would amuse Rolf.

'I will show you to your room,' Lusard said.

Rolf thought the man must have been in his seventies, he had a wrinkled brown face and a thick crop of grey hair. He wore thick black-framed spectacles.

They walked through a narrow corridor, hospital green wallpaper on the walls and a faded brown carpet on the floor. The proprietor showed him to a ground floor room, with doors opening out onto a small veranda. Rolf faked a limp as he followed. Lusard opened the door with a flourish as if presenting a breath-taking vista to an eager tourist.

The bedroom was large and had a bathroom adjoining it, across the polished wood floor. A cracked mirror hung upon the wall opposite an unmade bed with a lumpy, blue and white, striped, discoloured mattress. A battered-looking chest of drawers and an armoire occupied the right hand wall, opposite the glazed double doors. Grubby, thick, green curtains hung either side of them to ensure the blackout at night.

'I can bring you something? Breakfast?'

'That would be very welcome, thank you,' Rolf said.

'Chicory and petit pains? It is not good weather but maybe you would like to sit on the terrace. For your wounds? Fresh air…'

'Pneumonia?'

'Of course. I'm sorry. I can help you?'

'Yes, I need a taxi to take me to town later today.'

'This is a problem. No taxis around here, no one has gasoline.'

Rolf handed the man a twenty-franc note.

'I need to get into town,' he said.

The proprietor smiled. 'I will see what is available. Please wait and I will come back. My wife will come and make up the bed.'

Left alone, Rolf unslung his rucksack and sat on the bed setting the bag on the floor between his legs. Leaning forwards, he checked the contents, his guns, the ammunition, and the now creased German uniform. At the bottom of the rucksack, he rummaged for a moment and pulled out the dog-eared psalm book. A fleeting memory of his mother's face came to mind. He pictured her smiling. Sighing, he put the book into his coat pocket.

He needed to hide the uniform before he went out to meet his contact, but the room seemed spartan and bare, with nowhere obvious to secrete his things. Rolf remembered his instructor saying that to hide something, choose a place in full view if you can, so he decided to lay out the uniform flat under the mattress once the bed was made.

There was a knock on the door. Rolf, following an instinct, allowed his hand to jump to his back where his Luger sat in his belt.

'Yes?'

The response was a mumbled female voice, so he stood up and called '*Entrée.*'

The woman who opened the door reminded him of Charles Laughton in the Hunchback of Notre Dame. She looked wizened and had a bent back, from some disease of which he was ignorant. She wore a red, girlish dress and to Rolf, it seemed an absurdity for someone of her age. When she looked at him, she turned her head sideways and up as if it was impossible to elevate her head. He felt sorry for the woman, an involuntary response.

'I can make up the bed now?'

'Yes, thank you.'

The woman waddled to the mattress and, breathing hard,

pulled out the bed and began applying the sheets she had brought. Rolf, standing by the French window, began to feel guilty. He advanced and took the sheets from her.

'I can do this. It will take moments only.'

The woman frowned. He had irritated her.

'It is my job. I can do this easily.'

'Please at least let me help you.'

'You are the guest,' she said, placing a flat hand on his chest. 'Sit down please.'

She had a faint smell of old urine. Rolf sat in the chair by the window until the woman finished. From the pocket of her cardigan, she produced a short-stemmed pink rose and placed it on the pillow.

Turning to Rolf, she smiled, exposing her brown teeth. It was as if she felt she was the generous hostess of a famous St Tropez hotel; as if she had made a bed for a newly-wed couple and she wanted to savour the moment.

'Thank you,' Rolf said.

In silence, the old woman left, closing the door behind her.

Chapter 4

1

The truck bounced up and down despite the smoothness of the road. Rolf wondered whether the wheels might be square. Seated next to him was a man called Pepé. He was Lussard's cousin, a small man with quick moving limbs, a constant cheery smile and a cloth cap. He provided the only transport Rolf was able to enlist. The light faded as they entered Paris. A huge pink and yellow sun sank on the horizon, its last rays picking out rooftops and casting shadows across the road and the tramlines. The cab of the truck smelled of gasoline and exhaust fumes, but Rolf did not care. He was focussing on the task ahead.

'Two hours,' Rolf said, alighting.

Pepé smiled a toothless grin, nodding. Rolf had no way of knowing whether the man understood him, but he knew he spoke plain enough French himself, so he hoped the message went home.

He alighted in the rue Pasteur, walked down to the rue

de la Méricourt and turned left, seeking the café where his contact should be. There was a bottle-green awning overhead as he entered the café and he opened the glazed, wooden door with a slow left hand, flat upon the glass, his right behind his back, nudging the handle of his Luger.

Inside stood six tables, each with a white tablecloth and a candle burning in the murky dusk light that entered through the wide front window. He looked around, still uncertain. Mirrors lined the walls and behind the bar, a row of spirit bottles stood upon a shelf. A brown glass bottle modelled in the figure of a bear, sitting on its haunches with its arms up, drew Rolf's eye. He recognised it, since he had often drunk Kummel with Johan, in what seemed to be a century before, before all the evils pursuing him since his friend's death.

By the far wall sat an old fellow drinking chicory, or some such brew, and Rolf took a table by the window. The waiter seemed pleased to open and pour the first glass of a bottle of Bergerac, which Rolf began to sip, savouring the pleasant blackcurrant aromas, and thinking how it reminded him of Sandrine, that first night he had seen her. His glass of Kummel arrived next. He sipped it and thought its sweet cumin taste complimented the wine.

He waited but nothing happened. He glanced across at the old man, who smoked a large, yellow pipe and drank his "coffee". Presently, the man got up and approached Rolf.

'You are here for your health?'

'I have no swim-wear, but I would like to swim.'

'The Seine is too cold anyway.'

'Sit, please,' Rolf said, gesturing a chair.

The old man reached across the table and they shook hands. 'Brossolette,' he said.

'I am Rolf. It is all you need to know.'

He looked at the man's face. There were not enough wrinkles to support his initial impression of age and Rolf realised the man was younger than he seemed at first. Brossolette had a grey moustache and wore a dark suit. He had left an overcoat at the other table and Rolf estimated the man carried a pistol, from the bulge in his jacket. He called the waiter across and asked for a glass. When it arrived, Rolf poured from the bottle and Brossolette drank, savouring the wine and looking at Rolf with serious dark-brown eyes, the stare intense.

'You wonder,' Rolf said, 'whether I can do this?'

'I make no judgement. I have seen many unlikely people do incredible things. Like I said—no judgement.'

'You've been watching the target?'

'Yes. It would be a good idea to do the thing at his home. There are few other opportunities.'

'We tried that last time. I think he knew about it though. We were betrayed. I fought my way out. It was when Gautier and his group were taken. You know what happened to them?'

'Gautier? Yes. I know.'

'Well?'

'They interrogated them, tried them, and shot them. It can happen to all or any of us, anytime. You don't climb a ladder without being prepared to fall off.'

Rolf paused then. Brossolette still stared at him.

'There was a woman too.'

'Woman?'

'Yes. Sandrine Lebeau. What happened to her?'

'Lebeau? I don't know. All I heard was about Gautier. You know, he and I fought in the First War. We were in the same unit. What happened to him was a sacrilege.'

'You're a Catholic?'

'No. I'm a Communist. It was a convenient expression, loosely said.'

'The girl. How can I find out about her?'

'Why?'

Again Rolf was silent. He sipped his Kummel. Putting it down, he lit a cigarette, blowing the smoke into the still, cool air above Brossolette's head.

Presently, he said, 'She was a close friend. Can you find out what happened to her? I would consider it a favour.'

'So, like that. Yes, I will try to find out.'

'Perhaps Manouchian knows. He knew her too.'

'He's been arrested. I can't ask him'

'Arrested?'

''Yes. He's a poet and an intellectual. He's shut up in a fort outside Paris with other poets and the like. If you knew Gautier, you will understand how I feel about Special Brigade number two.'

'Yes. I understand. More wine?'

'Please. This woman. Tell me truthfully what she means to you.'

'Sandrine? Everything.'

'I understand. Don't let it get in your way.'

'How could it? No one seems to know where she is.'

'All the same.'

'Boucher will protect himself. Last time he had Milice and soldiers all over his apartment. No other place?'

'He often takes his son to school. He gets out of the car and goes in. It is possible.'

'I won't shoot a child.'

'You won't have to. Like I said, he drops him off and then comes out. We can get him when he comes out. There are

259

two men in the car as well as the driver, but we can take care of that. All you have to do is get past the school gates. There are guards there.'

'I have a uniform. It would be a shame not to use it.'

'Uniform?'

'Yes, German colonel. I could claim to be visiting the school before my child goes there.'

'It sounds stupid. Why don't you just shoot the guards?'

'Boucher would hear and he wouldn't come out, would he?'

'Why not do it outside as he comes back to the car?'

'His men will still be in the car and it's bulletproof.'

'When do we move?'

'Tomorrow. You understand what to do?'

'Fully. Back up?'

'Yes, I will have six men outside and one will come with you inside.'

'No. I go alone. What if he recognises me? He knows my face as well as I know his.'

'It matters? The second he does, you will have shot him.'

'As you wish. Where do you stay?'

'Small hotel. The Sovereign, in Gabriel-Péri, just outside the city.'

'Ha. I know it. A man called Lusard owns it.'

'You know him?'

Brossolette laughed.

'Yes. He is a sympathiser, a communist. You've told him anything?'

'No.'

'Good. He won't be at risk then. We need him. A man called Jules will pick you up at five o'clock tomorrow evening. You have all you need?'

'Yes. All I need. You will find out about Sandrine?'

'I will try. I'm going now. You?'

'I have no transport for another hour. I will eat and then leave.'

'Good. You will make a fine Colonel.'

Brossolette smiled, then stood up and crossed the room to his overcoat. Rolf noticed the man limped. They glanced at each other as Brossolette left. Rolf remained sitting and called the waiter. He ordered soup and bread. His appetite seemed to have gone.

2

Rolf, alone in his room in the Sovereign Hotel, knelt, leaning over the bed. The light from the single bulb threw shadows across the bare polished floorboards. He clasped his hands and closed his eyes. In a quiet voice he said the Lord's Prayer, then six Hail Marys. He thought about Sandrine. He hoped she was safe and that one day they might meet again. He said, still out loud, how he wanted to tell her. He wished he could explain that his love meant more than anything in the world to him, and how he did not care what she had done.

There was a knock at the door. He felt for his gun under the pillow. He picked it up and pushed it under his belt, behind his back. He glanced around the room to ensure there were no signs visible of whom he was and what he was here to do. He had been careful but now he was obsessional.

'*Entrée*,' he said, standing.

The old woman who had made his bed entered. She looked up at him, her bent back making eye contact difficult. In her hands she held a tray with a single coffee pot, a demitasse and a filled, small balloon of brown liquid which Rolf assumed was cognac.

Rolf smiled. He had ordered nothing.

'My husband thought you might like a cup of chicory and an Armagnac.'

'You are very kind.'

'I heard you praying.'

'I thought I was very quiet when I prayed.'

'My body is bent and failing. My ears are good.'

He looked at her face and imagined she had once been a beautiful woman. She had high cheekbones and retained full lips despite the furrows revealing her age. Rolf wondered what kind of life she and her husband led here in this little hotel. He watched as she crossed to the low table by the chair at the window. She drew the blackout curtains.

'You are in love. I can see it in your eyes. It is a wonderful thing to be in love. You may laugh when I have gone but Pierre and I still love. It is something we cannot change even if we wanted to; or if it didn't suit. True love is a wonderful thing. Isn't it?'

'Yes.'

'This girl of yours. She is where?'

'I don't know. It's why I prayed for her.'

'Keep praying for her. One day you will see her again, unless the Germans take her away. So many people deported. So many rounded up. You know about the Velodrome d'Hiver?'

'The Vel d'hive round up?'

'Yes. You know they had children there too. They starved them. There were no toilets, little food, some died. Your people did that. Why don't you pray for them too? Maybe it would be just.'

'I am no longer one of those people. Like I said, I was wounded and I'm not in the army anymore. I'm glad to leave it all behind.'

'Can I sit down? My back aches if I stand too long.'

'Please. Sit.'

'My name is Jeanne. You know? Like Jeanne d'Arc, my husband says. He says we should not judge others, though he does it all the time. When you came earlier, I wanted him to make you leave because you are German. Our country suffers because of people like you but he says, let him alone Jeanne. He says he can see in your eyes, you are not one of these men. Is he right? I want to believe him.'

'I am what I appear to be, Jeanne.'

She wagged a crooked finger at him. 'You know, there is more about you than a simple woman like me can see. Isn't there?'

'What are you doing here?' Rolf said. 'Spying on me?'

'No. I have done that already, when you were out. I saw the uniform, the guns. It is unusual for a German officer to hide these things, unless he isn't a German officer. Unless he is something entirely different.'

'You take a risk now.'

'Risk?'

Rolf pulled out his Luger and set it on the bed. 'You know if I was of a different kind, I would have to kill you.'

'If I know nothing else, I know you are not that sort. The kind of man who would do that would be cold. You are not cold. You love and that is your weakness. Whatever you are doing here, this love of yours will kill you. Love can kill as well as bring happiness. I think you are here to do something and it isn't for Germany. You must not be weak. My husband

and I would not tell anyone, you know.'

'If I killed you both the risk would go away.'

'We are both so old, it does not matter. Our son died of diphtheria when he was only four and our daughter moved to Algeria years ago. I came because I wanted to tell you that you have no need to fear, your secret is safe. How long will you stay?'

'I will go in the morning. I don't think I will need to come back.'

Leaning hard on the arms she hoisted herself up from the chair. She grunted with the effort. Rolf was tempted to help her but realised she would have resented it. She hobbled to the door and turned, her head tilted sideways to look up at him.

'I hope what you do tomorrow will make a difference. I hope you succeed. If you need to run afterwards, come here. We will hide you.'

'Here?'

'Yes. We are your friends. Do you believe that?'

'Yes, I believe that.'

'I mean it.'

'Yes.'

'Don't go anywhere else. No one can be trusted. Promise me.'

'If I have to, I will come.'

'We are friends. When do you go?'

'Early.'

'*Bonne chance.*'

The door closed and she left Rolf wondering what had transpired. Could he trust her? It was dangerous. Even if he could trust them the Special Brigade could make them talk. Even so, what could they say? There was a German who had a Heer colonel's uniform? They did not even know his name.

He knew what his instructors would have said. The mission is everything. Take no risks. They would have advised killing them both, for safety's sake. Rolf knew, however, that he could not. He pondered why he would not and began to realise, it was not their age, but what the old woman had said about love. To Rolf, killing people who truly love is a sacrilege. He could never dishonour love in such a way. He thought about Sandrine and the way seemed clear now. He knew he could never condemn her, whatever the reason for her betrayal.

He slept well that night, his mind at peace.

Chapter 5

"A lie gets halfway around the world before the truth has a chance to get its pants on."

Winston Churchill

1

As Brossolette had promised, the car stopped outside the hotel at six in the morning. Rolf wore the uniform. It was a little too small but he knew no one would question him even if he had returned to his own barracks, since it was genuine and had belonged to a prisoner of war. It was dark outside, the spring mornings had not yet returned to early sunrises and he felt cold. He stood on the flat, grey paving stones as the green Renault stopped beside him. There were two men inside. One in the front and one in the back. Rolf stepped forward and gave the phrases that bonded them together as wolves of the same pack.

The driver, who introduced himself as Jules, smiled as they moved forward, even before Rolf had time to slam the door. He was a man of average height, wearing a black beret and a dark overcoat. As they set off, he uncorked a bottle of what Rolf could smell was brandy of some kind.

'Nice to see a German ready to kill another,' Jules said,

smiling as if he were on a picnic outing in the country.

'I stopped being German long ago.'

'And now you are what? English?'

'Never mind. Just drive.'

'I've upset you. I'm sorry.' He leaned back and said across his shoulder, 'Jean-Paul. Don't annoy this fellow, he's tetchy.'

'I'm not bad–tempered. I just do not like to give information to people I do not know. You would be wise to do the same.'

Jules wagged his head from side to side. He said, 'He knows it all, this one, eh?'

Silence came then and Rolf watched as the Paris streets sped by. Rows of shops, boarded up, small squares where opportunistic sellers hoped to ply their wares and men pulling or pushing handcarts, laden with goods; all seemed ready for the city to awaken and pour forth its eager customers. A dog ran out in front of the car and Jules screeched to a halt, then they set off again at a modest pace so as not to attract attention, Jules cursing.

Rolf put his hand into his overcoat pocket and felt his psalm book. In his mind he repeated, "*The Lord is my shepherd…*"

It was no use, nothing would calm him down. His heart thumped inside his ribs, and despite the cold he felt sweat beginning to form on his forehead by the time they crossed the Pont de Saint-Cloud.

'Where are we going?' Rolf said.

'Montparnasse. It's a posh school. Very private and secure. You know this man is French?'

'Yes. I know. He has turned on his own people. He deserves to die.'

'Maybe. Paul has made this his mission in life and he seldom fails.'

'Paul?'

'Brossolette. You don't know him?'

'I've met him once, that's all. You know him well?'

'He is a master of disguise. You met him as a young or old man?'

'What?'

Jules chuckled. 'He changes shape like flowing water. It's why they have never found him. He runs an underground press and co-ordinates whole groups of men, but the SD are no closer to finding him than they are to conquering the Rosbifs. You heard about Africa?'

'Yes.'

'They wiped their arses with Rommel. It was a great moment. You see? They will never find him.'

'You and your friends will take out the occupants of the car?'

'We have some British guns. We will do the bodyguards. Paul said you would do the necessary with Boucher as he comes out.'

'There are two guards at the gate?'

'There are enough of us for you not to worry about the guards. Just do your part and we'll all be happy.'

2

The car drove up the Boulevard Edgar Quinet and turned left into Rue Huyghens. It was a narrow street, and halfway along it Rolf spotted two guards seated at the entrance of a high, wrought-iron railing with open barred gates. They drove past and Jules said, 'This is the place. We go round again. There is a side street, you noticed? We park there until it is time.'

'The others?'

'You won't see them. They hide in doorways and some of them aren't here yet.'

They parked the car in a side street diagonally opposite the private school. Ten yards from the gates, a series of stone steps ten or so feet across, rose to the wooden double doors of the entrance, and beyond Rolf could see a courtyard. It was all he could see. He did not know the geography of the school but since he would wait until Boucher came out it did not seem important. The steps in front of the school and the area before the gates were his killing ground. He recalled one of his instructors explaining how this kind of job required thorough knowledge of the area and where to run to, as a failsafe, but Rolf also knew there had been no time for him to look around.

London wanted this done fast, before the Special Brigade caught their man. And after? They had seemed evasive when he asked. 'Find your way back, you'll get instruction before you leave,' was all Foy had told him. On the aircraft, before the drop, he wondered whether he was so expendable they might have known he would meet his maker on this mission. This mission, on foreign soil, whatever nationality he considered himself allied to, was intended to be a success. He knew London saw him as a renegade German and not much more. Rolf didn't care. At that time, to him, losing Sandrine meant he was as expendable in his own mind as he imagined London saw him.

Rain began to fall. It began with tiny droplets, but within ten minutes the drops enlarged and a downpour ensued. It became impossible to see through the windscreen, and despite the wipers Rolf thought they might not see the car arrive.

'Look,' he said, 'we have to get out. I can't see anything.'

'In this? You're crazy. He isn't due for another fifteen minutes. No sense in getting soaked. If you look like a drowned rat, they won't believe who you are.'

Rolf could see the sense in that and he calmed. He looked at his watch. Eight-forty. Boucher usually arrived at ten minutes to nine. Perhaps Jules was right. He lit a cigarette and Jules opened the window, winding with all his strength.

'Do you have to do that? I have asthma. I can't stand the smoke.'

Rolf wound down his window and threw the Gauloise out. It extinguished in a puddle as soon as it landed. It was still raining hard.

'Look, we need to be closer.'

'Will you relax? There is plenty of time.'

'If we get it wrong by a minute, the plan will not work. I'm going closer.'

Rolf got out. As the door closed, he heard Jules swearing at him. He wrapped his heavy raincoat around himself. At a run he crossed the road and walked past the school entrance. Both guards carried rifles, and no doubt side arms. Neither of them looked his way and he ducked into a doorway, sheltering from the rain, but still able to see the roadway in front of the school.

He lit another cigarette. The smoke seemed to calm him and at once, he regretted getting out of the car. It put him out of touch with Jules and his comrades. Anything could happen.

Chapter 6

"Without courage all virtues lose their meaning."

Winston Churchill

1

Sometimes plans needed to be fluid. When the black Mercedes pulled up he realised it was five minutes early. To Rolf it made no difference. He knew what he needed to do. He peered around the doorway entrance and watched as Boucher left the car. He held the door open to a boy of perhaps seven or eight and took his hand as they approached the school entrance protected from the diminishing rain by an umbrella. Rolf waited. The thoughts uppermost in his mind were still reminiscences of Sandrine. He knew it was inappropriate, but she was never far away from his thoughts. He pictured a scene of Boucher, striking her across the mouth. He visualised the man threatening her with the blowtorch. Anger stirred and he knew it would be enough to allow him to complete.

He gave it five more minutes then approached the gates. He had papers. London station had assured him the documents would pass muster and he felt confident in that. They seldom made mistakes. The guard to his left saluted, though he was not a German soldier, and Rolf felt sorry for him. He was admitting defeat. He saluted as if he wished to ingratiate himself and Rolf knew it was demeaning. He would never have done that to a foreign invader.

The man to his right examined the papers. He looked up at Rolf. 'I do apologise, Colonel. Why are you here?'

'My little boy needs a school. I have an appointment with the head of the school.'

'Of course.' The man stood up then and saluted. 'Heil Hitler,' he said.

Where was Boucher?

Rolf smiled and said, 'My dear fellow, there is no need to be so formal. This is not a military matter.'

The man smiled at Rolf, who turned to the other guard. 'You there.'

'Me sir?'

'Yes. How long have you worked here?'

'Three months sir.'

'Is there ever any trouble? You know—partisans and the like?'

'No sir.'

'Good, good,' Rolf said.

He felt uneasy. Boucher had not reappeared. He strolled towards the broad stone steps, walking as slowly as he could, as he pocketed the papers SOE had given him. He was too early. A few minutes. That was all.

Still no Boucher. He realised he could not delay walking up the steps towards the entrance. He hoped the others would be in position. If they were not, then he would be on his own in dealing with the gate guards.

Boucher had not emerged. If he had to kill the man inside the school, he would do it.

Still no Boucher. Rolf swallowed hard. Tension rose in his mind. It was all going wrong. Boucher was supposed to be descending the steps now. Rolf began walking up; he could delay it no longer. The thought he could miss Boucher entirely, crossed his mind. The man might be upstairs in the school or could have gone to see a teacher.

Each step seemed too high. Each time he placed his feet, he wished he could slow down, but he had to play the part, fulfil his acting role. He reached the top step wondering what he could do now. He turned and looked down at the two guards and saw no activity of any kind. One of them smiled at him. He wondered where the partisans could be, though of course, they would not act until he shot Boucher; there would have been no point.

He came to the wide, oak, double door. It was open and he could see a courtyard beyond, cloisters surrounding it. A lectern stood to his left and a book for signing in lay upon it. A nun approached as soon as he crossed the threshold.

'Yes?' she said. She had a pleasant but serious face. He imagined how she would look with make-up and lipstick, but scolded himself at once, shutting away the unwelcome thought.

'I am Colonel Muller. I came to look around the school. I was hoping for my son to go to this school.'

'You have an appointment?'

'No, but perhaps I could make one if today is inconvenient.'

'Please sign in and then wait here. I will ask Reverend Mother if she will see you. Muller, is that correct?'

'Yes. Correct.'

He was beginning to sweat again, despite the damp, cold air but he clicked his heels and bowed as if nothing was wrong. Rolf was playing his part well.

The nun scurried away, her black habit swirling, and the long wooden rosary hanging from her waist clicking as she walked. Time ticked away. Rolf imagined how she would look without clothes. This time he allowed his thoughts to pursue the image. He knew it was only a way of defusing the tension in his mind.

A bell rang, loud and clear and it brought back memories of his own school days. A small boy of perhaps seven or eight, in a bottle-green uniform ran past him, holding a blue file, no doubt late for a class.

Rain still fell into the quadrangle, pooling in grey, cold puddles in places. The flags reflected the morning light and Rolf felt uneasy again. What if the Reverend Mother did have time to show him around? He might even miss his chance to kill Boucher, the torturer and killer of women.

In his mind, he related Boucher to his father. His father's shoes would have fitted Boucher very well, whether he was smaller in stature or not. The nun returned, followed by another who seemed to be old and frail. She had a walking cane in her right hand and leaned upon it every time she put her left foot to the ground. Behind, walking at a slow pace, was Boucher, his son next to him. They were at the far end of the cloister, a matter of fifty yards. He knew it was an impossible shot for the Luger, an inaccurate pistol at best, and he would have to wait until they were closer.

The boy wore school uniform, but he was not in class. Rolf found himself wondering why, unless Boucher was negotiating a day off for some reason. He noticed his heart still beating fast inside his chest. His collar felt tight and he was sweating. His target held the boy's hand. Rolf felt inside his coat for the Luger. He had nine rounds. He would make them count.

2

At thirty yards, Rolf was still too far away for a certain head shot with a pistol. His heart beat faster and he had a vague feeling of wanting to flee, though he recognised it was only the effects of the adrenaline surging through his body.

Twenty yards and his fear left him. He had a job to do and he knew he would do it. He stood still waiting for the nun at the front to be close enough to be out of the way. Rolf looked at Boucher. The man was smiling and looking down at this son. He spoke in soft, easy tones and Rolf found himself wondering what they were talking about.

At fifteen yards, Rolf moved. He ducked fast, sideways. He drew his gun. Running first to his right out into the yard then towards the walkway, he shortened the distance between himself and his quarry. The sudden movement must have alerted Boucher. Rolf saw him shove the child behind him with one hand. He reached inside his coat. Rolf fired a two round burst. Boucher fell. The nuns screamed and the younger of the two made for Boucher. Rolf approached uncertain whether he had completed his task. The Special Brigade Commander turned over fast. He held a Luger machine pistol like Rolf's. He fired. Rolf responded. Ricochets resounded around the cloisters. The nun ducked back behind a pillar. A bullet struck Rolf in the thigh, just above his knee. His leg buckled. He was down.

He lay there and cursed. Frantic, he felt the leg. There was pain but he could still feel his foot. He rolled and tried to stand. His good leg did most of the work but he limped like the Reverend Mother without her stick.

Boucher was not on his feet. He seemed immobile this time. Rolf levelled the pistol. He had him now. He knew it. A walking stick hit him on the shoulder. It was the older nun's. He ignored it and limped forward. It was then all his buried thoughts came to the fore. The child stood in front of Boucher. He was small even for his age.

'Get out of the way,' Rolf said, still limping forward.

'No.'

'Get out of the way or I'll shoot you too.'

'No. I won't let you hurt my papa.'

Rolf was an arm's length from the child. He reached out to push him away. The boy pushed his hand away and backed up. He lay on his father's body. Tears crawled down his face. The grimace on the face, the wetness of the tears brought something out from deep inside Rolf. He recognised what the boy felt. He knew. The empathy was perfect.

In his mind, he pictured Max's face, screwed up, contorted by drunken rage as Rolf stood in front of his mother. He would not let him hurt her. The backhander came so fast he had not seen it. He had recalled nothing else of the next two days, but the mental picture of his father's face became burned like an indelible scar into his mind.

Rolf froze. He heard shots fired outside. He could not take the shot unless he manhandled the child away. No man could kill a child like this. He turned away then. He limped, in pain, past the two squatting, terrified nuns, who were trying to hide behind the pillars of the cloister, their hands covering their heads. He sat down on the top step, dizzy and unsteady. He was breathing fast and a terrible thirst consumed him. He eased himself down the cold steps on his backside. He grabbed the railings and pulled himself up. His mind would not allow him to take in the carnage around him, though later he did recall the two dead guards, the black car's open doors, and the three bodies inside. Rolf could feel the blood trickling into his shoe. Warm and sticky it must have left a trail all down the steps. He staggered unsteady and weak. Someone grabbed his arm and tried to help him walk, then another came on the other side. A car engine screamed, tyres screeched, and he felt jolted as if they pushed him hard into a car. Then all was dark. He could hear, but saw nothing.

Then he heard no more either.

Chapter 7

"Courage is going from failure to failure, without losing enthusiasm."

Winston Churchill

1

Surfacing, there was a smell of disinfectant. The light hurt his eyes when he tried to open them, so he kept them shut. His leg ached and his heels felt sore where they contacted the sheet beneath him. He shifted and sharp, lancinating pain came from his left leg, above the knee. His fading consciousness evaded taking in his surroundings and he drifted off, watching with mesmeric fascination as a pair of heavy, blood-spattered, black shoes, swung from side to side in front of him. He could hear angry voices, echoing and shouting.

Rolf came to again. This time someone was wiping his face with a soft, damp cloth. Opening his eyes, the light from the bulb above him seemed so bright it stung. He heard himself groan, then he was awake. Visions of Boucher, the boy and the nuns flashed though his mind. He tried to sit up.

'Don't struggle,' a cracked voice said and he noticed who

was swabbing his face.

'Jeanne D'Arc,' he muttered.

He heard the woman chuckle. The sound seemed merry and out of keeping with the old lady from the hotel.

'Yes, it's me. I told you we were friends.'

'Friends. Yes.'

'You lie quiet. I have some soup for you. You've been in and out of the waking world for a night and a day.'

'My leg…'

'Yes, you let someone shoot you. You must have been careless.'

'Boucher?'

'I don't know any Boucher. They just left you here and told me to look after you until they came back.'

'The bullet? You removed it?'

'Went clean through. The bone isn't broken either, my husband said, so the problem has been bleeding and muscle damage. It will get worse for a few days, but you are as strong as an ox.'

Rolf pulled himself up the bed. The pain was excruciating. Once it began to settle he took the bowl of soup from her gnarled, arthritic hands. The clear soup was dark-brown and smelled of onions laced with garlic. His hands were unsteady, and although they shook he managed to finish the bowl without adding burns to his injuries.

The room looked no different from when he had left the morning before, if it was the morning before and not the day before that. He felt confused but reluctant to ask.

'I don't think you can walk on that leg for another day or so. There is a bottle on the table, here,' Jeanne said, gesturing to the object. 'I have left a bell too. If you need us, ring it, but be patient, we are busy people. A hotel does not run itself.'

Rolf smiled to her.

She said, 'I found this in your coat. I will get another book for you, to keep the boredom away.'

Rolf said, 'Thank you. It was a gift from my mother, many years ago. A different world. You are Catholics?'

'Ha. No. We are Marxists, it is enough to believe in. Maybe I'll get you *Das Kapital*, instead?'

'No thanks, I've read it.

'You have?'

'I have a degree in philosophy. I've read many such things.'

'Then you perhaps understand us. There is no place for God in this world.'

'I won't argue. I'm too tired.'

'Yes, get some sleep maybe. I will come back later. I'm tired too.'

'You sat with me?'

'Naturally.'

'Then I am even more grateful to you.'

'It was because it was necessary. My husband and I believe in the cause of liberation. Many others do too. I'll come back later with hot water and you can wash.'

She scuttled from the room, bent and old, but her movements seemed animated, surprising Rolf with their speed. The door slammed behind her leaving him alone. The room was silent though a faint sound of cars or trucks came to him from time to time. He wanted more soup but did not want to disturb the old woman so soon. He shifted in the bed and the pain was less, though still severe.

Rolf wondered whether Boucher was dead or not. He knew he had shot him but without the head shot to finish it, there would be some chance he could survive. Perhaps Brossolette would know. He needed to get up but he felt weak and dizzy even propped up in bed. He would have to wait. Patience was not one of his virtues and his mind mulled over the scene in the school repeatedly. He could not have killed the child, nor could he have struck him. If Boucher survived the attack, Rolf felt sure it was God's wish, not his.

One tiny corner of Rolf's mind welcomed Boucher's survival, if that was the consequence of his own weakness. He had spared the child, not even struck him and if the price of that was failure, then he was happy it should be so. Damn SOE and damn Brossolette, he wanted only peace now.

He thought about Sandrine and wondered where she could be. She might not even be alive as far as he knew. He hoped Brossolette would keep his word and find out, but after the fiasco at the school he knew the partisans would not regard him as useful. He had failed and that was that.

2

The train rattled on the track making a loud danke schön—bitte shön—danke schön—bitte schön sound to Rolf's ears. He smiled at the thought. It would only be appropriate at home and this was not his home. The landscape seemed flatter than he had imagined it would be. People's descriptions of Scotland were always about mountains and rolling green hills but he saw none of these as his train journeyed north taking him further and further away from home, from France, from war and from Sandrine. His handcuffs rattled like the train and he shifted position often, disliking the restriction of movement, as it caused pain from his healing leg. The single guard opposite him also stared out of the window and he seldom spoke, making the monotony of the journey even worse.

He fiddled with the white cloth patch on his coat, a symbol that showed his interrogators had not felt he was a staunch or intransigent Nazi. If they had thought he was entrenched, the patch would have been black. To Rolf there was a passing similarity to the yellow star worn by Jews. The implication they might treat him badly hovered then disappeared. Britain was not Germany nor was Churchill a Hitler.

He mused over Sandrine too—a now familiar habit. Rolf had missed her more than anyone in his life. At first he prayed for her, kneeling at his bedside, but he realised her absence from his day to day life eroded his feelings, her betrayal vying with his love, and sometimes now, winning the day. With the passage of time, he had started to become angry. The feeling was deep inside, like his anger with Max. His religious beliefs assuaged neither his own feelings of guilt at his lack of success as an assassin, nor his growing anger. His disappointment with the woman he once loved, and her absence, were combining to replace his feelings of love with anger.

He closed his eyes and reviewed the interview SOE had called his "debriefing".

'We sent you because you were trained. You knew you had to finish the job,' Foy had said.

'It was not possible.'

Foy thumped the desk that separated them in the small office on the corner of Baker Street and Dorset Street. Rolf looked out of the window; outside it began to drizzle. SOE now used the whole block. They were expanding it seemed to Rolf, while his world was contracting.

'Not bloody possible? You shot him once in the stomach and then left. You've ignored your training, let us all down. Have you any conception of what you've cost us? Years of manoeuvring, years of risk for our people.'

'I'm sorry. I told you about the child.'

'Yes. Because you spared one boy, Boucher is now free to torture and kill any number of people. He's caught our operative. He's even sent twenty four of his prisoners to the death camps in the east already. All because you didn't do what you were supposed to do.'

'I know. Maybe I wasn't the right man for the job.'

'Trouble is, those who make the decisions here have decided to alter your status. I can't even send you back. They're bloody furious.'

'Status?'

'Yes, they now regard you as a POW.'

'But that is not fair. I came here of my own wishes.'

'Either way, you will have to sit out the war in a camp in Scotland.'

'But…'

'It wasn't my decision. I'm just telling you. If I had got my way, I would have sent you back. There's nothing I can do for you.'

Foy had rung a buzzer and two armed police entered.

As the train left Arbroath, he began to feel cold. Spring it seemed was slow to evolve in Scotland. They continued to Aberdeen and then changed train to Peterhead. It was a strange flat place, farmland to the left and to his right a wild seascape, in places interrupted by wide yellow, misty dunes and beaches, though Rolf could imagine they seldom saw the sun. The grey sea in the distance, layered with mist, was flat calm and seagulls flitted along the shoreline as the train made its way north.

Alighting on the platform, he looked up and down the station. Pigeons cooed in the eaves of the station building and he could smell coke burning somewhere nearby. His guard took his arm and guided him towards a low red brick building adjoining the stationhouse. The black, pitched roof sat perched on top like a cumbersome hat and a tall wire fence surrounded the station itself. Inside the building, he sat on a wooden bench. His breath steamed as he looked around. There were posters on the wall proclaiming "Dig for Britain" and another inviting him to join up and fight the Hun. The Hun indeed. He was the Hun, and the irony did not escape him. Two windows broke the monotony of the walls and thick iron bars protected them. If he had wished to escape, it would have been impossible. He held no such wishes: all he wanted now was an end to the war and return home, though there was nothing there for him. For all he knew the war would last for the rest of his life and he would die here an old man in a POW camp.

Presently, the guard returned, and holding Rolf's arm guided him out onto the frosty concrete steps at the station entrance in silence. There seemed to be no one around. A green canvas-covered truck stood outside with its engine running, and the guard whose name Rolf did not know, lifted the brown tarpaulin rear flap indicating for Rolf to enter.

It was with relief Rolf found there were other prisoners here, seated on wooden benches either side of the truck. They looked dishevelled and gaunt. A small dark man to his right shifted up and Rolf took his place on the board. The guard passed a chain through the handcuffs and padlocked it to the tailgate.

The guard remained at the station and Rolf could see his boots as the truck pulled away, diminishing into the distance. There had been no need to say goodbye, they had only exchanged three sentences all day.

Rolf turned to the man next to him and introduced himself in German. The man stared at him, a blank look on his face. He replied but Rolf realised this man was Italian, not German. Neither of them understood the other.

Rolf passed the rest of the journey in silence although the other prisoners spoke in hushed tones from time to time. No one smiled. Subdued disgruntlement was all Rolf could see on their faces and he wondered where the British took them prisoner. He was unable to ask, and after a few minutes he ceased to be curious, knowing he might never find out. He smiled once to himself. If the war lasted long enough he might not only improve his English, he might learn Italian too.

The journey ended after half an hour. They disembarked onto a roadside, where their new home stood. A battered road sign indicated to his right with the word "Fetterangus" and a small arrow showing the way. To his left, tall wire and concrete fences reached for two hundred yards around a series of rounded metallic grey buildings. There were doors at either end and small wire-covered windows at intervals along one wall. Wooden steps gave access at either end. Between the huts, the ground was churned into a brown mire of mud and there were no walk-boards.

A gun turret stood next to the gateway though no one seemed to be in evidence inside it. Two soldiers in buff uniforms opened the gates and the twenty men found themselves ushered in. The gates clanged shut behind them and the guards escorted them across the mud to one of the Nissen-huts. As he mounted the steps, it began to dawn on Rolf that this would be his home for years to come, unless the war ended very soon and he thought that would not be the case.

The hut was long and wide. Bunks lined the walls and a central, wood-burning stove stood in bleak remonstrance in the centre. Rolf could see no wood however, and assumed they would have to cut their own or freeze, though there was nowhere he could see where they might do so.

First in, he selected a bottom bunk to his right, near the stove. His leg was too painful to climb into or out of a top bunk after all. Each bunk had a mattress but no blankets and he felt relief at having a blanket in the kit bag they had allowed him to bring. They had searched it many times on his way here.

The Italians sat or lay on their bunks. No one spoke. An air of gloom descended. So this was the end of Rolf's war.

Chapter 8

"An appeaser is one who feeds a crocodile—hoping it will eat him last."

Winston Churchill

1

Rolf found it hard to accept that years passed. For him, it was as if his life had concertinaed. In the first spring, he volunteered for duty, working on farms nearby the camp. He was never tempted to try to escape. Britain was an island, there was nowhere to go. Even if he did escape, where would he run to? He had no desire to go home to Dortmund. He knew he could never find Sandrine until the war ended. So what was the point? No. Better stay here and do what he knew. The farm work suited him in a physical sense. It was familiar. He understood it and it felt as if it brought him back to real life, after a nasty and unpleasant experience, which his nature insisted to him, the war had become. He helped bring in harvests, he helped on the road gangs in the autumn, and he felt at the end of every day when he worked, as if the tiredness in his limbs was cathartic.

They fed him well and he learned later that the Compo rations were the same as they gave the British fighting men, though the monotony of it destroyed his appetite most of the time. When he thought hard, he was shedding the past, Sandrine, Gautier and Boucher; they all seemed to fade somehow. What it left within him, was a desire to be part of the land, part of real life as his own personal philosophy painted it.

Yet sometimes, when he was alone the past visited him. Often it was in dreams where he could see his father. At other times, it came to him when he was awake, lying on his back in the Nissen hut; when pictures of Sandrine arose. The vision of her most often was of her back—bony, slim and perfect. The jagged points of her vertebrae marching down to the cleft above her bottom; it excited him and disturbed him, but he could no more reject her body than he could reject his dwindling love for her.

And his love was dying. It was like a plant crying out for the watering sustenance of her presence. The more time he spent away from her, the more he became aware of her betrayal, her seeming infidelity. It was as if all that remained were shabby, time-ravaged memories. As the years passed, he hated her at times and at others he wished with a gravid desperation to see her face, as if it might salvage him from the utter boredom and depression filling his mind, here in the flat, Scottish farmlands, so familiar, yet so foreign to him.

He was cold too. Each winter that came seemed colder than the last. Snow fell on the hills in autumn and in the spring; it still came, as if it visited him to draw warmth not only from his body, but from his mind. That chill took over his thoughts in the end. His love was withering in the cold of the Scottish winters, where mist and freezing wind grabbed at his body, mirroring what happened in his heart.

He would not have described himself as bitter. Some might have suggested that, but Rolf knew, deep inside, he would come through this time unscathed. He felt like a man at the end of his life, looking back yet wanting to laugh at the absurdity of it all. It was because, to Rolf, it was truly absurd. His weakness in capitulating to the Nazi principles he had hated, his readiness to desert the army for a woman, his failure to kill Boucher. He felt ridiculous when he thought of these things. The prime example of the absurdity of his life, was his love for Sandrine.

It irritated him too, in the end, that Italians were his only companions. No German compatriots joined him in Camp 110. The Ministry of Defence seemed to have decreed that Mintlaw in Aberdeenshire was a province of Italy and he a German, could only ever be a guest, a visitor, whom no one expected would become part of it all. He broke that by learning to converse with his neighbours. At first, they showed caution. No one spoke to him since they thought he might be a British spy or some other unusual fish in the tank in which they all found themselves swimming.

2

Once he learned enough Italian, Rolf set up lectures in English language and a separate course in philosophy. Both were well attended, though Rolf knew it was because there was nothing else in the camp to stimulate anyone's intellect.

He made one friend though. Sotto-Tenente Pietro Dragoto, from Sicily, was younger than Rolf, but he had fought in the Dolmites—the Via Ferrata, where he was captured and transferred south and then to Britain towards the end of the war. They became friends because of the philosophy class.

Rolf gave forth his understanding of Anaximander's concept that life changes, like the water flowing in a river, so that the descending foot never touches the same water ever again. As he attempted to draw parallels to their life in the camp, Pietro stood up.

'It's stupid.'

'What is?' Rolf said, responding to the only question anyone had asked him since the course began.

'It has nothing to do with rivers. Life changes, but our thinking, it is the same. The experiences stay in our minds. They don' flow away, we keep them. This fellow was a Greek, right?'

'Yes,' Rolf said, perplexed.

'In those times, the Greeks did nothing but fuck each other. Stupid. What his name again?'

'Anaximander.'

'Huh. Stupid name. He oughta learn some decent philosophy.'

'Like what? Mein Kampf? Like speeches by Il Duce?'

'No. No. Like this German fellow. Nooch?'

'Nietzsche, you mean.'

'Yeah, that guy. He had good ideas.'

'Like what?'

'Like we all got a super-fellow in us.'

Rolf smiled, and that impressed him, because he realised as soon as it happened, he had not smiled—truly smiled with humour, since he came to the Camp. They continued the conversation for the rest of the evening, and next morning, when it was time to leave the camp to work, Pietro still argued.

In fact, Pietro argued all the time. He argued for more than a whole year. Rolf always recalled how they spent their time together arguing, until after the war ended.

'Pietro,' Rolf said one day. 'Ever thought about escaping?'

'No. I don't think about that.'

'Why not?'

'You see? You always come up with some stupid idea.'

'I was wondering whether you might like to go without me and leave me in peace.'

'Why you say that? We are brothers. Long after this war is finished, we still friends. You see that girl in the village?'

'What girl?'

'We was walking past the post-office. That girl, she look out at us and she look in my face. Beautiful girl. She wants me. I can't sleep at night because she wants me.'

'Shut up, Pietro.'

'No. Really. I don't sleep at night. You don't think about women sometimes?'

'Of course I do. It's just…'

'Just what?'

'I loved a woman once and she betrayed me.'

'Hah! You silly, German, Sauerkraut. All women betray you if you give them chance. If you keep them happy in bed, they never leave you.'

'It wasn't like that. She betrayed me to the French security police.'

'So maybe she needed to. The war is ending. The Americans come and they enter France. Go find her. We'll be out of here soon. You go find her. Tell her it's all better now. Make love to her, it will be fine.'

'She betrayed me to the French police. You think it's as easy as that?'

'Yeah. Think with you dick, not your head. It's much better life that way. What else is there? We fight, we sweat, and in the end, we die. If you love this girl, go find her and fuck her.'

'Shut the fuck up,' Rolf said and turned to look out of the window.

Pietro chuckled.

Chapter 9

"Success is not final, failure is not fatal: it is the courage to continue that counts."

Winston Churchill

1

By 1946, Rolf waited for the British to repatriate him. His only letter from Annika told him how she had married a farmer near Elsa's farm and she remained happy. She asked him to come home. She explained how she missed him and how her life would never be complete if he did not come to her.

Rolf could see between the lines. She needed him no more now than she ever did since their parents died. Had she not said so herself?

He wanted more in his life than a simple return to the farming community where he grew up. He wanted to teach and England seemed to him to be ideal. There were opportunities here and he saw them. First, he registered his interest in staying. The authorities denied him initially, of course. When he applied for the lecturer's job at Goldsmith's College and passed the interview, they insisted he produce proof of asylum.

Rolf told lies. He explained to the panel how the area he came from was in the Russian sector and the Soviets would arrest him and torture him if he returned. In the post-war confusion no one questioned him, and they granted him leave to stay. It was not a carte blanche. In three years, he would have to apply for citizenship and make sure they removed him from the 'Prisoners of War' list. He had no concerns. Rolf had learned that whatever happened, patience and application solved most difficulties.

2

Thick smog drifted across the tussocks on Blackheath as the dusk light began to fade, and Rolf drew his scarf up to better cover his nose and mouth as he walked. It was a Tuesday and he always worked late on a Tuesday. There were lectures to plan and scripts to mark but the day had been productive, so he had nothing to do now apart from feed himself and listen to the radio. Settling into his new job had taken him no time. He was now, at last, doing something he loved and he delighted in it. Over the past three years, his nightmares continued, but they never prevented him from functioning like any of the others who had come home scarred by the war years.

He lived now in Blackheath Village in a two bedroomed third-floor flat that suited him. People left him alone up there. Seeking the company of others gave him little pleasure but he was seldom lonely. He thought about Sandrine less now and he found the memories less painful too. Sometimes he wished he had gone back to France to look for her, but what was the use? She had betrayed him like Judas, like

Quisling. She could not have loved him after all. He had fooled himself. He attended church in a mechanical way as if it was necessary but he found even his religious convictions were dwindling. He wished he could be devout, but they had never brought him happiness, nor had they served his mother well either. Her miserable death at the hands of his father would have happened anyway, whether she was deeply religious or not.

He checked the mailbox and rifled inside, finding two bills and a letter from Pietro, who still kept in touch, though his communications were less frequent than before, when their incarceration was fresher in both their minds. Climbing the stairs, he noticed the carpet was loose and it brought back a memory of the Paris apartment house where he first came across Boucher. His mind flashed back to the moment when Johan entered and how different he had been in those days. He had felt then there was a future. Not so now. All that was good was his work and he wanted nothing else. He felt like a hollow and empty receptacle of a man in whom no real emotions stirred any longer.

The flat was in darkness as he opened the door. Switching on the light, he shut the door and sighed. It was not company he wanted, it was regression. He wanted to be back there, in Paris, holding hands with Sandrine, in a different world where there were no soldiers, no Special Brigade and no war. But he knew he should not dwell upon it, even those memories could be painful if he did. Betrayal does that to a man, he thought.

In his kitchen, he opened the refrigerator and removed a shepherd's pie left over from the day before. He lit the oven. He placed the dish on the top oven shelf and as he shut the door, the telephone rang. It could not be anyone to whom he would have wished to talk. Perhaps a wrong number. It happened so often these days.

'Blackheath 2016,' he said.

There was silence for a few moments, so he said, 'Hello. Who is this?'

'Rolf, is that you?'

It was a female voice. There was a trace of French accent.

'Yes. Who is speaking?'

Again silence.

'Hello?'

'It's me. Sandrine.'

This time Rolf had nothing to say. His mind raced. Nothing he had experienced before equipped him for this. He realised his heart was beating fast and he felt dizzy. He sat down on the stool by the telephone, pressing the black resin to his ear as if he could keep the sound of her voice closer that way.

'Sandrine? Where are you?'

'Don't hang up. Rolf, you have to let me explain.'

'Explain? Explain what? How you betrayed me? If they had caught me that day in Dieppe, they would have shot me.'

She lapsed into French, speaking fast. 'Rolf, I can't do this on the telephone. I must see you. I have things to tell you. Important things. I have to see you.'

'No. There is nothing to explain. There are no excuses you can make. Think of Gautier, think of the others. You can't excuse what happened to them.'

'I thought you might at least see me once. For old times' sake. The war is over. There were reasons for all of it. Please.'

'I can't trust myself with you. You take a risk with your own life here. I could hand you over as a traitor and collaborator.'

'No. I know you too well. You would never harm me. I trust you.'

'Well, I don't trust you.'

'Please say you'll meet me.'

'I don't know.'

'I beg you. There is a café in town opposite Charing Cross station next to the News Cinema. Tonight at eight. Please say you'll come.'

Rolf said nothing. He replaced the receiver. It dropped into the cradle with a soft click. He sat still, staring at the shiny black resin surface and wondered for a moment whether he had imagined the whole conversation. He had always believed that if he heard her voice again he would hate her. Those feelings did not come to him. Rolf realised he wanted to see her. He wanted to touch her. Then he rejected that. The betrayal hung in the air in front of him.

Getting up, he began to pace the floor. He came full circle. He wanted to see her once more. To look in those eyes, touch that soft skin, but the fact of all that went before stifled those feelings again.

How did he feel? Desire again replaced the rage he thought he would feel. But she betrayed him to Boucher. She could never explain that away. Never. It was ridiculous.

Yet he wanted to see her. He could not understand why he felt like this. He looked at his watch. One hour. He crossed to the kitchen, his shoes clacking on the bare wooden boards. Switching off the oven, he went through to the hallway and grabbed his coat and scarf. It was beyond his control. He knew now he wanted, despite everything, to see Sandrine again.

Chapter 10

"The Fault... is Not in Our Stars, But in Ourselves..."

William Shakespeare

1

Rolf alighted from the train, stepping onto the dull platform in the cold, misty station. Looking up the glazed dome was shrouded in the smog of the London winter. Few people had been on the train. A woman, dressed in a brown fur-collared coat and a brown hat, clicked along in high heels in front of him. He watched her swinging hips, and had it not been for his appointment he would have admired how they swayed with an enticing to-ing and fro-ing. A man in a grey suit pushed past him carrying a suitcase, in a hurry. A black-uniformed man in a peaked cap approached.

'Porter sir?"

'Yes, thank you. I've got ten minutes to catch the train to Penzance.'

The uniformed man accepted the suitcase and they were off down the platform. To Rolf's right, a billow of steam emerged from the train engine and he imagined it adding to the smog which lay like a blanket over every corner of the city. He showed his return ticket to the guard at the platform entrance who nipped it with his clippers.

'Cheers, mate,' the man said and handed it back.

Pocketing the ticket in his tweed overcoat pocket, Rolf advanced into the foyer of the station and made for the entrance, directly ahead, past the ticket office on his left. A newspaper seller stood outside as Rolf exited through the tall archway.

'Eeve-nin Standard… Eeve-nin Standard,' he called.

Rolf glanced at the man. He wore a light coloured scarf, tucked into a brown woollen jacket and a cloth cap perched upon his head. He saw Rolf looking.

'Paper sir?'

'No. No thank you,' Rolf mumbled as he made towards the ornate, black iron railings at the station entrance. Standing on the pavement, he leaned on one of the stone pillars adorned above by a white orb in its wrought-iron enclosure. He gazed across the Strand but the smog was now so thick he could barely distinguish the other side of the roadway. He waited for a hackney cab to pass and crossed behind it. Turning left towards Trafalgar Square, he thought he knew where the café was. It stood on the corner towards the end of the block.

He passed the News Cinema with its bright red and blue posters announcing "Mickey Mouse" and "Betty Boop". Rolf felt a strange desire to enter and watch the cartoons but he shrugged off the feeling, knowing he was simply trying to avoid what was ahead of him.

Ten yards away, he saw her. She was leaning against the stone wall of the Lyon's Corner House, smoking a cigarette. His familiarity with her movements made his heart skip. He even knew it would be a Gauloise. The smoke she exhaled seemed part of the surrounding smog, for it disappeared as if camouflaged, as soon as it left her lips. She was not looking his way and it was not until he was five yards away that she noticed him.

Sandrine turned to face him. He saw she was as beautiful now as the first day he laid eyes on her in that Paris restaurant. Only the faint crow's feet at the corner of her eyes attested to the years since he last touched her. She wore a long, blue, thick woollen coat and a hat with a medium brim. Around her neck, she wore a white scarf and she had folded her coat collar up for warmth. She looked anxious and said nothing.

Rolf slowed as he approached. At this moment he had no idea what to say. Their eyes met. He did not understand what he felt. Anger, hatred and love seemed mixed in equal proportions, but his strongest impulse was to take her in his arms. He fought the desire and stood three feet away, silent, immobile.

'Well?' was all he said.

'Rolf.'

'Yes. We both know my name. What is all this about? You must know how I feel. Boucher nearly got me. You stabbed me in the back. You think it is as simple as saying the war is over? All is forgiven? It isn't. I loved you. You never loved me, only pretended.'

Rolf turned around and began walking away. He had said what he wanted to say and his heart was breaking because of it. Somewhere inside him, a voice seemed to say, '*Fool!*'

Her hand scrabbled at his elbow. She took hold of his coat sleeve and he turned back. He looked down at her face. There was an unfamiliar vertical crease between her eyebrows. She was on the verge of tears. He hated himself then, but he knew that being with her was being complicit. People had died because of her, yet there was something more in his heart which he could not access.

'Rolf, please. I need to talk to you.'

'You need to talk to me? You need to be shot for what you did.'

'You would do that? Then do it.'

'Don't be stupid.'

'Can we go somewhere?'

'Why? I've said what I needed to say.'

'There's more.'

'More? How? You were a collaborator all along and you betrayed everything you believed in, even after I saved your life and we made love. I loved you. Don't you understand what that meant to me?'

'Not here. The café.'

She tugged at his sleeve and he followed her, his reluctance betrayed by the strength of her grip.

2

The Corner House had no windows apart from its frontage, and there was a smell of deep fried potatoes as they walked in, but it was warm and the worn, soft, brown carpet seemed to offer welcome. There must have been forty tables, white tablecloths with small bouquets. White porcelain saltcellars and pepper pots stood beside the drooping flowers in the centre of each. A young couple sat at a window seat to the left, discussing something with serious expressions. Further back, two soldiers dressed in buff battledress uniforms talked with loud voices and even louder gesticulations. Rolf assumed they were drunk.

A waitress in a black dress and a white, lace-edged apron greeted them as they entered. Her black and white hat perched on her head seemed ridiculous to Rolf. She showed them to a table in the rear. She was middle-aged and her greying permanent-waved hair bounced before them as she walked.

'I'll be with you in a moment,' she said, smiling.

Rolf realised they had not spoken since entering and he removed his coat, hanging it on the back of his chair, determined not to be the one to break the silence between them.

'I don't know where to begin,' she said.

'I'll bet you don't.'

'Rolf. Life can be more complicated than you see on its surface.'

'I loved you. You betrayed me to Boucher. How can there be anything else? It isn't complicated.'

'You know, if I could have given my own life to save you I would have. I found myself in a Hell without end, because of Boucher. Remember that first time I sat down with you at that tiny café? I was on my way to meet my brother. He was sixteen at the time and both our parents were dead. He needed me. I supported him. I loved him.'

'So? You say that, but I'm not sure you even know what love is.'

'Please. Let me finish.'

Rolf glared at her.

Bitch.

'Boucher was always in the background. He knew our father. He was a friend of the family for many years and after my parents died he helped us with money and other things.'

'Like sex?'

'No. Nothing like that. He got me the job at the restaurant for example.'

'Lovely man. We should all forgive him the torture and sending Jews and partisans to the death camps. You've seen the pictures from Auschwitz? What a nice fellow.'

'No. He wasn't a nice man. He heard rumours that I was in with Gautier. He arrested my brother. Then he brought me in. In front of me, he flared a gas-torch across Maurice's stomach. Then they started beating him. They beat him until he begged me to do something. He begged me. They broke me then. Nothing in the world meant as much to me as my brother—until you came.'

'You're lying.'

'No. I swear. They held him prisoner and made me work for them. Boucher is evil; he deserved to die. You know he got away?'

'I don't know anything about what happened to him. I tried to kill him in forty-three, but failed, so they sent me to a POW camp in Scotland.'

'Forty-three? It was long after you escaped.'

'Yes. They sent me back. They knew I could identify him and they trained me to do the job. I failed; it's a long story.'

'I did it all for Maurice. You have to believe me. What would you do? A choice between me and your sister? What would you do? Tell me.'

Rolf remained silent. In his head he realised her explanation gave him the perfect excuse to be with her again. Once more, he rejected the thought.

'It doesn't matter what I would have done. It is the fact of it. You told Boucher where I was. You lied to me when you said you loved me.'

'It was the only thing I never lied about. I still love you.'

The waitress appeared. They ordered coffee but there was none, so they settled for tea.

'Scones?' The waitress enquired.

'Thank you, no,' Rolf muttered.

As the waitress walked away, Sandrine said, sitting forward in her chair, 'I never lied to you. I struggled with the fact of my love for you. You don't remember?'

'Yes, I recall your tears. When crocodiles open their mouths really wide to engulf you, they shed the same kind of tears.'

'Rolf, I need you to forgive me. I love you.'

'You come here and expect absolution for your weakness? I loved you. I don't think I do now. I think of Zedé and his kindness to us. I think about how he faced the special brigade coming for him. He was brave. You showed only cowardice. How can you expect me to take you back after all the blood on your hands? What happened to your brother, anyway?'

'Boucher sent him to Treblinka, in Poland.'

'And?'

'He died there.'

'So it was all a waste of time then? You should have had the courage to suffer like him and remained loyal.'

'And what do you care? You're not French. You're German. How can it matter to you what happened to the partisans? They weren't your people, they were mine. It is for my conscience to examine and bleed for. I did what I could for love. For Maurice.'

'Hah.'

Rolf waved his hand across the table, his impatience showing.

She looked down at her tea and said, 'Boucher promised not to kill you or send you away. It was the only reason I gave in.'

'If I couldn't trust you then, how can I trust anything you say to me now?'

They finished their tea. Rolf wished he had succumbed to the scones.

Chapter 11

"To sleep, perchance to dream — aye, there's the rub..."

William Shakespeare

1

'Come in,' Rolf said.

He opened the door to his flat. She was breathing hard from the climb up the six flights of stairs. They took off their coats in the hallway and he hung them side by side on the double hook on the back of the door. She walked into the room and fumbled in her bag. Lighting a cigarette, she sat down on the red velvet sofa and pulled an ashtray towards her where it stood on the low table in front of her. She crossed her legs and looked up at him.

'You live alone?'

'What?'

'Sorry. Of course you do. I...'

'What happens now?'

'I don't know. You have a drink?'

'I have only this bottle of grappa. A friend sent it from Sicily.'

'Grappa then.'

306

Rolf poured two glasses of the pale yellow liquid. He passed one to Sandrine and sat beside her. She turned to him with lips parted, her eyes searching his and it became uncontrollable. He reached for her and their lips met. He felt warm inside, but it was as if some tiny voice taunted him again. He wanted both to push her away and he wanted to make love to her.

They began touching, familiar yet unfamiliar at the same time. His thoughts became like a chimera: as if action and reaction were inexplicably merged inside him and he moved inside his thoughts, mechanical and passive. He stood up and led her to the bedroom in silence. Neither of them spoke as they undressed in the shivery cold. They came together under the covers, touching, kissing—a lingering sexual contact. Minutes later, Rolf got up.

'I'm sorry. It's never happened before.'

'I understand. It is all too much to take in for us both. Maybe this was a mistake.'

'Yes,' he said, dressing. 'Maybe it is too soon or maybe too late. I don't know.'

Rolf walked through to the lounge and lit one of Sandrine's cigarettes. Thoughts raced through his brain. He drank more grappa then took his head in his hands. A vivid picture of his father's shoes came to him. Max had betrayed him too, in his way. Even his mother had betrayed him by staying with the man who would kill her. Life was a sea of shit.

He stood up again and went through to the bedroom. Sandrine lay on her side. Her eyes were closed and he thought from her breathing, she slept.

2

Rolf balanced in a delicate pose on the window ledge. The air, thick with smog felt icy and still. In his mind, he found his hatred for Sandrine; in his heart, his love for her was an integral part of his life. He could no more separate the two than he could continue with it. They were all the same; his father, his mother and this French girl.

Yes, he forgave her. He understood her motives and he understood her pain. Those things in her made no difference to the torture he was experiencing. Should he stay and wait to find someone else? Should he commit and take all his miserable thoughts with him.

Still he teetered on the brink. It reminded him of the day in the hayloft, before Berlin; before the great evil of which, in the end, he had become a part. He looked down. Three floors up. Over in seconds. He could not see the paving stones below or the black iron railings with their spikes and prongs. Max's face came to mind. Was this what went through his mind too before he kicked the stool away? Had he also found he could not face the duality of his life? The good man. The bad man. The drunk. Neither and both.

What was he leaving behind in the world? There was nothing and now there never would be. Nothing marked where Rolf Schmidt had been. Nothing indicated to anyone what he had done. Nothing at all. Any good thing he might have done would go to the grave with him. Like in that Shakespeare play.

What remained of his life was like the smog.

Impenetrable.

He knew it was time to go.

Her voice startled him. It cut through his determination

like fire melts ice. Teetering, he held onto the window frame.

'You can't do this, Rolf.'

Her voice was quiet and calm.

He said nothing.

'Rolf you can't just desert us.'

The word "us" screamed in his ears.

'Us?' he said.

'Our son needs you.'

Rolf clambered back into the room. He stumbled and staggered as he jumped down, then he stood looking at her face. He recognised her beauty but there was still a barrier between them. It rose like the wall they were building in Berlin. A cold wind lifted the floral curtain behind him and he shivered.

'What are you talking about? You...' he grabbed at her naked arm. She too shivered and goose bumps appeared beneath his fingertips. They stood facing each other; she naked and he barefoot and in his trousers.

'Yes. Boucher knew soon after you fled. He let me go. He knew my brother would die. He let me go.'

'You... You were pregnant?' Rolf sat down. He looked up at her. He grabbed the grappa bottle and drained the last dregs into his mouth. It burned his tongue as he swallowed. He wished there was more of it. He needed something to ground him as he listened and the words became part of him.

'I fled to Alsace and had my son in a hotel there. A woman helped me at first but I had to get a job. I was alone after that. In the war, no one cares, you know. I thought about you all the time.'

'You never told me.'

'No.'

'Why?'

'There was no time. I wanted to tell you on the road to Dieppe, but couldn't.'

'I don't understand.'

'Think about it. We were traveling to Dieppe for me to hand you over. Boucher said he would keep you locked up and not hurt you. I believed him. I was afraid you would fight; they outnumbered you by so many. If you had known, you would have fought, wouldn't you?'

'Where is he?'

'I left him in France. He's with an aunt of mine.'

'Is he really mine?'

'There was no one else. Only you, Rolf.'

'How old is he?'

'Here,' she said. Sandrine picked up her bag from the table. She scrabbled inside and then proffered a battered photograph.

The smiling face of a child aged seven or eight stared out at him from the photograph. The smile on the young lips seemed somehow familiar. The boy wore a tattered, sleeveless jumper and shorts; he held his right hand up as if waving. His other hand held a woman's whose grey gabardine raincoat hung next to his cheek. His hair was fair and Rolf could see his own mother's eyes as clear as if he stood facing her, looking up, on the day she gave him the psalm book.

'Rolf, we can still make a life together. I love you still.'

'Love? Can love grow with roots in a soil of betrayal?'

'I don't know, but I know that without hope of that I might just as well join you on the window sill.'

Somewhere inside him a rough, brown, hessian rope gave way and snapped, severed at last.

Find more writing by Fred—including a blog, free chapter downloads and details of upcoming public appearances, at:

www.frednath.com

THE CYCLIST

A World War II Drama
by Fredrik Nath

"The story is brilliantly executed... Nath's biggest success is the sustained atmospheric tension that he creates somewhat effortlessly."
-LittleInterpretations.com

"A haunting and bittersweet novel that stays with you long after the final chapter—always the sign of a really well-written and praiseworthy story. It would also make an excellent screenplay."
-Historical Novels Review—Editor's Choice, Feb 2011

www.fingerpress.co.uk/the-cyclist

FAREWELL BERGERAC

A Wartime Tale of Love, Loss and Redemption
by Fredrik Nath

François Dufy, alcoholic and alone, is dragged into the war
effort when he rescues a young Jewish girl from the Nazi
Security Police.

Then the British drop supplies and a beautiful SOE agent
whom Dufy falls in love with. But as the invaders hunt
down the partisans in the deep, crisp woodland, nothing
works out as Dufy had hoped.

www.fingerpress.co.uk/farewell-bergerac

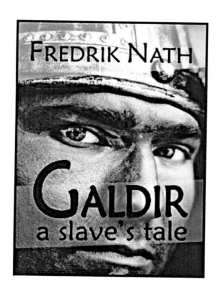

GALDIR: A SLAVE'S TALE

Barbarian Warlord Saga, Volume I
by Fredrik Nath

"Highly commended"
-Yeovil Literary Prize

A tale of love, brutal battles and conflict, in which a mystical prophecy winds its way through an epic saga of struggle against Rome.

www.fingerpress.co.uk/galdir

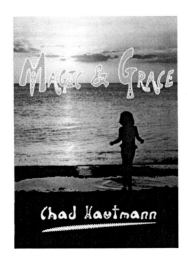

MAGIC AND GRACE

A Novel of Florida, Love, Zen, and the Ghost of John Keats
by Chad Hautmann

"Quirky and funny and heartfelt and rich"
-Ft. Myers News-Press

"A compulsively readable mixture of fast-paced plot, likable
protagonist, and subtly deep theme"
-Magdalena Ball, CompulsiveReader.com

"Highly entertaining, often thoughtful, and strategically
humorous"
-Ft. Myers & Southwest Florida Magazine

www.fingerpress.co.uk/magic-and-grace